Favors come back to haunt you....

And it was payback time for Ash Cain.

He'd hardly looked forward to the prospect of seeing Jillian again. He remembered all too well how one encounter with her fifteen years ago had left him feeling.

But he thought of the way she had looked this morning, peering through the crack in the door. Her skin had been rosy from sleep, her long hair tangled around her shoulders. Images had materialized in his brain—vivid images of twisted sheets, crumpled pillows and long, hot nights.

He knew right then that he never should have taken this job. His odds of survival were better staring down the barrel of a gun than making it through a summer with Jillian.

Dear Reader,

Welcome to another month of top-notch reading from Silhouette Intimate Moments. Our American Hero title this month is called *Keeper,* and you can bet this book will be one of *your* keepers. Written by one of your favorite authors, Patricia Gardner Evans, it's a book that will involve you from the first page and refuse to let you go until you've finished every word.

Our Romantic Traditions miniseries is still going strong. This month's offering, Carla Cassidy's *Try To Remember,* is an amnesia story—but you won't forget it once you're done! The rest of the month features gems by Maura Seger, Laura Parker (back at Silhouette after a too-long absence), Rebecca Daniels and new author Laurie Walker. I think you'll enjoy them all.

And in months to come, you can expect more equally wonderful books by more equally wonderful authors—including Dallas Schulze and Rachel Lee. Here at Silhouette Intimate Moments, the loving just gets better and better every month.

Happy reading!

Leslie Wainger
Senior Editor and Editorial Coordinator

Please address questions and book requests to:
Reader Service
U.S.: P.O. Box 1325, Buffalo, NY 14269
Canadian: P.O. Box 1050, Niagara Falls, Ont. L2E 7G7

LAWYERS, GUNS AND MONEY

Rebecca Daniels

Silhouette®

INTIMATE MOMENTS®

Published by Silhouette Books

America's Publisher of Contemporary Romance

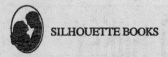 SILHOUETTE BOOKS

ISBN 0-373-07563-4

LAWYERS, GUNS AND MONEY

REBECCA DANIELS

will never forget the first time she read a Silhouette novel. "I was at my sister's house, sitting by the pool and trying without much success to get interested in the book I'd brought from home. Everything seemed to distract me—the kids splashing around, the sea gulls squawking, the dog barking. Finally, my sister plucked the book from my hands, told me she was going to give me something I wouldn't be able to put down and handed me my first Silhouette novel. Guess what? She was right! For that lazy afternoon by her pool, I will forever be grateful." That was eight years ago, and Rebecca has been reading and writing romance novels ever since.

Born in the Midwest but raised in Southern California, she now resides in Northern California's San Joaquin Valley with her husband and two sons. She is a life-long poet and song lyricist who enjoys early-morning walks, an occasional round of golf, scouring California's Mother Lode region for antiques and traveling.

TYVMFE! —For Bill Fattarsi
My favorite lawyer,
big gun
and main money man.
When I look at you, I understand
the mark of Cain.
Oh, you know.

Chapter 1

"Freeze!" Jillian Hughes clutched the smooth wood grip on the butt of the 9mm SIG P226 automatic pistol with both hands and focused the tritium sight between the shoulder blades of the stranger prowling the roof of her house.

The man paused abruptly. Slowly, he began to turn.

"I said *freeze,*" Jillian demanded again. "Now let me see your hands—slowly." Carefully, the man lifted his arms. "Now turn around and walk to the ladder—keep it slow and easy."

He was tall, well over six feet, and his bare chest and shoulders looked well-developed and strong above the faded Levi's. He pivoted around, moving cautiously to keep his balance on the slanted surface. As he turned, his gaze searched until it found her standing on the lawn below.

Jillian felt a chill run the length of her spine when she peered up into those cold, steely blue eyes. Surprise was evident on his face, and she knew that seeing her standing on the lawn in her short pajamas and thin robe was not quite what he'd expected.

"Look, lady, I think you've made some kind of mistake," he said, stopping and lowering his hands a little. "I don't—"

"Get those hands back up," she directed, cutting him off and gesturing with the nose of the gun. "Keep moving."

His blue eyes narrowed, the icy gaze shifting from her to the gun, then back to her again. Slowly, he moved to the aluminum extension ladder propped against the side of the house and started to climb down. His heavy work boots gripped the rungs of the ladder, and the tools hanging from his leather belt swayed and clattered against it.

Jillian watched his every move with a cautious eye, her hands flexing and releasing nervously on the gun. Her entire body wanted to cry out, to tremble and release her fear, but instead she concentrated on keeping the gun steady. She had no idea who the man was, but she knew he had no business being on her roof. At this point, she wasn't about to take any chances. Just the fact that he was a stranger was reason enough for her to be careful.

On the ground, he looked even taller, and Jillian's hold on the gun tightened still more. His straight black hair was long, hanging to his shoulders, and the red bandanna tied around his forehead held it out of his face, and out of those startling blue eyes.

"Look, lady, I'm not looking for any trouble," he told her, his hands coming up in a helpless motion.

"Good. Then you won't mind telling me what you were doing up there." Jillian was glad her voice betrayed none of her alarm.

"I'm supposed to paint and fix the roof," he explained, taking a step forward. "The owner hired me—"

"*I'm* the owner," she corrected, cutting him off, "and I didn't hire you for anything. And if you take another step toward me, I'll blow your head off. Are we clear on that?"

"Okay, easy, I'm sorry," he conceded readily, halting where he stood. "Look, I guess there's been a mistake. I thought the Iverses owned the place."

The gun lowered a fraction. "What do you know about the Ivers?"

"They hired me," he told her, his gaze drifting to the gun again, "to patch the roof and paint the place."

"So you won't mind if I give them a call."

His eyes narrowed, and his gaze shifted back to her. "You're the one with the gun, lady. You're calling the shots."

Jillian thought for a moment. If he knew the Iverses, there was a good possibility he was telling the truth, but something about him made her uncomfortable. He didn't look like any roofer or housepainter she'd ever seen before, but then she was hardly an expert. Living in New York City, she didn't exactly run up against too many roofers and painters. But if she'd learned nothing else in the last two years, she'd learned never to leave anything to chance.

"This way," she ordered, motioning toward the house's back door. She followed him through the screen door, through the small porch and into the kitchen. "That's far enough," she said, freeing one hand from the gun and reaching for the telephone. It wasn't easy balancing the gun and the telephone receiver while using the old-fashioned rotary dial, but she managed.

In her small kitchen, he appeared even bigger and more threatening, and she wouldn't allow her eyes to drift away from him for more than a second. It was obvious he didn't like the gun pointed at him, and he watched it intently with a cold gaze. She half expected at any moment he would try to make a run for it or attempt to knock the gun from her hand, but he did neither. He merely stood there, leaning his massive frame against the kitchen counter and watching her every move.

"Hello, Tess. It's me—Jillian," she said when the phone was finally answered. "Look, I'm sorry to be calling so early but . . . uh . . . Tess, I've got someone here. He was up on the roof and he says—"

But Jillian never had a chance to finish. Tess Ivers gasped loudly and immediately launched into an apology. She'd completely forgotten to tell Jillian about the arrangements for the painting and roof repairs which had been made weeks ago.

As Tess explained about chipped paint, broken shingles and summer storms, Jillian unconsciously lowered the gun farther and farther down. Her gaze awkwardly shifted from the stranger's face to the floor, then back to his face again as it slowly began to sink in that he'd been telling her the truth, and it appeared she'd overreacted . . . just a little.

The stranger watched Jillian as she listened to Tess on the phone, quietly folding his strong arms across his powerful, bare chest. He knew he was being vindicated by Tess Ivers's explanation, but he seemed to take no satisfaction in that fact. There was no sign of pleasure in his eyes at being ex-onerated, no smug expression of righteousness in his face. She would almost have preferred that, or at least under-stood it.

Instead he merely continued to stare, that icy gaze of his almost penetrating through her. The way he stood there, the strange manner in which he watched her, made it seem un-important that Tess was able to corroborate his story. To Jillian, the man still looked dangerous.

"Your story checks out," she said simply after hanging up the phone, carefully avoiding his gaze.

"You sound disappointed."

"Look, I'm sorry if I frightened you. It was a mistake." She took a deep breath and pulled her robe closed. She felt foolish for having overreacted, but she wasn't about to start offering up a lot of excuses. She just wanted him to go away and leave her alone. She wanted to go back to bed and start the day all over again, try to forget this whole thing ever happened. "I'd like you to leave now, please."

"What about the roof?"

"Forget the roof."

"But I was hired to fix it."

"Well, I'm firing you."

"You sure? You've got a mess up there, lady. One good summer storm and you're going to float away."

"Look," she said, not able to hide her exasperation or her discomfort any longer. "Just forget about the roof, would you? I'm sorry you were inconvenienced. Submit a bill for today with the Iverses and I'll see that it's taken care of. But now—" she stopped and motioned towards the door "—please just go?"

For a moment she thought he might not have understood, for he made no attempt to go. He merely stood there, staring at her. Had he forgotten she was still armed? When he finally did move, pushing himself lazily away from the counter, it almost made her jump. Slowly, he moved across the small kitchen to where she stood.

"Cain," he said, offering her one of his massive hands.

"W-what?" she stammered, then immediately became furious with herself. What did she have to be afraid of? She was the one holding the gun.

"I'm Cain," he repeated, lifting her free hand into his and holding it rather than shaking it.

At the touch of his hand, Jillian felt a strange strangling sensation in her throat, and the whole situation changed.

She understood in that moment just why the man was so dangerous, just why he made her so uncomfortable. He wasn't afraid of her. He was the type of man who knew exactly the kind of threat he posed to a woman, a man who possessed a raw sensuality and basic animal magnetism that cut through social barriers and conventions. She was suddenly uncomfortably aware of the bareness of his chest, of the flimsiness of her pajamas, of the remoteness of their location, the emptiness of the house.

"Cain," she repeated, her voice barely above a whisper.

She felt the pressure of his hold on her hand increase just slightly when she spoke his name, and a quiver of anticipation traveled the length of her spine. In the space of a millisecond, her mind had created images, concocted crazy scenes. They had nothing to do with violence and guns, or of bodily harm or mortal danger. She wasn't imagining those massive hands choking and wounding her—she imagined them holding and caressing. She felt those roughened palms moving and seeking, she saw that penetrating gaze cold and unrelenting, and she was struck with an entirely different kind of fear. He disturbed her, she realized, more than he should, more than she should allow him.

The hand at her side squeezed tightly around the butt of the gun, but a gun didn't offer her the kind of protection she needed from a man like Cain. Only her anger and indignation did. *He* wasn't putting those images in her head—*she* was. And she was going to make them stop.

"Okay then . . . *Cain,*" she said sarcastically, pulling her hand free and pushing past him. She walked to the back door and opened it for him. "I won't keep you any longer."

At the door he paused and looked down at her, his eyes drifting purposefully down her body to the gun at her side. "You know, you should be careful with that thing, lady. That's a lot of gun you've got there."

"I know how to use it," she said, ignoring his insolence and holding her ground.

A slow smile moved across his lips, but it did nothing to soften the hard lines of his face. "I'll bet you do, lady. I just bet you do."

She watched as he walked out the door, then she sagged heavily against the frame. She let out a long, slow sigh and closed her eyes tight. It was only then that she felt the pounding coming from inside her head.

Opening her eyes, she looked at the daisy-faced kitchen clock on the wall above the stove. It wasn't even seven o'clock yet. What a morning.

The sound had awakened her from a dead sleep. Of course, now she understood it had been him—Cain—on the roof above her, but at the time she'd thought the noise had sounded like a gunshot. Just one lone blast, but it had shattered the stillness of her sleep like fireworks on the Fourth of July. Her terror had been immediate, and fear had tasted bitter on her tongue and in her throat. Even though it had been years since she'd last heard the sound of a gunshot, it was a sound she would never forget. One single gunshot had ended her father's life twenty-one years ago, and the blast from his assassin's gun would remain in her memory forever.

Assassins. Executioners. Hit men. Nameless, faceless purveyors of violence and death…. And they were after *her* now.

Pushing herself away from the door, Jillian ran a tired hand through her long, tangled hair and started back to the bedroom. The sun streaming through the faded lace curtains felt like little needles against her tired eyes, and she rubbed at them wearily. All in all, her first morning back in Lighthouse Landing was turning out to be quite interesting. She'd not only been awakened at dawn by a half-naked stranger pounding on her roof, but she'd nearly blown his head off in the process.

She looked down at the gun in her hand. Maybe she had come on a little strong, but given the circumstances, could anyone blame her? After all, how were you supposed to act when you had a hit man on your trail?

Jillian Hughes had a right to be nervous. She'd spent the last three years of her life working to make her case against flamboyant crime boss Alfred Donelli stick, and the road to conviction had been a long one. She and her team at the U.S. Attorney's office in New York had dealt with everything from hung juries and retrials to allegations of jury tampering and death threats. But it had all paid off. Five weeks ago, she had sat in a courtroom and listened as the jury came back with verdicts in twenty-three counts of racketeering and tax evasion charges. Guilty on all counts.

The Donelli case had been plagued with an atmosphere of intimidation and innuendo from the very beginning, but threats and warnings were nothing new to a federal prosecutor. They were part and parcel of the job. So when FBI informants came forward with news of a plot by the vindictive don to seek revenge against those responsible for putting him behind bars, she hadn't taken those threats too seriously. After all, Donelli had a flair for theatrics. He liked to read his name in the headlines. She'd assumed this was just more posturing on his part—the act of a desperate man going down swinging, but still going down.

But when trial judge Bruce Andrews car had exploded ten days ago, with him in it, Jillian began to take those threats very seriously. Since his sentencing, Donelli had been cooling his heels in a holding facility, awaiting his permanent move to the level-six maximum-security federal penitentiary in Marion, Illinois, but that move was still months away. Once he was housed within the walls at Marion,

Donelli would be powerless to operate his underworld empire, but until then, the man could still reach the outside world, and still reach her.

Jillian opened the top drawer of her nightstand beside the old four-poster bed and slipped the SIG back inside. She looked down at the gun lying on one of her grandmother's lace hankies and shook her head. She had reacted a bit like Dirty Harry this morning. But then, stress had a way of making a person act a little crazy, and God knew for the last three years she'd been living with her share of both stress and crazy. Still, guns had a way of upping the ante, and overreacting could have dangerous consequences. In the future, it would be wise to try and relax just a little.

She walked into the bathroom and turned on the faucets in the big, claw-foot bathtub, adjusting the water flow. As the tub began to fill, she thought about the arguments she'd had in her office with the FBI agents assigned to investigate the Donelli threats. They had wanted to assign agents to her for protection, but Jillian had spurned their suggestion. Growing up a member of the politically powerful Hughes clan had robbed her of enough private life, and the Donelli trial had only made that worse. The thought of giving up any more of her privacy and placing her life in the hands of some federal watchdog was not her idea of protection—especially since she doubted their ability to actually keep her safe. As a kid, she'd seen firsthand just how ineffective so-called protection could be.

Jillian had been only eleven when her father had tossed his hat in the race for the U.S. presidency, but she was old enough to remember all the security and precautions her whole family had been forced to endure for the next two years. And yet all those elaborate precautions, all those strict safeguards, had failed to protect her father. The night before Senator Collin Hughes had been expected to win his party's nomination as their candidate for the office of President of the United States, one lone gunman had pushed past security forces and shot her father in the head—killing him instantly.

Jillian slipped out of her robe and pajamas and into the cool, soothing water in the tub. No, she hadn't been about to assign her safety to a system she didn't trust. She could take care of herself. Ron had taught her how to handle a gun, and she wasn't afraid to use it. So instead of federal protection, she had put in for a leave of absence, circulated a convincing story about spending the summer in the Yucatán's tropical resort of Cancún, and instead set out for Lighthouse Landing.

Lost in the remoteness of the more than one thousand miles of waterways in Northern California's San Joaquin delta, Lighthouse Landing was about as far away from Donelli and New York as Jillian could get. No one knew about the little one-story house with its heavy wisteria vine that twisted over the porch and its neatly trimmed lawn that her grandmother had left her six years ago, or about the long summers she'd spent here as a kid. But when she'd pulled her rental car into the driveway yesterday afternoon, she felt as though she'd come home. The whole place had been endearingly familiar. She'd driven from the airport in Sacramento, through the intricate labyrinth of levee roads and drawbridges, and to the small community as though she made the commute every day.

Nothing had changed. The place was exactly as she'd remembered it—the same cluster of houses, the same trailer park, the same small marina and boat ramp, the same dock and gasoline pumps, and the same country store fashioned like a miniature lighthouse. Hank and Tess Ivers, who owned and operated the small marina and market and who'd been looking after the house since her grandmother had died, had been surprised, but delighted, to see her again.

Lighthouse Landing had been the perfect solution for a lot of reasons. Its remoteness and isolation offered her protection from Donelli and his threats, but it also provided her the solitude she needed to heal from the pain of her failed marriage.

Jillian knew she had neglected a lot during the Donelli trial, but her marriage to Jeff had begun to crumble even before that. It was her fault—she took full responsibility for the failure—but that didn't make it any easier to accept.

Her marriage to Jeff had started out with two strikes against it. She had known Jeff felt threatened by her family's wealth and position, and he was uneasy about her own success as a prosecutor. But more important than any of that, he'd known from the beginning she had married him on the rebound.

Ron had only been dead three months when she'd accepted Jeff's proposal, and she'd still been reeling with grief. At the time, though, marrying Jeff had seemed like the answer to her prayers. As a lawyer, he was staid and dependable. He didn't take the kind of chances Ron had as a tough, streetwise New York City vice cop. How many times had she begged Ron to quit the force and marry her, pleaded with him to turn in his badge and take a desk job—anything that would get him off the streets and out of danger? But it hadn't worked. Ron had died as he had lived—fast and furiously.

But life with Jeff posed none of those risks. With him, she didn't have to worry about thugs and thieves, about gangsters and guns. She'd have the kind of safe, steady, secure life she'd always wanted—or at least thought she'd wanted. There had only been one thing she'd forgotten about, one thing she hadn't considered. She didn't love Jeff, and he never could quite forgive her for that.

It was understandable Jeff would have wanted to strike out at her. He loved her, and he was angry and resentful that she couldn't return his love. But his anger and resentment had turned to cruelty. And he did more than hurt her—he'd been determined to humiliate her, as well. Knowing how important her privacy was to her, he'd lashed out in the one way he knew would hurt her the most—publicly. Betraying her with another woman hadn't been enough for Jeff. He'd set out to betray her with as many other women as he could. It had been devastating for her, humiliating—especially when she discovered most of the other women were workers in her own office.

But all that was over now. She had to accept the fact that her success in life would be relegated to the courtroom, not with men. She'd had little luck there. Her relationships with Ron and Jeff had been difficult and complicated, and she didn't want any more complications in her life.

Cain. She closed her eyes and thought about the giant of a man she'd discovered on her roof. He wasn't her type at all, but there had been something about him that had gotten all her hormones going. She'd never been attracted to that beefcake-Chippendale-construction-worker type. It wasn't that muscle and brawn repelled her exactly. Actually, she found something very…basic in the appeal of hard bodies and well-developed physiques. What generally turned her off those "physical" types were their overblown egos and runaway chauvinism. She was too strong a woman to tolerate those kinds of frailties in a man. Besides, she liked to think of herself as too tough for men like that. She liked to think she could chew up men like this Cain character and spit them out.

But maybe it was time she started rethinking some of those old biases. After all, she'd already tried and failed at emotional relationships. Maybe it was time to concentrate on a purely physical thing with someone like Cain. After all, she was over twenty-one, a consenting adult. Women she knew had affairs all the time. What did it matter if she liked him or not? She was talking one summer here, not forever. Just a simple exchange of physical gratification—no strings, no ties, no promises to make, none to be broken. What harm would it do?

Jillian suddenly remembered the feel of Cain's rough palm against her hand, and a little chill ran the length of her spine. She remembered how his skin had gleamed in the sunlight, and how blue his eyes had looked behind those thick, dark lashes—so dark, so enigmatic, so—

She felt a sudden, curious twinge of excitement, a rush of familiarity—déjà vu. There was something about Cain, something about his eyes, something in their color, in the way he'd looked at her. Something she knew but couldn't quite remember....

But the moment was fleeting, the feeling soon gone. And it was just as well. She had no business thinking about the man in the first place. She hardly wanted to be reminded about what had happened this morning, and the debacle she'd made of it. Besides, when she thought about the way he'd looked at her, how uncomfortable he'd made her feel, something told her nothing with a man like Cain would be easy or uncomplicated.

After her bath, Jillian dressed and spent the rest of the morning unpacking and exploring the small house. She hadn't been in the house since her grandmother's death six years earlier, so she spent the time poking through closets and searching through boxes. She found albums of family photos and dozens of mementos that brought back a flood

of memories—a bittersweet collection of happy and sad re-
membrances.

In the afternoon she walked to the small marina and to
the Iverses' country store, where she stocked up on some of
the basics—bread, milk, eggs, etc. Tess apologized again for
the mix-up about the roof repairs and fussed about the in-
convenience, but Jillian waved off her concern. She was
uncomfortable talking about it. She wasn't sure Tess was
aware she'd actually held the unsuspecting roofer at gun-
point while she'd checked him out, and she just wanted to
forget about the whole unpleasant incident.

Unfortunately, that didn't turn out to be a very easy thing
to do. Later that night, long after she'd gone to bed, a sudden thunderstorm tore open the sky. The downpour was violent and unexpected, and the roof of Jillian's house sprung
to life with hundreds of small, fresh water streams. The call
she made to Tess Ivers the next morning was one she'd
dreaded making.

"I was afraid that would happen," Tess lamented over the
line. "But don't worry. I'll get someone over there as soon
as I can."

"Thanks, Tess." Jillian shrugged sheepishly, looking at
the dozen or so pots and pans that were scattered about the
kitchen and living room, catching the drips from overhead.
"I appreciate that. Oh, and Tess? Do you think you could
find someone other than that fellow from yesterday—that
Cain?"

"Was there a problem with Cain?"

"Uh . . . no," Jillian hedged. "Not really. I just
thought . . ." Thought what? Jillian asked herself as her voice
drifted off. What was she supposed to tell Tess? That she
was embarrassed and she'd rather not see the man again
without a gun in her hand? That she thought she'd rather
not have somebody around who looked at her like that,

whose blue eyes made her nervous and had a way of making her think crazy things?

"Jillian, sweetie? You there?"

"Hmm—what? Oh! Yes, yes I'm here."

"You were saying about Cain. You had a problem?"

"Uh...no, Tess. No problem." Jillian closed her eyes and felt her whole body cringe with embarrassment. "Anyone you think can do the job would be fine."

"All right, honey, I'll get right on it then. We'll get somebody out there as soon as possible. 'Bye."

Gratefully, by midmorning the rain was gone, and the sun moved out from behind scattered clouds. By midafternoon the temperatures had climbed to the century mark, and the hot, dry heat had parched all evidence of the storm. Jillian spent the rest of the day cleaning up, drying rugs in the sun and mopping up the floors. No one showed up to begin repairs on the roof, and Jillian began to hope that meant that Cain character had moved on to another job, and Tess was finding someone else to fix her roof.

The night was hot and still, and the air thick with humidity. Jillian lay in bed, staring up at the ceiling, convinced she would never fall asleep. She was too uncomfortable, too tense. Outside, behind the house, Lighthouse Slough flowed lazily along the levee, but even the gentle breeze off the water failed to cool her overheated body.

She lay in the darkness, listening to the sounds of the night—the quiet delta so dissimilar from the noisy sounds of New York City. But the peacefulness she sensed had nothing to do with the quiet silence of the night or the absence of city sounds. It came from a feeling of solidity that was there, a stability that could be relied on.

"You can never step in the same river twice," Jillian whispered into the darkness. She remembered hearing her grandmother say those words, and she knew them to be

true. Life changed constantly, but the delta had a sameness
to its ever-changing landscape, and Jillian took great comfort in knowing the waters always flowed.

The first loud blast woke her up; the second had her
yanking open the drawer on the nightstand and pulling out
the SIG. She stopped then, blinking her eyes and trying to
clear the fog in her head, trying to come to terms with the
fact that it was no longer dark, that it was morning, that she
had been asleep and someone was knocking on her front
door.

"It's all right. Calm down," she mumbled to herself as
she fumbled for her robe. Her chest rose and fell with giant
gasps of air, and the sound of her heart echoed through her
entire body. She glanced at the clock on the nightstand. 6:00
a.m. *Chill out just a little. It's not gunfire. You're fine, you
were just startled.*

But she still kept the gun in her hand as she slipped out of
bed and tiptoed across the living room to the door.

"Who is it?" she asked, but when she pulled apart the
curtains on the door and looked outside, her question was
already answered.

Cain saw the curtains part and glanced down at her
through the glass. "Just making sure there are no *misun-
derstandings* this time."

Jillian let the curtains close, looked down at the gun in her
hand and cringed. She'd nearly done it again. Hiding the
gun behind her back, she unbolted the door and cracked it
open.

"Mrs. Ivers told me you were coming," she announced,
trying to sound as businesslike as she could after having just
awakened from a deep sleep. "You're here to fix the roof
and paint."

Cain looked at her through the narrow opening, his brilliant blue gaze traveling the length of her. He wore a white T-shirt tucked into the same tired Levi's he'd worn the other morning, and his chest and shoulders looked just as strong, just as massive covered as they had bare.

"I'm going to try," he corrected. "Unless, of course, you decide to pull a gun on me again."

Jillian's gaze shifted nervously away, and the hand behind her back flexed around the butt of the SIG. "I thought I'd apologized for that the other morning."

"Oh, you had," he assured her. "I just wasn't taking any chances this time."

"You took me by surprise, that's all," she offered awkwardly, by way of explanation.

"Well, if it makes you feel any better, you surprised me, too," he said dryly, then turned and started down the steps of the porch. "I'll just be getting to work now, if that's okay with you."

Jillian nodded and closed the door. Pulling the gun out from behind her, a small giggle welled up from inside. Covering her mouth with her free hand, she squeezed her eyes closed tightly and tried to hold back the laughter. She felt a little like a kid who'd just stuck her hand in the cookie jar—and gotten away with it.

Chapter 2

The gun had pissed him off. He didn't like having guns pointed at him, and she had coolly and proficiently stood down on the ground and pointed that cannon up at him as though it had been some kind of fashion accessory for this year's chic businesswoman.

A SIG. Who'd talked her into that? The Secret Service used SIGs. What did she want to do—stop a train? She'd practically be able to do it with that twenty-round magazine she'd had the thing loaded with.

Cain looked down to the spot on the lawn where she had stood the other morning. He had to hand it to her, though, she had meant business. Even in the skimpy outfit and the tousled hair, he didn't doubt she would have pulled the trigger if he had given her the provocation. But damn, he couldn't help feeling just a little foolish. She'd gotten the drop on him—*him!* He should have seen it coming.

Yeah, the gun had pissed him off.

Cain listened to the sounds of the woman moving about inside the house below. So far, so good, he thought to himself as he quietly labored away. There had been no sign of recognition in those stormy brown eyes of hers—just anger, indignation and maybe a little chagrin. Of course, he had changed a little in the decade and a half since she'd last seem him. He would be forty in a few weeks, and the long hair and dirty Levi's were a far cry from the precision hair cut and three piece suit he'd been wearing when they'd first met.

But the lady had gone through some changes herself. Fifteen years ago she'd been a nineteen-year-old college sophomore—perky, innocent and spoiled as hell. At thirty-four, Jillian Hughes didn't look quite so perky, and he knew for a fact she wasn't innocent. Still, she was beautiful—tall and shapely with that smooth, golden skin and long, flowing black hair. But it was her eyes that he recognized. He'd have known them anywhere. Those eyes, and that one kiss they'd shared, were something he'd never forget.

The Kennedys, the Rockefellers, the Hugheses and others like them were about as close to royalty as one got in this country, but Cain had long ago lost his fascination for their special brand of status and style. As crown princess to a dynasty, Jillian Hughes barely spoke the same language as he did. Once he'd been impressed by the power, the extravagance and the special advantages of people like her, but over the years he'd seen too much indulgence, too many squandered lives, too much lost hope, to have anything but contempt for those bestowed with so much.

But overindulgence and pampering didn't change the fact that Jillian Hughes was a beautiful woman—more beautiful now than she'd been as a teenager, when she'd waltzed that shapely bottom of hers past him time and time again. She'd had all the cockiness of youth back then, and the charm and charisma of the Hughes clan. They were so special, so different from ordinary people. He remembered wondering if they ate and drank and slept like everyone else. And if they were cut, would they bleed?

Only...he knew they bled. Collin Hughes had bled all over his young daughter. Photographs of her kneeling beside his dead body in a blood-splattered dress had run in newspapers around the world.

Cain thought of the kiss. Over the years that's how he'd come to think of it—the kiss. The one and only. The one, brief, innocent moment in his life when he had reached out and hadn't gotten burned. Was that why he'd always remembered it? Was that what had him remembering the taste of her, the feel of her lips, that funny little sound she'd made when her breath caught in her throat? He had reached out to her fifteen years ago as a man, and she had responded as only a woman could.

Sweat streamed down his face, and he wiped it away with a swipe of his arm. He'd thrown off the T-shirt, and the midmorning sun grew harsh against his back. Below, inside the house, he heard the sound of water running. Jillian Hughes was taking a shower.

The thought of the cool water pouring over her tall, slender frame had his body reacting. Suddenly the sun seemed hotter and unmerciful, and the rush of heat did crazy things to his head. He began to wonder...if he were to climb down the ladder, if he were to open that squeaky screen door and find his way into that small, old-fashioned bathroom, if he were to touch that wet, seemingly flawless skin of hers, would she respond to him again?

He slammed the hammer down hard against a rotting shingle, sending wooden splinters flying in all directions. It was happening already. He thought he'd gotten all that out of his system long ago, that he was no longer susceptible, no longer vulnerable. He'd hoped that time and contempt would have changed the way he felt, would have stopped any reaction, destroyed any appeal. After all, he was hardly a rookie any longer. He was older, wiser, maybe even a little jaded by all that he'd seen and been through. And yet it seemed she still had a way of getting to him.

Fifteen years ago, fate had stepped in. Things had ended before they'd had a chance to start. Circumstances had allowed him to walk away, to take cover, to find the shelter he needed to lick his wounds and to persuade himself that what he'd seen in her eyes and what he'd felt in his heart hadn't been real. He'd convinced himself that what had happened had been a fluke, an accident.

But he'd have no such luxury this time. There was a long, hot summer ahead. There were no dark corners, no places to hide. There was only the blazing sun, and a job that needed doing. The fever may have started in his brain, but it was his job this time to make certain no one got burned.

Cain had become a master of finding dark corners, of lurking in the shadows, of getting beyond half-truths and omissions, and of watching his back. Working undercover for the FBI, you either mastered those things or you ended up dead.

Jillian Hughes might have thought she was taking charge of her own fate when she'd spurned the bureau's offer of protection, but United States Senator Graham Hughes, chairman of the powerful ways and means committee, wasn't about to take any chances with his dead brother's only daughter. He was going to make sure his niece didn't get in the way of an assassin's bullet, even if that meant he had to twist every arm in Washington. From his office on Capitol Hill, Graham Hughes had begun calling in favors, and Cain had been one of the first he had called. Cain owed Graham Hughes a favor—a big one. And it was this favor that had landed him in Lighthouse Landing on Jillian Hughes's roof pretending to be a handyman.

Fifteen years ago, Cain had been a young marine at Quantico when Graham Hughes announced his intention to take up the torch his brother, Collin, had assumed eight years earlier and make a run for the presidency. Cain knew that he had been hand-chosen by Hughes to join the Secret Service team assigned to the senator's protection because Cain's father had served as Hughes's commanding officer in the Pacific during World War II. Cain had never been comfortable with the special favor, but it had been an opportunity of a lifetime.

Only, the trouble with favors was that they had a way of coming back to haunt you, and it was payback time now. Hughes had described as willful his niece's unwillingness to cooperate with FBI agents and accept their protection, Cain called it just plain stubborn. He'd hated like hell being pulled from his current assignment, working to bring down a major drug operation in the Sacramento area, simply to baby-sit a headstrong, obstinate woman, but personal preference had nothing to do with it. When Hughes had called, Cain hadn't been able to refuse the request.

Still, he'd hardly looked forward to the prospect of seeing Jillian again. He remembered all too well how one encounter with Graham Hughes's niece had left him feeling fifteen years ago, and the thought of spending an entire summer hanging around the woman hadn't exactly sounded inviting. But it was his job, and Ash Cain always did his job.

He thought of the way she had looked this morning, peering through that crack in the door. Her skin had still been flushed and rosy from sleep, and her long hair fell mussed and tangled down her back. Immediately images had materialized in his brain—erratic, random images of tangled sheets, crumpled pillows and long, hot nights. He knew right then he never should have left Sacramento. He should have told Graham Hughes no deal. His odds of survival were better staring down the barrel of a drug dealer's gun than making it through a summer with Jillian.

How many times as a college coed had Jillian Hughes, along with her entourage of Hughes cousins, breezed past him during those early months of Graham Hughes's campaign? Dozens? Hundreds? It didn't matter. It could have been a thousand times, and yet she still wouldn't have given him more than a passing glance. To her he'd been invisible, just another of the nameless, faceless army of minions assigned to the security she'd grown up around.

Cain had noticed Jillian, though. It would have been hard for any man to miss her long hair, and those short skirts and gorgeous legs. He'd never seen anyone like her before—rich, confident and achingly beautiful. He'd been dazzled by her. And when a pushy reporter had gotten fresh with her during one of their campaign stops, he'd rushed to her rescue like a charging bull. While the others in the team had escorted the senator on to his speech in the banquet hall of the hotel, Cain had carefully guided Jillian down the elevator to her uncle's waiting limo.

But, of course, that had been before—before he'd become cynical, before life had developed a hard edge. Before Vicki. Vicki—his beautiful, ambitious, bitter wife. By the time Cain had left the Secret Service—and Vicki—for the FBI ten years later, he'd seen enough of the Washington power brokers, and the women who wanted them, to last him a lifetime.

Cain stopped, taking a deep breath and reaching for a shingle from the stack piled beside him. Putting it into place, he reached into a small pocket of his leather tool belt for a long, galvanized nail. He thought about Jillian again, about that summer, about that night in the quiet underground garage. He'd never forget the look in her eyes when he'd reached into that elevator and grabbed that reporter off of her. She'd been terrified, and she'd looked at him as though he were some kind of knight in shining armor.

It was pathetic really, now that he thought of it, but after weeks of having Jillian look right through him, he'd been flattered and thrilled to have her attention. And when he'd led her through the underground garage to the waiting limousine, she'd clutched at him so tightly. Opening the door for her, she seemed nothing like one of the smug, cocky Hughes brats. She'd looked up at him with those eyes of hers, and to this day he would swear he had seen sadness in them, vulnerability. It had been so real, his heart had flipflopped in his chest. If it hadn't been for those beautiful eyes, he never would have done what he had. He never would have leaned down into that car and kissed her long and deep on the mouth.

Cain pounded the nail down into the roof, securing the shingle in place and reaching for another. It had been a stupid thing to do, kissing her like that. He'd crossed the line, and that wasn't allowed. But fate had stepped in and saved him from himself, changing everything. Because of his wife's sudden illness, Graham Hughes had dropped out of the race soon after that night in the parking garage, and Cain never saw Jillian Hughes again after that. It had been just a moment in his life, a brief interlude, and he should have forgotten it a long time ago.

Only, he didn't forget it. He'd thought of her again and again after that. And he'd been thinking of her six months later when he met Vicki at an embassy reception. Of course, Vicki's family was hardly as powerful or politically connected as the Hugheses had been, but they'd wanted to be. They'd traveled in the same wealthy, privileged circles. But unlike Jillian Hughes, who had barely looked at him until the night in the limo, Vicki had teased and flirted with him from the first moment they met.

Because Cain had been young and caught up in the lure of the wealth and power of Washington, he'd been easily taken in. An American royal princess had taken a fancy to him, and he'd let it go to his head. He and Vicki were married before he'd known what hit him. But after nearly a decade of watching what overindulgence, rampant ambition, alcoholism, and stubborn arrogance had done to his wife and to their marriage, he'd had enough. He left the Secret Service for the FBI. Busting drug dealers and infiltrating smuggling rings might not be as glamorous as looking after Washington's elite, but at least it was *real*.

Cain stood up, stretching the aching muscles of his back and arms. Squinting up at the merciless sun, he guessed it to be about noon. He'd had enough of this for the time being. After all, the bureau was paying him to watch the woman, not actually reroof her house.

From his perch high on the roof, he had a clear view of the landscape in all directions. In the distance he could see the languid activities of boaters and fishermen at the marina, poised at the confluence of Lighthouse Slough and the Mokelumne River. The waterways stretched wide and smooth out into the distance, the lazy current looking deceptively serene. But tides through the delta were known to be treacherous—rising and lowering in a matter of hours and creating powerful undercurrents that could pull down even the strongest swimmer.

But Cain's trained eye wasn't focused on undercurrents and refreshing waterways. He inspected the area, looking for anything that didn't belong.

He had to admit Jillian Hughes could have chosen much worse places to hide than this lost little oasis in the San Joaquin Delta. Life here was slow and relaxed. And even

though a variety of tourists, boaters and fishermen crowded
the rivers and sloughs during the summer months with their
armada of houseboats, ski boats, Jet Skis, sailboats and
luxury yachts, it would be hard for one of Donelli's hit men
to go for too long unnoticed. A New York wise guy would
stick out around here like Graham Hughes at a Guns n'
Roses concert.

Cain's eyes scanned the roads that cut through the farm-
lands, skirting the network of levees and crisscrossing the
countryside, until he spotted what he was searching for.
Along a lone levee road, a small, weathered VW bus was
parked, nestled in the tall tule grass, looking lost and forlorn. Lifting a hand, Cain signaled, and after a moment the
headlights of the bus blinked once, then once again in response.

Spence. His partner. Quietly watching from a distance,
running interference, canvasing the area and backing him
up. Spence protected him while he protected the woman.

Just then Cain heard the sounds of a television from inside the house, and the muscles in his neck and stomach
tightened again. He didn't have to worry about someone
sneaking up from behind as long as Spence was out there.
If he just could have figured out how to get someone to run
interference on the other end, he'd have been all set. But
unfortunately, Jillian Hughes was all his.

He walked across the roof to the ladder, climbing down
into the cool shade of the house. It had to be over a hundred degrees already, and the heat of the day wouldn't peak
for several hours yet. On the ground, he unhooked the
leather utility belt from around his waist and looped it over
his shoulder, then bent down to pick up the small ice chest
containing his lunch. Crossing the backyard and climbing
the levee behind the house, he walked out onto the dilapi-

dated dock built out over the cool waters of Lighthouse Slough.

Setting the ice chest down, he slid the tool belt off his shoulder and down beside him on the dock. Reaching up, he pulled off the red bandanna, shaking out his long, straight black hair. Kneeling down, he carefully rinsed the sweat-soaked bandanna in the river, squeezing out the excess water and draping it over a roughened post to dry, which in this heat would require only a short time. Reaching down into the water again, he splashed handfuls of cold water against his face, his hair, and against his bare chest, letting the droplets roll to his jeans and down to his boots, soaking them.

The water felt good against his overheated skin, soothing and peaceful. Maybe it was just the heat getting to him—making him think crazy, making him remember things he should have forgotten long ago. He sat down on the dock, leaning back against one of the posts, and reached for the ice chest.

Pulling out a cold can of ice tea, he took a long drink, emptying it in one gulp and crushing the can against the dock. He began to feel cooler and more in control. That's what he needed to concentrate on—not only *staying* cool, but *keeping* his cool, as well. Protecting the woman was a job—nothing more. Old memories weren't important. Besides, didn't they say familiarity bred contempt? Maybe after a summer with her, the mystique would finally fade and he'd be able to put those old memories to rest once and for all.

Jillian moved back a step, shifting her weight onto her tiptoes to get a better look over the top of the ruffly gingham kitchen curtain. After her fiasco the other morning with the gun, she wasn't about to risk his spotting her peeking at him through the window.

But she'd worried for nothing, she realized, peering out across the lawn to the levee that held back the waters of Lighthouse Slough. He wasn't looking in the direction of the house, anyway. He was too busy reaching down and splashing water into his face and down his chest.

She watched as the water made hundreds of tiny rivulets down his shiny, tanned skin and soaked the denim of his Levi's dark and wet. He'd taken the bandanna off, and his hair fell free and loose. With the water, he slicked it back away from his face.

She studied the dark brows, the thick, heavy lashes, and the cold, sapphire eyes and felt another faint twinge of familiarity. Brushing the feeling aside, she watched as he reached to splash another handful of water. Only, this time, his hand moved with the water across the hard, developed plane of his chest. For a moment she forgot about everything, unconsciously taking a step closer to the window and leaning over the sink for a better view. She had become mesmerized by the movement of his hand, following it across the dark skin, imagining the feel of that hot, smooth chest and wondering just how it would be to touch that kind of power and strength.

It was only when Cain suddenly straightened up and stretched his back that she realized how close to the window she was actually leaning. If he were to have looked up just then, he would surely have spotted her ogling him from inside.

Jillian reared back away from the window so quickly that she knocked her drinking glass from the tile counter and into the kitchen sink. The glass clanged noisily against the sink's porcelain, but luckily didn't break. Gratefully Cain made no sign of having heard the disturbance, or of having seen her spying at him through the window, and Jillian felt herself go weak with relief. She blushed hot all over, embarrassed and angry with herself. What had her so intent on making a fool of herself in front of this man?

She'd sat inside the house all morning, listening to him hammer and pound on the roof above her. With every bothersome bang, every swing of the hammer, he seemed to invade her thoughts. It had made her furious. She'd tried to busy herself, tried to get her mind on something else. But it seemed that no matter what she did, no matter where she went, she heard the steady rhythm of his hammering above her, as though he were driving himself deeper into her thoughts with every pounding blow.

Watching as he crushed his ice tea can against the dock, she squared her shoulders. She needed something to do, she decided. She couldn't spend her days watching this guy. She'd come to Lighthouse Landing to rest and relax, not peep on the hired help. She had to find something to occupy her time; she was used to being busy, used to having something to do. No wonder she couldn't keep her mind off the man outside—she had nothing else to think about.

"Well," she mumbled aloud, her hands planted firmly on her hips. "We'll fix that."

She stepped out onto the back porch, surveying the backyard with a thoughtful, critical eye. The brick walkway that ran the length of the yard and ended at the steps leading up the levee was orderly and meticulously maintained. The lawn had been edged neatly along its path, the huge valley oaks bathed the yard in shade, and the grass looked lush and green. But the large section of yard at the back, closer to the levee, looked neglected and unkempt. It was the plot that had once been her grandmother's flower garden, but it had long since been left to seed.

That was the answer, Jillian decided in a sudden burst of inspiration. She'd restore the garden. It would be the perfect summer project for her. Her grandmother had loved that garden and would be heartbroken to see how it had been neglected and overgrown. It wouldn't be an easy job, but it would keep her busy—busy enough, at least, to keep her mind off broad chests, strong arms and startling blue eyes.

She started out the screen door, then hesitated for a moment. She wished he wasn't sitting there. She didn't like the idea of poking around in the backyard with him watching. And even though the white cotton shell and khaki bermuda shorts she wore were hardly what she'd call alluring, she didn't want to do anything that might give him the idea she was hanging around trying to start something up with him.

She shook her head angrily. What was she thinking? This was *her* house, for heaven's sake. She wasn't about to let some man make her a prisoner in it—no matter how bare his chest was.

Taking a deep, determined breath, she swung the screen door open and marched down the back steps and out across the lawn. She tried to ignore Cain sitting on the dock, keeping her eyes focused instead on the small shed behind the garage, but she felt his gaze on her every step of the way.

The shed was run-down, and the paint along its weathered walls was peeling badly. Her grandmother had used it to store all her tools and garden supplies, but Jillian doubted if anyone had even been inside the place since Grandma Wells had died. Aware that Cain was watching her, she pulled at the door, but it didn't budge.

Wonderful, she groaned to herself. *Now what?* Grasping the rusted handle tighter, she pulled again. The last thing she wanted was for him to come down there and offer to help her. She pulled harder, causing the hinges to groan ominously. Finally, amongst the squeaking and groaning, the door flung open.

A musty cloud of dust and cobwebs billowed out into the light. Jillian reached about blindly in the darkness for the string of the light bulb that she remembered hung from the ceiling. Finding it, she gave it a jerk, and the small shed flooded with light.

The wooden shelves were lined with the dusty remains of clay pots, seed packets, fertilizer boxes and plant-food tins. On the dirt floor in the corner, there were large sacks of peat moss and potting soil, and a variety of gardening tools hung from the ceiling and lined the walls.

A rush of emotion choked Jillian, and tears stung her eyes. She suddenly had a clear vision of Grandma Wells with her wide-brimmed hat and gardening gloves, rustling through the small shed, transplanting seedlings and repotting plants. Clara Wells had been her mother's mother. She hadn't been wealthy or socially prominent, nor had she been part of the Washington political establishment like her father's family was. Grandma Wells had merely been a woman who had worked hard all her life, raised her family, and who had loved her grandchildren with all her heart.

Jillian remembered how she had felt when her mother had called to tell her Grandma Wells was dying. It had come as such a shock. Jillian couldn't imagine her grandmother ill. She had always been so vital, so full of life. Jillian had dropped everything in New York and caught the first flight to California, but it had been too late. Her grandmother had died an hour before the plane landed.

It had been a painful blow for Jillian. She'd shared a special bond with her grandmother, and that was no doubt the reason Grandma Wells had left the small house to her. But even though there had been family and friends to greet her when she'd arrived from New York, Jillian remem-

bered how empty the little house had felt without her
grandmother's presence. That was probably why she'd
stayed away for so long. She hadn't been able to stand the
emptiness.

Grandma Wells had been the only person Jillian could
remember who had never asked anything from her, who had
simply offered her love—no strings attached. And memories of that wonderful woman, and their summers together,
were some of the sweetest she had from her childhood.

Maybe that was why she felt so safe in her small house
now. It was as though Grandma Wells was still there, still
watching over her.

Brushing back the tears and the memories, Jillian surveyed the contents of the shed. Mindful of spiders, she
poked through boxes and checked on the condition of tools.
In her head, she made mental notes of what supplies she
would need, and began to chart how she would start work
on the garden.

Spotting an old, wide-blade hoe hanging on the wall, she
carefully lifted it down. Taking it with her, she left the shed
and carried it across the lawn to the overgrown garden. She
was aware of Cain still sitting on the dock eating his lunch,
and the interest with which he watched her. But she continued to ignore him—taking a special effort to appear nonchalant.

Jillian examined the garden, realizing the weeds and
overgrowth were even worse than she thought. But looking
closer, she was able to make out signs of the brick pathway
that had once twisted through the garden, and hidden beneath the mangy, overgrown vegetation, she found the small
stone bench she remembered sitting on as a kid.

Weeds had invaded everything, twisting and tangling, but
she found the thick stocks and flourishing limbs of wild
bushes and shrubs that had once been so meticulously at-

tended to by her grandmother. Halfheartedly, she lifted the hoe and brought it down on the dry, thick weed bed.

"You need to soak it first."

The sound of Cain's voice made her jump. Turning around, she squinted against the sun's glare to find him standing on the levee looking down at her. Lifting a hand, she shaded her eyes. "What did you say?"

"The ground," he explained. He stood silhouetted against the sun, his feet apart, his arms at his sides, and his hair hanging loosely about his face. "It's too hard." He slowly began climbing down the levee toward her. "You need to soak it first—get the ground good and wet—like it was the other day after the storm. Soften it up, then you do your weeding."

"I'm aware of that," Jillian said with authority, as though that was exactly what she had been doing. What was he, some kind of expert? "I was just checking things out—seeing how bad it was."

Cain stopped in front of her and let his blue gaze survey the disorder. "Pretty bad." His eyes moved to the hoe in her hand. "You're going to need a lot more than that to clean up this mess."

"I wasn't aware you were proficient in landscaping as well as roof repair," she snapped, not even attempting to hide the sarcasm in her voice.

"Don't have to be to figure that out," he shrugged, seemingly unaffected by the biting comment.

"Well, thank you for the suggestion." She bristled, picking up the hoe and turning to leave. "I think I know what to do."

"But then, I'd probably think about clearing away some of this brush first, before I even thought of hoeing," he mused, continuing with the thought as though she hadn't even spoken. "Get rid of some of the tangle, see what I had under there."

Jillian glared back at him, then stalked across the yard. *Typical,* she snorted as she headed for the back porch. *Just like that macho, know-it-all type to have to climb down from his perch and give the little lady advice, to assume she didn't know what she was doing. What a chauvinist. Why doesn't the man just mind his own business? What does he know about it, anyway?*

Chapter 3

"I've soaked the ground, got it good and wet, but I'm going to concentrate on clearing away some of the brush first—you know, see what's under all that before I even think about hoeing," Jillian explained casually to Tess as she waited for her purchases to be rung up. "I'm going to start in on that this morning."

"Well, it certainly sounds like you know what you're doing," Tess said, punching the keys of the cash register. The small store was empty, except for one other customer who browsed through a tabloid newspaper at the magazine rack. "Sounds like you inherited your grandma's instincts for gardening."

"Oh, I don't know about that." Jillian shrugged modestly. But inwardly she cringed, hoping Tess never mentioned anything like that to Cain.

"You know," Tess said, stopping suddenly and snapping her fingers, "I've got some nice garden gloves in aisle two. You might want to take a look."

"Thanks, I will," Jillian said, strolling down the aisle and finding them. Walking back, she added a couple of pairs to the rest of her things.

"I remember Clara out there in her floppy hat and garden gloves. She sure loved those flowers of hers." Tess smiled, shaking her head. "And her roses—I swear, I never saw any prettier."

"Yes, she had the touch all right," Jillian agreed, her eye catching the rack of magazines near the counter. Picking up a tabloid newspaper, she smiled at the other customer who stood nearby thumbing through a magazine. Just then, she glanced up and spotted a row of brightly colored sun visors hanging from a nearby display, Delta Daze emblazoned across the bill. Slipping the magazine back into the rack, she reached up and tossed one of the visors on to the pile, as well. She shrugged to Tess. "It's no floppy hat, but maybe it will help."

"Then you'll want some of this, too," Tess said, reaching up to a shelf behind the counter and pulling down a plastic bottle of sunscreen. "Otherwise you'll end up with a bad burn. And believe me, nothing makes these hot nights of ours worse than a sunburn."

"That reminds me, there's an air-conditioning unit in one of the living room windows. It ran when I switched it on, but it doesn't seem to cool the air. Is there someone around here who might be able to fix it? I wouldn't mind having some air-conditioning.This heat really gets to me."

"Why don't you have Cain take a look at it as long as he's out there," Tess suggested, searching a jar of mustard for the price tag. "Maybe he could get it working, and guys like him are always looking for ways to pick up a few extra dollars."

"No," Jillian said cautiously, wondering just how much Tess knew about her first encounter with Cain. "I don't think so."

"It might not take much," Tess went on thoughtfully. "You know, ours stopped working a while back and it turned out to be something really simple. Hank was able to fix it himself. I'd ask Cain if I were you. He'd probably be able to get it running. I'm sure he wouldn't mind." She hit the total button and read the results. "That's twenty-seven sixty."

"I don't know," Jillian said, making a face as she reached inside her purse. "We didn't exactly get off on the right foot. I don't think he'd be interested in doing me any favors."

Tess gave her a curious look and started to say something but was interrupted by the customer from the magazine rack. "Thanks," she said, as the man slid the money for his magazine across the counter. Turning back to Jillian, she started packing the groceries into a canvas shopping bag. "Why don't you ask him? All he can say is no. If he won't do it, tell me and I'll send Hank over to take a look." She tossed the receipt into the shopping bag and started to hand it to Jillian, then hesitated. Tess Ivers had dutifully followed the orders given to her by the FBI; she had sent their man Cain over to do work on the house, she'd agreed to the restrictions and to the secrecy—especially when they'd explained Jillian's safety could be at stake. But she couldn't help being curious. "How are things...with Cain I mean. The work going all right?"

"Fine, I guess," she said, opening her wallet and pulling out some money. "He seems to work hard enough."

"It's hard work," Tess lamented, slipping the money into the register and handing Jillian her change. "Especially in heat like this. I'm just glad you decided to go ahead and have the painting and repair work done now, though. Summer storms can be a nuisance, but it's the winter I was worried about. I don't think that roof would have lasted the year."

"Yeah, well..." Jillian mumbled, letting her words drift. She didn't like talking about Cain, even indirectly. The fact of the matter was, just thinking about him made her uncomfortable. They hadn't spoken as much as a word in the two days since that afternoon in the garden. He had mutely gone about his work, and she'd made a point of staying out of his way. She was still a little piqued by the way he'd stepped in uninvited and started giving her advice about the garden. Of course, the fact that she'd come to see the wisdom of his suggestions and was following his advice didn't change the fact that it had been a pushy and nervy thing to do.

Jillian visited with Tess awhile longer, then started the short walk back to the house. It was only a little after ten, but already the morning temperatures had started to climb. The sun was hot, and even the light exertion it took to walk the couple of blocks to the house had her body reacting. Beads of perspiration formed on her forehead and upper lip, and the thin material of her sleeveless cotton shell began to feel damp and clingy.

Reaching into her purse, she pulled out a tissue and patted at the moisture on her face. How did people stand this kind of heat? It zapped her energy and made her miserable. If only the small air conditioner at the house worked, it would make her life much more pleasant.

She thought of Tess's suggestion about talking to Cain. She really hated the thought of asking him. Besides, the way he felt about her, he would probably enjoy the thought of her being hot and uncomfortable in the stuffy little house.

He would no doubt get a perverse sort of pleasure in knowing she was miserable.

She grimaced and wiped at her face again. The heat was pretty bad, but it would have to get a lot hotter before she'd be willing to give him that kind of satisfaction. Besides, people around here got used to heat. She would, too.

As she walked, Jillian could hear the sounds of hammering in the distance, and she immediately pictured Cain on the roof. How he could stand being up there in the blazing sun, she'd never know. Even though he arrived early every morning and had several hours to work when the sun's rays weren't quite so harsh, for most of the day he labored in scorching heat. It was little wonder his skin had been baked to a dark mahogany.

She thought about how he had splashed himself with the cool river water the other afternoon. He'd taken to cooling himself in that fashion several times during the workday. Could she help it that she just happened to be looking out the kitchen window whenever that happened? It wasn't as though she wanted to watch him. Of course, what would be so wrong if she did? The last time she looked, there was no law that prevented a healthy American female from admiring the sheer physical beauty of a healthy American male— even if he was pushy, arrogant and unfriendly. But despite the rationalization, her voyeurism still embarrassed her.

Reaching the house, she turned up the drive. Cain appeared over the peak of the roof—tools dangling, jeans dirty, boots scuffed and chest bare. Already the red bandanna around his forehead was soaked with sweat, and his bare skin gleamed, dark and shiny.

Spotting her, he stopped, staring down at her with clear blue eyes. He looked almost surprised to see her standing there, and immediately his expression changed. The muscle at his jaw clenched tight, and the line at his brow deepened.

"Hi," he said suddenly, making it sound more like a challenge than a salutation.

"H-hello," she answered back, clearly startled. For the last two days he'd all but ignored her, content to go about his business in a purposeful silence and barely giving her so much as a passing glance. She hadn't expected him to take any notice her, much less have anything to say.

"Need some help with that?"

Jillian actually felt her jaw drop as she followed his gaze to the canvas grocery bag in her hand. "No, no it's fine. I've got it, thanks," she answered vacantly, feeling a little dazed. Her surprise had moved a full degree closer to incredulity. What was she suppose to do now? Clearing her throat, she daintily wiped at the perspiration on her forehead again. "Uh...how's...uh...the work going?"

"Okay," he said easily, drawing an arm across his forehead. He rested a hand on his hip, and did something then that was the biggest surprise of all. He smiled. Well, almost. It wasn't a broad, full, easy smile. It was more like a small, cursory attempt—as if his face was unaccustomed to such activity. But despite the pitiful attempt, it was enough to soften the rugged features of his face. "Actually it's slow and hot. I guess I better get back to it."

Bending down to pick up a stack of shingles, Cain gave her a small nod and walked over the peak of the house and went back to work. Jillian stood in the driveway, staring up at the spot where he'd stood and wondering if she'd just imagined the whole thing. She remembered the old saying about being knocked down by a feather, and knew it had never been more true than at that moment. She was flabbergasted. If he'd leapt off the roof, swept her up in his arms and danced her around the driveway like Fred Astaire, she couldn't have been more surprised.

Bewildered, she walked slowly into the house and began putting her groceries away. What had happened? What had caused the sudden turnaround?

Paranoia suddenly struck. Had Tess talked to him? Had they been discussing her? Had Tess told him she'd been complaining about him? Had she told him to be nicer to her? But even as possibilities popped into her head, she dismissed them as outlandish. Tess wasn't meddlesome, and Jillian had a feeling no one could intimidate Cain into doing anything he didn't want to.

But she still couldn't help wondering what had caused the sudden change in Cain's behavior. Had something happened while she was at the store? Did he want something from her? Time off? More pay?

Finishing up in the kitchen, she walked back to the bedroom and searched through her drawers for something that would be more suitable for work in the garden. None of the clothes she'd brought from New York were particularly old, and when she'd been planning her trip and packing, she hadn't exactly anticipated she'd be working in a garden. But eventually she found a bright, oversize fluorescent green T-shirt she wasn't particularly crazy about, and the matching pair of cotton shorts, and decided to designate them as her work clothes.

Changing quickly, she listened to the hammering on the roof above her. She had to admit that a decrease in the hostilities between her and Cain would make the atmosphere around here a little better. But the sudden shift in attitude still made her uneasy.

She pulled her hair back into a long ponytail and secured it with an elastic band, then headed back through the house. In the kitchen, she stopped long enough to slather her arms and legs with the sunscreen, then pick up the new garden gloves and visor she had just purchased and head outside.

She still didn't trust him, she decided as she pushed open the screen door, but that funny little smile of his had been rather nice, and it was a lot nicer than the icy glares she'd been getting for the last two days. Still, she couldn't help wondering: What did he want from her?

"It's a perfect opportunity," Spence pointed out again, pausing to take a deep breath. "I think it might be worth considering."

Cain didn't have to see his partner's face to know that he struggled to hold in his frustration—his voice was filled with it. Not that Cain blamed him, really. If the shoe were on the other foot, Cain wasn't so sure he could be as calm, or so diplomatic as Spence. But that was Spence—easygoing and tactful. Only, Cain knew even Spence had his limits, and Cain was pushing them.

From a pay phone at the marina, Spence had called him on the small cellular phone he kept hidden in his tool belt along with the Glock 17 automatic pistol he kept with him at all times. Spence had called to let him know Jillian was on her way back to the house. While browsing through the magazine rack in the Iverses' store, he'd overheard a conversation between Tess and Jillian, and he thought something he'd learned from that conversation could prove useful to them.

Cain had listened to Spence's information, but found himself reluctant to act upon it. He'd liked the way things had been the last couple of days, and wasn't anxious for them to change. Cain and Jillian had settled into a comfortable pattern—he did his job, and she stayed out of his way. Sure there was some strain between them, but he was comfortable with it. It allowed him to watch over her, protect her, do his job and not let his personal feelings of hostility or antagonism get in the way.

Normally when he worked undercover, he was on the lookout for any excuse that would bring him closer to his subject, anything that might enable him to get to know them better and get them to trust him. It just made the job easier.

And now Jillian needed her air conditioner fixed. It seemed like a perfect opportunity. Cain could step in and save the day, come off smelling like a rose. She would trust him, rely on him, and that would just make the job of protecting her a lot easier. But Cain wasn't looking for anything that would put him closer to Jillian Hughes. When it came to *this* particular subject, *this* particular woman, he preferred to keep his distance. Unfortunately, there was no way he could make Spence understand that, short of getting into the past and talking about a lot of things he'd rather not talk about. Besides, he wasn't convinced what Spence was suggesting would work.

Of course, Cain wasn't exactly surprised when Spence told him Jillian had said the two of them had "gotten off on the wrong foot." Yeah, you might say that. He remembered that damn SIG all too well, and looking down the barrel of a cannon like that hadn't exactly done much to get things started on an up note. And it had been hard enough for him to accept that he'd lowered his guard long enough for her to have gotten the drop on him like that, but the fact that Spence had watched the whole episode through binoculars from the VW bus had only made it worse. Spence hadn't stopped ribbing him yet.

But despite the fact that their first encounter had been less than desirable, he wasn't sure Spence's plan would work, anyway. Some people you just couldn't be friendly to, and he was beginning to think Jillian Hughes was one of those people.

The woman was stubborn and bullheaded, and he doubted she would ask for anyone's help. He'd tossed down an olive branch two days ago, but she'd all but spit in his face. He'd tried to be nice when he saw her whacking away at the dry, hard ground with that puny hoe. He'd offered her a few friendly suggestions on how to go about starting work on the garden, and her cool, unfriendly response had practically left him frostbitten.

"You don't know the woman like I do, Spence," Cain said, leaning back against the side of the house. "It just won't work on her."

"Well, you never can tell," Spence reminded him. "You know what they say about a little kindness."

"I'll think about it," Cain mumbled finally, flipping the mouthpiece on the small phone closed and slipping it into his tool belt. He climbed back up the ladder and walked out across the roof. Waves of heat rose up off the composition green and he squinted up at the blazing sun. It wasn't even noon yet, and already the sun was scorching.

So, she wanted her air-conditioning fixed. That surprised him. He wouldn't have thought the heat bothered her. She had looked so cool and collected when she'd left the house earlier, not a hair out of place. It was as though she were impervious to the warm weather and hot sun. Everything about her screamed money and class—from the clothes she wore, to her long, shiny hair and lush, rich complexion. Creamy white shirt, white shorts, leather sandals, tortoiseshell sunglasses and skin so smooth it made him want to salivate.

How many times in the last two days had he sat on this roof and listened to the sounds of water running in the tub or in the shower? Pictures had come alive in his brain, and his thoughts had run rampant. As the sun pounded down on him, his mind had been pummeled with images of Jillian in a bath or in a shower—of the cool water swirling around her, beading and sheeting against her smooth, golden skin. He pictured her hair, dark and long, falling wet and slick down her back.

The heat suddenly became unbearable, and he felt his body's feeble attempt to safeguard him from it. Beads of sweat materialized all over, gathering at his neck and trickling slowly down his back. Weren't the sun's relentless rays enough without having to contend with the overheated images of her in his brain, as well?

Spence wanted Cain to get closer to her. Spence suggested he be nice, be friendly, get her to like him, to trust him. Couldn't Spence see what he wanted was impossible?

Of course he didn't, Cain realized as he swiped at the sweat running into his eyes. He picked up the hammer and angrily brought it down on a nail. He was suddenly unaccountably and uncontrollably furious—but not as a result of Spence's suggestions or his lack of understanding, but because he was right. Cain knew what he had to do, and whether he liked it or not, he would have to do it. He was a professional, and being a professional meant he had to put his feelings aside and concentrate on the job he had been assigned to do.

And his job was to watch Jillian Hughes. He was supposed to stick close to her, watch her and protect her. It didn't matter if the woman had a way of getting under his skin, if she invaded his thoughts and made him crazy. What mattered was that he did his job—and if that meant being nice to her, then so be it.

But when he stood up and walked over the peak of the house and saw her strolling up the driveway, his stomach twisted uneasily in his gut. He cursed Graham Hughes again and the circumstances that had brought him to her doorstep. And the job that made it impossible for him to leave.

*   *   *

Jillian reached into the camellia bush and grabbed at a handful of long, errant honeysuckle vines that had all but taken over the small shrub. Holding tight, she pulled the vines free, dragging them across the garden to the growing pile of refuse she'd collected.

Tossing the armload of vines onto the pile, she stopped and carefully surveyed the work she had done. She'd been laboring steadily for the last two hours, but it looked as though she'd barely made a dent in the overgrowth. Still, judging from the considerable pile of garden refuse beside her, she was definitely making progress.

Looking down at herself, she slowly shook her head. She was a mess, drenched in perspiration, clothes clinging to her overheated body. She couldn't remember ever having been so warm, and she knew she'd never perspired so much in her life—not even when she'd given her closing arguments to the jury in the Donelli trial. Still, she felt wonderful. There was something very satisfying about working in the garden, about clipping and weeding, getting her hands in the dirt. She hadn't thought about the trial, or Jeff, or Donelli, or hit men in hours, and the respite had been wonderful.

Slipping off her visor, she wiped an arm across her brow and crossed the lawn to where the garden hose hung on the faucet beside the garage. Turning the spout, she held up the end of the hose and let the water trickle down. When the warm standing water in the hose had cascaded out, and the flow turned cool, she carefully leaned over and put the water to her lips and took a long, slow drink.

The water felt even better than it tasted against her hot, dry lips. She let the cool and refreshing drizzle wet her lips, then moved it to dampen her cheeks, then finally threw caution to the wind and gave into temptation completely, turning the small, rejuvenating flow over her head and letting it trickle down her entire body.

Shaking off the excess water and pushing her wet hair back from her face, she slowly straightened. Water had poured everywhere, drenching her T-shirt and causing the wet material to cling tightly, but she didn't care. The water had strengthened and invigorated her, and she started back across the yard ready to begin work again.

Slipping the visor and garden gloves back on, she picked up a pair of long-handled clippers and went to work on the honeysuckle once more. Its leafy vines were by far the most densely overgrown, having invaded a good portion of the south end of the garden. By clipping and pulling, she slowly worked her way from one corner to the other. She stopped only long enough to drag the long vines free and add them to the refuse pile.

The mound had grown to be quite sizable, and after tossing the last armload on top, she picked up the clippers and headed for the garden shed. Returning the clippers to their hook on the wall, she rummaged through the shed until she found the ball of twine she'd seen earlier. Grabbing it, she tossed it into the old wheelbarrow and wheeled it back across the yard. She'd decided she would bundle what vines and foliage she could, then call it a day.

But bundling the pile and securing it with the twine turned out to be more difficult than she'd anticipated. The unruly vines sprawled in all directions, and she struggled and strained to contain them into parcels small enough to wrap with the twine. It seemed to take forever, and her tired arms became scratched and scraped. She was grappling with a particularly large bundle, when she felt her hold starting to slip.

"Here, I've got it."

She spun around at the sound of Cain's voice. The whole bundle would have given way if it hadn't been for his arms reaching out and relieving her of the load.

"Thanks," she mumbled, flustered and surprised to find him standing there. She quickly reached for the twine and helped him tie off the stack. Watching as he tossed the bundle into the wheelbarrow with the others, she quickly reached up and ran a hand through her hair. She hated to think what she must look like with her flaming cheeks and damp, soiled clothing.

"You've done a lot," Cain observed, resting his arms on his hips and surveying the garden. He glanced back at her, trying hard not to notice how her heightened color made her eyes sparkle and her skin look smooth and satiny.

"It's a start," she said nervously, feeling ridiculously pleased by the comment. She was grateful that he'd put on his white T-shirt and she wasn't subjected to his bare chest at such close range. "Bundling this stuff is the worst part, though."

"Want some help?"

She was sure the look on her face must have been almost comical, for all she could do for one long moment was stand and stare. "Uh...no, that's all right," she stammered, pulling herself back to consciousness with a little shake of her head. "I'm just going to take it slow and easy."

"But we could have this done in no time," he said, unfastening his leather tool belt and carefully placing it in the shade of the tree. He reached down and gathered up an armload of the disorderly vines and neatly formed them into a bundle. Holding it out for her to tie off, he arched a brow. "Ready?"

Jillian vaulted into action, feeling clumsy as she struggled to wrap the twine around the bundle he held. "You really don't have to do this," she insisted, amazed at how easily he maneuvered the gangly vines into neat, tidy bunches. "You've been working on the roof—you must be exhausted."

He shrugged, tossing down the bundle and gathering up more vines for another. "I don't mind. Besides, it's getting too hot up there, anyway. I need a break."

Jillian nodded her head as though she understood, but the fact was she didn't. She hurried to keep up with him, cutting twine and tying off the bundles. She wondered if maybe there had just been too many people in her life who had wanted something from her, or that maybe it was just that she'd been a prosecutor for so long that she'd become overly suspicious, but she couldn't help wondering for the second time that day why he was being so nice to her.

Did he know who she was? Was that what brought about the sudden change in attitude? Was there something he thought her family's money and power could do for him?

She glanced at him out of the corner of her eye. Somehow she had a hard time picturing someone like Cain being impressed with the Washington social scene and big money politics. He didn't seem like the kind of man who would find much need to kiss up to anyone.

But he had been right about the bundling. With the two of them working together, the pile quickly began to disappear. Jillian marveled at how strong he was, how his muscular arms and shoulders managed the unwieldy job almost effortlessly. She hurried about, wrapping the bundles with twine and tying them off, all the while continuing to watch Cain.

"That wasn't so bad," he said when they finally finished. He tossed the last of the bundles into the wheelbarrow with the others and carefully lifted up the handles. "Where do you want me to put these?"

Placing a hand on the top of the bundles to help balance them, Jillian led him to an area behind the fence near an old incinerator and helped him unload the wheelbarrow.

"I'll burn these after they've had a chance to dry out," she said as she turned and started back for the garden.

Cain nodded his head, following behind her with the empty wheelbarrow. "That'll be a hot job."

Jillian nodded, blotting the top of her lip with the back of her soiled garden glove. She'd long since passed the point of being concerned about how she might look. "Yeah, maybe I should save that for some cool evening."

As they passed the shed, Cain stopped and propped the old wheelbarrow against the wall. He pointed to the worn rubber wheels and rusted bucket. "This thing has seen better days. It's been used a lot."

"It has," Jillian agreed, remembering all the times Grandma Wells had pushed her about the yard in it. "My grandmother loved gardening. When she was alive she used to keep the garden and the yard in meticulous condition."

"This was her place?" He knew her entire history by heart, but the questions were all part of the illusion he wanted to create, all part of the job.

Jillian nodded her head. "Yeah, she left it to me when she died. I don't get much of a chance to come out here very often."

"You're not from around here then?" He tried to picture cosmopolitan Jillian Hughes being satisfied living permanently in a little backwater burg like Lighthouse Landing.

She shook her head. Could it be he really didn't know who she was, that he hadn't recognized the name? "No, I live in New York. Tess and Hank look after the place for me. I'm just here for the summer."

Cain nodded his head. "That explains why I thought they owned the place."

Being reminded of the mix-up that led to their disastrous first encounter, Jillian stiffened. "Uh...yeah, look, I apologize again for that business the other morning. I guess I've been a little...jumpy lately."

"I guess," he said dryly, then shrugged. "But no harm done."

"Well, believe it or not, I don't usually go around pointing guns at strangers."

He looked at her, his clear blue eyes full of skepticism. "You looked awfully comfortable with that thing. Are you a cop or something?"

She laughed a little, feeling ridiculously pleased that he'd noticed her expertise. She reached up and slipped off the visor and pulled at the elastic band holding her ponytail. With a slight shake of her head, the long hair tumbled past her shoulders and down her back. "No, but a friend of mine was. He taught me how to handle a gun."

"Was?" he asked, watching as her thick hair fell down her back. He tried hard not to think about its rich color, or how soft it looked.

"I beg your pardon?"

"You said he was a cop."

"Yes, he was killed."

"I see," Cain mumbled, remembering the file. Ron Larsen, NYPD, the one great love of her life. "Well, this isn't New York. Hopefully you won't have any need for a gun around here."

"Yeah, hopefully," she said cryptically, the smile slowly leaving her face. Suddenly uncomfortable with having said so much, she cleared her throat. "Well, I really appreciate the help." She stuck her hand out, offering it for him to shake. "Thank you very much."

He gazed down at her extended hand a moment before covering it with his own. "Anytime."

Chapter 4

It had been such a nice dream, relaxed and quiet. Jillian had felt so comfortable, so at ease. She hadn't worried about what was proper or what was right, what she looked like or what would happen next. She'd just enjoyed herself, and after nights of dreaming about guns and trials and people lurking in the darkness, it had felt good not to be afraid.

But she was awake now, lying in the darkness feeling the perspiration gather along her hot skin. She pushed the sheet off her, staring up at the ceiling, thinking about the dream, wondering what had caused her to have it.

She'd been sitting on a beach, watching the ebb and flow of the waves. The breeze had been cool in her hair, and the sand warm against her bare feet. She hadn't been concerned about being out there in the open, hadn't been afraid of who might be watching from the cliffs, who might sneak up from behind. She'd felt safe, secure, and she'd felt that way because of the man who sat beside her.

Cain.

It wasn't as though he'd touched her or anything. He'd just sat beside her, occasionally glancing in her direction. She remembered the crystal blue of his eyes—a blue she had once thought so cold, so unfeeling. But there was nothing cold in them now. They were striking and clear behind his dark lashes. She'd remembered feeling that inkling of recognition again, but it had only been for an instant. What she really remembered had been that smile, that peculiar little half smile like the one he'd given her when she'd walked up the drive yesterday. That smile that had looked almost painful for him to effect, but had increased the steady cadence of her heart nonetheless.

She thought about him, about how he'd acted yesterday, his offer to help, the way he'd looked. To say he'd been friendly might be an overstatement. He'd been nice to her, in an awkward sort of way, but she suspected that to a man like Cain, those feeble attempts had been tantamount to being effervescent.

She didn't know him very well, but in her line of work she saw a lot of different kinds of people, and it didn't take a genius to figure out he was someone who operated on an economy of words. He wasn't the kind of man who would sit for hours and bend a woman's ear about what he thought or how he felt. He was the kind of person she hated to get on the stand, the kind she had to pull the information out of—bit by painful bit.

Jillian thought for a moment. Would Cain be that way about everything in his life? Would a woman have to pull the emotion out of him? Would she have to coddle and cajole him? Flatter and coax? Would he be free with his feelings, or was he the kind of man who would tell a woman he loved her once, and then never feel the need to say it again?

She shook her head, twisting her legs about restlessly on the bed. What was the matter with her? Why would she even bother to wonder about Cain and his emotions?

She pushed her hair up, spreading it across the pillow, and letting the faint dawn breeze cool the back of her neck. She thought about what Tess had said, about asking him to look at the air conditioner. At the time, things had been so strained between them, she wouldn't have thought it could get warm enough for her to consider asking him. But after yesterday... well, she'd think about it.

Sitting up in bed, she heard the steady hum of an engine outside. She actually *felt* the low rumbling before she heard it, thinking the gentle vibration might be the precursor to an earthquake or something equally devastating.

She glanced quickly at the nightstand drawer, considering the gun, but deciding against it. After the other morning, she thought it was probably wise to exercise a little more discretion when it came to the SIG.

Getting up, she tiptoed out of the bedroom and down the hall to the living room. Peeking outside, she looked out across the deserted driveway, realizing only then that the engine sound wasn't coming from the front of the house at all.

Moving quickly back through the house, she silently sprinted across the worn linoleum floor in the kitchen, and carefully peered out the back window. Outside, pulling up beside the old dock along the levee, was a boat. Its running lights shone brightly through the faint morning mist, and the low rumble of its engine sounded like the purr of some giant predatory cat.

"What in the world...?" Jillian mumbled aloud, blinking and hardly believing her eyes. She couldn't imagine who would be tying up to her grandmother's dilapidated old dock, but she didn't have time to wonder long. Even before her curiosity could turn to fear or concern, or even apprehension, she saw Cain step down from the deck and loop the tow rope around one of the weathered wooden posts.

Jillian didn't know much about boats, but she'd spent enough time water-skiing as a kid to know the engines on this one had sounded powerful. Somehow, if she'd had to picture Cain piloting something around the twisting delta waterways, she could have expected it to be something like this. The twenty-foot runabout had a small cabin in the bow, and was outfitted with a dark blue delta canvas enclosing the entire starboard end.

She watched as he continued to secure the tie lines and the moorings, feeling the muscles in her stomach tighten. Why would he tie his boat up to her dock? And from the way he was battening down the hatches, she got the uneasy impression he had every intention of keeping it there for a while.

Jillian ran back to the bedroom and quickly slipped into her robe. She thought about how helpful he'd been to her yesterday, how nice. Was this what he'd been after, a place to berth his boat? Was that why he'd changed so suddenly? Was that what he wanted from her?

She stormed back through the kitchen and out the back door. By the time she ran down the porch steps and charged across the yard, her anger had peaked and she was furious.

So, he needed a place for his boat, did he? He just thought he could throw a few nice words around and look at her once or twice with those blue eyes and she'd just give him what he wanted.

She pushed the hair back away from her face as she climbed up the levee and stormed out onto the deck. If he thought he was going to sweet-talk her with a few looks and a couple of half-smiles, brother, did he have another think coming.

Cain saw Jillian coming this time, and he was ready. She might have caught him off guard once, but he wasn't about to let that happen again. He looped the end of the rope around the post a couple more times, then slowly straightened up.

"What's this?" she demanded, hands on her hips and gesturing to the boat with a nod of her head.

"Good morning," he said quietly, wishing like hell he hadn't noticed how the morning sun behind her silhouetted her shapely form through the thin robe and pajamas.

"Good morning," she conceded with a deep sigh, thrown just a little by the simple, friendly greeting. "What's this thing doing here?"

"It's my boat," he told her, as though that answered everything.

"I assumed it was your boat. What's it doing here?"

"It's floating in the water next to your dock—what's it look like?" he said testily. It was stupid, but he'd actually forgotten just how much he disliked that spoiled-rich-girl manner of hers. Didn't she know it was hard enough for him to be nice to her without her copping an attitude? "Are you going to get your gun now and shoot it?"

Jillian bristled at the remark. "What's it doing here?"

"What do you mean?"

"I mean, what do you intend to do with it here?"

"Look, lady, I don't know what your problem is, but I have to get to work." He reached for his tools and ice chest from inside the boat and pushed past her.

"Wait a minute," she demanded, feeling a little foolish when she realized she'd actually stomped her foot. "You can't leave this thing here."

He stopped and looked back at her. Spence was a fool to think anyone could be nice to this woman for very long. "Why not?"

"Why not?" Jillian repeated, taking a deep breath, wanting nothing more than to tell him exactly why not. Unfortunately, at the moment she had no idea why not. "Because...because you didn't ask me. *That's* why not!"

"Oh, I get it," Cain said sarcastically, putting his hand on his hip and nodding his head. "I didn't get your permission. Is it okay if I just ask, or would you prefer that I get down on my knees?"

Jillian crossed her arms over her chest and gave him a cool look. "I don't know what kind of women you're used to dealing with, but this is not going to work with me."

Cain's forehead wrinkled in the middle as he scowled at her, confused. "What's not going to work?"

"That pathetic attempt of yours yesterday to be charming."

"My pathetic..." He shook his head and nearly laughed. "Lady, I think you need to go back to New York. We're not used to crazy people around here."

"Oh, and all that nice stuff, helping me and everything? That wasn't just to soften me up so I'd let you keep this boat here?"

Cain dropped his chin to his chest, shaking his head slowly. "You're paranoid, you know that, lady? Paranoid and neurotic."

"I'm also the one paying you."

Cain's head reared up, feeling as annoyed and as insulted by her suspicions as he would if he really were just the roofer and handyman she believed him to be. "You want to fire me?"

Jillian held her ground against his icy gaze, but she flinched inwardly. "I want to know what this boat is doing here."

"Fine," he said, turning around and stalking back out onto the dock where she stood. Staring down into her eyes, he suddenly realized what he'd thought was stubbornness was really apprehension, and his mind flashed back to a moment in that underground parking garage fifteen years ago. Seeing the same softness, the same vulnerability now as he had then, had every defense mechanism in his entire body going off. He wasn't about to let himself be taken in by a pair of velvet-brown eyes again.

"Okay, look," he said, making no effort to keep the displeasure from his voice. "I brought the boat because I live on it. I usually like to tie up at job sites when I can because it's just a lot more convenient. I can get started earlier in the mornings, work some in the evening. It's just easier, and it makes the job go faster. I guess I should have checked it out with you first, but I didn't think it was any big deal. But if you don't want it here, fine, I'll move it. If you want rent, I'll pay it. If you want to fire me, I'll leave. But whatever you want, lady, make up your mind quick. That sun isn't getting any cooler."

Jillian wished at that moment she would wake up and find this whole thing had been just another dream. Unfortunately, that wasn't going to happen. She'd done it again, she'd gone off half-cocked, she'd overreacted, and she'd made a mess of everything. She'd made a complete fool of herself, and the only thing that surprised her was that she'd managed to do it this time without a gun in her hand.

Cain had called her crazy, neurotic, paranoid. And standing there at dawn in her pajamas, stomping her feet and acting like some kind of indignant prima donna, she'd have to agree about the crazy part. What else could the man think? She'd acted like a suspicious, gun-toting lunatic ever since she met him. And if the proud Hughes tradition of believing everyone was out to get something from you wasn't neurotic and paranoid, what was?

The way she felt was beyond embarrassment. And there wasn't even any way she could begin to explain it all to him. What was she supposed to say? She was a little on edge because some creep rotting away in a holding cell somewhere had ordered a hit on her? Or that he'd have to forgive her for acting a little nutty but she was having difficulty dealing with the fact that her husband had slept with every woman he could get his hands on?

Amazed at her own stupidity, she dropped her hands to her side and drew in a deep breath. She couldn't look right at him just yet, preferring instead to focus her gaze on a spot somewhere beyond his left shoulder. "The boat's fine, Cain. Look, let's just forget all this, okay? Go to work."

Cain watched as Jillian walked past him and headed back to the house. He wasn't sure what he'd expected from her, but this quiet capitulation hadn't been it. Right or wrong, Jillian Hughes was a fighter, but there had been no fight left in the woman who'd just passed him.

Of course, if he had any brains at all he'd be breathing a sigh of relief. He had no right taking those kinds of chances, no right putting the assignment in jeopardy. He'd acted like an inexperienced rookie just now, getting insulted and letting his personal feelings get in the way. He'd let her get him angry. If she would have actually fired him just now, if she would have told him to take his boat and his tools and get the hell out of here, the whole assignment would have gone up in smoke. It had been a stupid thing to do—stupid and unprofessional.

Taking his tools and starting down the dock to the levee, he cursed quietly under his breath. He knew this would happen. He knew if he let his feelings start getting in the way, he'd screw up. It had been a mistake to just show up here with the boat. All he'd managed to do was put her on the defensive and destroy any progress he'd made yesterday.

He shook his head, thinking how she'd described his efforts to be friendly. Pathetic, she had called them. Damn, the lady had a way with words. She had a way of taking them and plowing them right into the dust. No wonder Donelli had ordered a hit on her. He'd probably been little more than hamburger after she'd finished with him on the stand.

Cain climbed up the ladder and walked across the roof of the house. As he fastened his leather tool belt around his waist, he glanced across the yard to the boat moored at the dock. Yeah, the boat had been a mistake. They never should have tried to surprise her with it like that, but it wasn't as though there had been a lot of time to consider all the ramifications.

Late yesterday evening, word had gotten to them that a drive-by shooting had occurred at the home of the man who had served as jury foreman at the Donelli trial. There was nothing that would indicate this had been anything other than what it appeared—a random act of violence. But it had gotten Graham Hughes edgy. Despite Cain's continued assurances that their peripheral surveillance and night stakeouts were sufficient to ensure her safety, the senator had decided he wanted someone close to his niece twenty-four hours a day. Cain and Spence had spent most of the night scrambling to come up with a way to do that, short of going to the woman with the truth. Showing up with the boat had been risky, but they hadn't much choice.

He looked down at the roof, surveying the work he'd already completed. As a roofer, it was probably a good thing he worked for the FBI. He reached for a stack of new shingles and carried them to the spot on the roof where he'd stopped yesterday. His workday was only beginning, but already his back protested the hunched position and his arms cramped and stiffened. He was beginning to think he was actually going to finish reroofing this house.

Cain fitted a new shingle into place and reached inside his belt for a nail. Hammering it into place, he thought about how he had worked in the same spot the day before and watched as Jillian quietly labored away in the garden below.

When she'd first waltzed out there looking so cool and together in that stylish outfit, he wouldn't have given her fifteen minutes in that sun. But he had to hand it to her, she'd pruned and trimmed and chopped for most of the afternoon, and she'd looked anything but cool by the time she'd walked across the lawn and took a drink from the hose.

His jaw clenched tight, remembering how the water had trickled down the smooth column of her neck to her shirt, soaking it and making the material dark. It clung to her body, outlining with aching clarity just how lovely a woman she had become. She was a far cry from a blossoming teenager now. She had bloomed to full splendor, her breasts soft and full, her waist narrow, and her hips curved and round.

She'd reveled in the cool stream of water, drenching her face and hair. It had surprised him to see her behave that way. She'd always seemed so cool, so restrained, but there had been nothing restrained in her enjoyment. He wouldn't have expected her to be so uninhibited.

And he hadn't exactly been ready for his reaction to seeing her, either. He knew when he took the assignment, he was still vulnerable to the lady. There were old memories there, old haunts. And one of the same things that had attracted him to her fifteen years ago still made him susceptible to her now. She was—then and now—a beautiful woman. Men are attracted to beautiful women, and he was, after all, a man.

But it wasn't until he'd seen her impetuously—almost wantonly—enjoying the cool stream of water against her overheated skin that he realized what he felt for this woman was nothing like what he'd felt for that young college coed all those years ago. He'd been infatuated with her back then. She'd represented something to him, something he thought he wanted, a life-style he thought he admired.

But standing on the roof yesterday and watching as the cool water from the hose splashed against her silky skin, watching as the color rose in her cheeks and the bracing wetness soaked through her shirt to reveal the true beauty of her, Cain realized what he felt now had nothing to do with infatuation.

He wanted her. His entire body had reacted to the picture of her standing there. He'd wanted to climb down that ladder and grab her to him, pull her into his arms and lick those sparkling droplets from her skin. He didn't care anymore about political power and family wealth; he was no longer impressed by the name or the recognition. All he'd wanted at that moment was her, Jillian, in his arms—touching, kissing, stirring those ageless flames and finding her special magic.

Cain slammed the hammer down hard on the shingle, which splintered and cracked. He wished he could splinter and crack the image of her in his mind as easily, shatter it so that he could no longer make it out.

Pausing a moment, he rubbed his tired eyes. He'd barely gotten any sleep last night. Things had been a little frantic after they'd gotten word about the shooting and Hughes's insistence that they step up their surveillance. He and Spence had stayed up most of the night keeping lookout over the house.

But at the same time he'd been almost relieved by all the upheaval in the night. There had been very little time to be alone, very little time to rest. The image of that wet shirt clinging to Jillian's body kept coming back to him when he'd tried to catch some sleep. He'd lain in the back of Spence's old VW bus and tried to catch a few winks, but it had been no use. Every time he'd closed his eyes, she'd been there—skin wet, clothes clinging. So he'd welcomed the chaos and confusion. It had helped him to keep his mind off the image of her—the image, and the memory of how it had made him feel.

Maybe that's what had him reacting so stupidly this morning, what had him forgetting his training, his professionalism, his job. She'd come storming down that dock in those flimsy pajamas with the sunlight at her back filtering right through them, and every cell in his body had come alive. After the night he'd had, that was the last thing he'd needed to see.

Inside he heard the water in the bathroom running, and his mind shifted suddenly. His whole body tensed as he imagined those flimsy pajamas—tossed and crumpled in a heap on the bathroom floor—and that smooth, perfect skin of hers made wet and slick from the water.

His mouth went dry, and despite the fact that the morning sun was mild, his body broke out in a full sweat. He picked up the hammer and slammed it against the broken shingle again. Damn Donelli for his threats and intimidations, damn Graham Hughes for getting him mixed up in all of this, and damn the job that demanded he stay close to the woman. How was he to talk with her, be nice to her, spend time with her, when every instinct told him to run for cover? How was he supposed to ignore his feelings and forget the woman when he was practically tied to her side by duty?

But the same instincts that made Cain want to run also made him know that just running from the woman wouldn't get her out of his head. It would be a long time before he forgot the image of her in the T-shirt, before thoughts of her and fantasies of her would no longer interfere with his sleep. And the longer he spent hammering nails into her roof, the longer he spent being nice and making small talk, the longer he spent watching and waiting, the longer it would take him to forget her once this was all over.

Jillian reached into the small stall shower built into the tile bathroom beside the old-fashioned tub and turned on the faucets. She wasn't in the mood for a bath. Baths were meant for lingering and relaxation, and she was too keyed up for either of those things.

She heard the sound of Cain's hammer on the roof above, and every muscle in her body wanted to flinch. She thought of how she'd stormed out to the dock, how demanding and unreasonable she'd been, and a wave of humiliation and remorse engulfed her.

What had ever possessed her to go charging out there like that? To overreact with such severity and make such a complete ass of herself? Where was all her professional reserve? Where was her lawyer's sense of patience and control? If she had behaved with such little control in the courtroom, she'd have been held in contempt and slammed in a holding cell so fast she wouldn't have known what hit her. So what had it been about the sight of Cain's boat tied up at her dock that had sent her through the roof?

Slipping out of her pajamas, she let them fall to the floor and stepped into the tiny stall. The sting of the spray felt cool and refreshing against her skin, and closing her eyes, she rested her head back against the tile and let the water flow against her.

What did it hurt if he tied his boat to her old dock? With his long days working on the roof and the plans to paint the house, his reasons certainly seemed valid enough, and she didn't doubt that given the rural locations in the delta, this activity wasn't unheard of. When she'd confronted him, he hadn't appeared the least bit defensive or sheepish, like someone who'd been caught in the act. He'd looked honestly stunned by her behavior.

What an egomaniac he must think she is, considering herself so important that she believes everyone is out to get her, and everyone wants something from her. She cursed again the spotlight her family's politics and her father's candidacy had thrown her into. All her life she'd had to deal with people who were interested in her only because of her last name, because of her family's connections. Was it any wonder she was cautious with new people, suspicious of their motives?

Cain had spoken with her yesterday, had helped her, been nice to her. There had been nothing in his manner or speech that would have given her the impression he'd had ulterior motives for his behavior. There had been no phony compliments, no bogus flattery, no unaccountable friendliness. He'd merely spoken his few words and offered his considerable help in that honest, straightforward style of his.

So why, then, had she jumped to such an erroneous conclusion this morning? Why had she immediately assumed he'd wanted something from her, that he was trying to use her, take advantage of her?

Jillian let the cool water pour over her head, pulling her long hair flat and causing water to stream down her face. She knew why. She'd enjoyed Cain's friendliness towards her—maybe too much. She barely knew the man, knew nothing of him. They were from different worlds, led completely different lives, and yet she couldn't seem to stop thinking about him. She felt foolish, maybe even a little embarrassed. After all, she was a professional woman, a lawyer with a brilliant career, a member of one of America's most prominent political families. She'd been wined and dined by senators, diplomats, judges and tycoons. She was no simpering plaything. She could challenge a man—intellectually, professionally, economically.

And yet no man—not even Ron—had made her more aware of being a woman than Cain. His appeal was elemental, powerful, able to smash the barriers of convention and protocol, of family name and social status, capable of tearing away the civilized trappings of formality and custom and bring it all down to the basics. Man and woman. None of the flowery accolades—not one of the refined compliments she'd received from all those cosmopolitan and urbane companions—had stirred need in her as much as one look from those cool, clear eyes had done.

Jillian stepped from the shower and toweled herself dry, then hurried to the bedroom to change into her work clothes. She'd laundered them the night before, but stains from the garden had left permanent marks. She could hear Cain moving around on the roof above, and she thought again of their encounter on the dock.

He was like no one she'd ever met—raw, wild, unpredictable. With him, there would be no flowery words, no pretentious flattery, there would be only need and action. Was believing he wanted something from her easier than admitting the truth?

She pulled a comb through her long, damp hair. She knew the truth all right. She had from the first moment she'd laid eyes on him. But admitting it... Well, she wasn't sure she was ready for that just yet.

Chapter 5

Jillian rubbed her forehead wearily against the arm of her T-shirt. The sun above was blazing, and the constant heat and perspiration had all but drained her energy reserves.

She glanced down at her watch. Two-thirty. No wonder she was exhausted. She'd worked through the morning and nearly half the afternoon.

Looking back across the garden, she assessed with satisfaction the progress she'd made. It was impressive. With the brush gone and most of the overgrowth cleared away, it was actually beginning to look like a garden again. Beneath the tall grass, she had found the stone borders around the flower beds and had spent the last several hours clearing the grass and weeds from them. But enough was enough. Dropping the clippers and trowel to the ground where she'd been working, Jillian slowly stood and started back for the house.

Every muscle in her body seemed to protest, and she rubbed at the tightness at her neck. Glancing up, she saw Cain on the roof working steadily away in the glaring sun.

He'd reverted back to a sullen silence again. Since their incident on the dock this morning, he'd deliberately stayed out of her way. Not that she blamed him. He probably didn't want to take the chance of setting her off again.

She stopped for a moment and watched as he hammered a shingle into place. His skin baked in the sunlight, wet and brown. How did he stand it? she wondered. The heat was oppressive, and yet he worked on, seeming almost invulnerable to it.

He'd made only one concession to the heat today. Sometime during the morning, he'd climbed down the ladder and walked back to his boat. When he'd returned a few minutes later, he was wearing a pair of olive bermuda shorts instead of the faded Levi's she was accustomed to seeing him in. Of course, with the long socks and heavy work boots, he reminded her more of a mountain climber than a roofer, but seeing his hard, muscled thighs and well-developed calves, she didn't doubt those strong legs could have easily carried him over a mountain if he'd wanted them to.

Cain's dark hair was pulled back in a short ponytail at the base of his neck, and a weathered baseball cap kept the sun off his face. But aside from the small adjustment to his wardrobe, there had been nothing to break his dogged concentration today. There had been no lunch break, no cooling off in the river, and not even so much as a glance in her direction.

Taking a deep breath, Jillian walked to the porch steps, stopping to pick up the jug of sun tea she'd set out to brew earlier. It looked dark and inviting now, having steeped in the sun for hours, and she looked forward to pouring it into a tall glass filled with ice. Carrying the jug with her into the kitchen, she set it down on the tile counter and headed to the bathroom for a quick shower and change of clothes.

The cool shower refreshed her, but the air inside the house felt warm and still. She thought about the broken air conditioner again. It seemed hard to believe that only this morning she had considered asking Cain to look at it for her. That was impossible now. The fragile thread of friendship he'd extended to her yesterday had snapped after the way she'd acted on the dock this morning, after the way she'd overreacted.

She stared at herself in the beveled-glass bathroom mirror. She'd made a mistake this morning. And as the reflection of the sad woman in the mirror stared back at her, she had a feeling it was a mistake she was going to regret for a very long time.

A strange, heavy sadness seemed to hover over her as she slipped into a light cotton tank-style sundress and stood combing out her long, wet hair. The feeling settled about her like the hot, oppressive air, but she did her best to overlook it. She couldn't go back and relive the morning again. What was done was done, and she'd just have to find some way to live with it.

With the heat and the dry air, her hair was nearly dry by the time she walked back into the kitchen to prepare a glass of tea. As she dropped the ice cubes into a tall glass and reached for a small lemon wedge, she listened to the pounding of Cain's hammer above her. She thought about how hot he must be working up there on the roof, and how cool the dark amber tea looked splashing over the ice.

She brought the glass to her lips, taking a long drink. The brisk flavor of the cold tea tasted smooth mixed with the slight bite of the lemon. She swallowed, and was about to take another long swallow when a sudden thought popped into her head.

She set down her glass and reached high into the cupboard for a large, clear glass pitcher. She paused for a moment, staring at the pitcher in her hand. The last thing she wanted to do was to make a fool of herself again, but he had to be burning up out there. Maybe offering him a cold drink wouldn't make him forget about what happened this morning, but it might help him to see how badly she felt about it.

Jillian set the pitcher down on the counter and walked quickly to the refrigerator, pulling out the ice. She worked quickly, filling the pitcher with ice cubes, slicing the lemon and reaching for a small plate to put the wedges on. She wanted to hurry and get out there before she had too much time to think about it, before she had time to back out.

Pouring the sun tea into the pitcher, she set it on a small, round tray along with the lemon wedges and two glasses. Balancing carefully, she headed outside.

Walking out across the backyard, she spotted him on the roof, hunched down and laboring at one of the valleys formed by the roof's contours. He seemed to be concentrating so deeply, she hesitated to disturb him. She'd even considered going back into the house when suddenly he looked down and spotted her.

"Uh, tea," she blurted out, gesturing by lifting the tray just a little. "I...uh...I made some ice tea. It's so hot out I thought maybe you..." Her voice faded, her mouth too dry to continue. He wasn't exactly making it easy for her. He hadn't so much as batted an eye. He merely stared down at her, his eyes cautious and full of suspicion, as though he half expected her to start ranting and raving again...or maybe pull a gun. Taking a deep breath, she swallowed hard and looked up at him helplessly. "I thought you might like some."

For a horrifying second, Jillian thought he was just going to ignore her, leave her standing there looking and feeling foolish. But after a moment, he slipped his hammer into the loop on his tool belt and slowly came to his feet. Her heart began to pound nervously in her chest as she watched him walk across the roof and slowly descend the extension ladder.

As he made his way across the lawn, she turned to the shade of the old scrub oak nearer the garden, setting the tray down on the grass and quickly pouring a glass of the tea. Still holding the pitcher in one hand, she offered up the glass to him with the other.

Taking the glass from her, he lifted it to his lips and drained it in one gulp. She quickly refilled it with more tea and watched as he took the glass again for another long drink.

What was it about him? she wondered as she stood there watching him drink. What kind of magnetism or charisma did he have that made her so aware him? Whatever it was, whatever sort of power he had or magic he possessed, it seemed to work on her. He didn't seem to need the usual trappings to get her attention—flashy cars, high-powered career, expense accounts and corner office. There was a recklessness about him, a fierceness that made him exciting and that she found almost irresistible. She suspected that nothing—not custom, not convention, not politics or prestige—would keep him from whatever he wanted.

"Thanks," Cain said, taking his cap off and wiping an arm across his brow. He allowed her to fill his glass again, then waited while she poured a glass for herself, as well.

"Oh wait, I forgot," she said suddenly, lifting the small plate from the tray. "Would you care for some lemon?"

Cain looked down at the neatly arranged lemon wedges on the petite plate. As he stood there in work boots and shorts, sweat pouring off him, and with a tool belt dangling from his waist, she primly offered him a lemon wedge as though they were attending the same fashionable garden party.

He stared down at the fine bone-china plate and the precisely sliced lemon wedges. They only served to remind him just how her whole crowd operated. They had a duty, after all, to be benevolent to those under them. Noblesse oblige. Fly into a nasty rage and fire all the servants one minute, then graciously welcome them back into the fold the next.

"No thanks," he said tightly, shaking his head.

"It…uh…looks warm up there." Jillian closed her eyes and cursed the nervousness that had her saying such stupid things. The man was drenched with sweat, for God's sake, and she'd said it looked *warm?* What an idiot. He already thought she was crazy—did she have to make sure he thought her witless, as well? She laughed nervously and shook her head. "I mean, the heat, how can you stand it?"

"Used to it, I guess." Cain shrugged, thinking that grappling with the heat wasn't nearly as hard as coping with the images of her in his head. Just looking at her now made him mad. She looked so fresh and composed in that creamy blue-green dress. She had that kind of cool and calm so-together look, like nothing would ever dare get her hot and bothered.

Suddenly he remembered the image of her standing in the grass the day before, the cool water from the hose drizzling down her neck, her hair, her face, soaking her shirt, causing it to cling. He wanted to find her attitude and her cool appeal patronizing and condescending. He wanted to look on her with scorn and contempt. He wanted to block all those images in his head and never be plagued by them again. That's what he *wanted,* but instead all he could think about was how soft and smooth her skin would feel, how cool her lips would be against his.

"Well, thanks for the tea," he said curtly, draining the glass and shoving it back into her hand. He slipped his cap back on and turned to leave.

"Cain."

He stopped, slowly turning to face her. It was only then that he noticed a fine sheen of moisture along her upper lip, the slight tremor in her hand and the nervous smile she flashed him. Immediately he felt himself weaken, and that only made him more irritable. "What?"

Jillian looked up at him, the water condensing from the sides of the tea glasses sending little droplets running down her hands. "Cain. This morning—"

"I don't want to talk about this morning," he said abruptly, cutting her off and turning back to start across the lawn.

"Cain, please," Jillian said, dropping the glasses to the ground and stopping him with a hand on his arm.

He paused, drawing in a deep breath, and turned to face her. "Just forget it, okay?"

"I can't forget," she confessed. "I behaved very badly. I said some really stupid things. I would like to apologize."

The look in her eyes stopped him—a look filled with need, with sadness, with regret. It was the same soft, vulnerable look he had seen in her eyes that night in her uncle's limo. The same look that had haunted him for fifteen years.

Damn her, he swore to himself. Damn her for being soft and vulnerable. And damn him, too, for caring.

"Look, we both said things we didn't mean," he told her, noticing for the first time that her hand was on his arm. "Let's just forget about it."

She breathed out a small smile. "I know you must think I'm a complete basket case, but it's just that there are some things in my life right now that are . . . well, they're rather . . . involved."

"You don't have to explain to me," he said promptly, wishing she would stop. Seeing her struggling to explain made him feel guilty. After all, he already knew all the ''involvements'' in her life inside and out. And watching as she laid pride and vanity aside to try and make him understand had his hard resolve turning to jelly.

"But I think I do," she insisted with a little nervous laugh. "Believe it or not, I don't usually go around accosting people with guns or subjecting them to temper tantrums. I know you might find this hard to believe, but normally I'm a rather sedate person."

"Sedate," he repeated drolly.

"And I almost never lose control like that."

"Almost never?"

"Or overreact."

"You overreacted?"

"And I . . ." It took a moment before she realized he'd almost made a joke. She looked up at him, her smile hopeful. "You understand then?"

Cain shrugged, telling himself setting things right between them would only make his job easier. Unfortunately, as he watched her face fill with relief, the job was the last thing on his mind. "I know crazy things in your life can make you act a little crazy sometimes."

She hadn't realized until that moment she'd actually been holding her breath, or that she was holding his arm with something close to a death grip. Releasing her breath in a long sigh, she immediately dropped her hand to her side. "Thank you."

"Don't thank me, I haven't done anything."

"You're willing to excuse my behavior—that's a lot," she pointed out. As though responding to the same silent command, they both turned and picked up the glasses and tray, then started slowly back across the lawn together.

"Well, back to the salt mines," Cain said, when they'd reached the ladder. He pulled out his hammer and put a boot on the first rung, ready to make the climb up.

"I don't see how you can stand it," Jillian said, fanning her face with her free hand. "The heat, I mean. It really gets to me."

Cain had decided last night to forget Spence's half-baked idea about the air-conditioning, but with the opportunity having dropped in his lap, it seemed too perfect to let pass.

"I noticed the air conditioner in the window," he said, gesturing with the hammer. "How come you never use it?"

Jillian glanced at the weathered exterior of the air conditioner protruding from the living room window and shrugged. "I can't get it to work."

"Do you have any idea what's wrong with it?"

"Not a clue," she sighed, shaking her head and glancing down at the ground. She hesitated, trying to work up the courage. There would be no better time than now to talk to him about fixing it, but she couldn't bring herself to ask. She was too chicken, and the peace between them too fragile. She didn't want to do anything that would threaten it.

"Would you mind if I took a look at it?" Cain asked.

Jillian's head snapped up in surprise, and she looked at him almost guiltily. "Uh . . . you mean try and fix it?"

"Yeah, if you wouldn't mind."

"Uh, no. No, of course not. I'd appreciate it. Thanks."

"I'll come by maybe later this evening then, if that's okay? Take a look?"

She nodded her head. "Sure, that would be fine."

He stood for a moment longer, looking at her and thinking how cool the creamy blue-green color of her long, narrow sundress looked against her skin. Despite the heat, despite the sultry delta afternoon, she looked as inviting and as mouth-watering as a cool, creamy mint—refreshing and rejuvenating.

If he were to lean over and press his mouth against those inviting lips of hers, would she rejuvenate him? Would she taste cool and bracing, and would she work her special magic on him? Would her fragrance and her elegance make him forget all his disdain and reservations, make him forget all the anger and intolerance he'd tried so desperately to hang on to? Caught up in his thoughts, caught up in the moment, he impetuously reached out and brushed her cheek with the back of his hand.

"Thanks for the drink," he murmured, slowly dropping his hand.

Jillian stared after him as he climbed up the ladder and disappeared over the top of the roof. She felt shaky all over, and her knees trembled beneath her. Slowly, her hand came up, touching the spot on her cheek where his hand had made contact. It had been such an innocent gesture, casual and unimportant. And yet the way it made her feel, the way she had reacted, had been anything but casual.

She turned around and walked back into the house feeling a little dazed and uncertain. She set the tray with the pitcher and glasses on the kitchen counter and stood staring down at them. But it wasn't them she was seeing at all— it was the look in his eyes, the expression on his face, the feel of his fingers along her cheek. She wandered back through the house, walking into the living room and collapsing down onto the sofa. She wasn't sure what it was she was feeling— relief, satisfaction, happiness, contentment. She probably should feel foolish, reacting so strongly to a simple touch on the cheek. But it really didn't matter. The only thing that mattered was that they were talking again. Cain was talking to her.

* * *

Cain dove off the dock into the cool river water, mindful of the often deadly currents that moved swiftly just below the surface. The feel of the cold water against his feverish skin caused a momentary shock, but it lasted only a few seconds. By the time he'd surfaced to replenish his air supply, the water had cooled and refreshed his exhausted body.

After several strong strokes through the water, he reached the back of his boat where a ladder on the rear diving platform hovered just above the surface of the water. Grabbing it, he climbed out of the river and onto the deck of the boat.

The sun had sunk low in the sky, and the oppressive heat of the day had passed. It had been hours since he'd shared that cold drink with Jillian, hours since he'd looked into her eyes or heard her voice.

It had been a stupid thing to do, touching her like that. He would have to watch himself, and be more careful in the future. He was supposed to be her roofer, for heaven's sake, her housepainter—not her boyfriend. It was not only inappropriate to touch her, it was unprofessional and highly unethical.

Still, he remembered how her eyes had flashed alive when his fingers had reached out and made contact with her skin. She'd looked at him with surprise and wonder, but there had been no sign of indignation or offense. He'd almost wished there had been. It would have made keeping his hands off her in the future a lot easier.

He toweled himself off, slipping out of the wet shorts and draping them over the back of the boat to dry. Climbing down into the small cabin, he pulled out a clean pair of shorts and a T-shirt. At least the wardrobe on this job was consistent.

He'd had a hell of a day. All the emotional turmoil churning inside of him had propelled him to work like a

Trojan. If he didn't slow down, he'd have the work around here finished in no time, and that would put them in a real mess.

He slipped the white T-shirt over his head and pushed his wet hair back away from his face. His body ached, having been pushed nearly to its limits today, and he wanted nothing more than to collapse on the narrow bunk in the boat's cabin and rest his weary muscles. But his day wasn't over yet. There was still the air conditioner to look at.

Cain reached down into the small refrigerator that was neatly secured in a bottom cabinet and pulled out a can of beer. Not that it would do much good. What he knew about air-conditioner maintenance and repair was not exactly impressive. But then, a month ago he hadn't known a hell of a lot about roofing, either. How quickly things changed.

He popped open the can of beer and tilted it back for a long drink. Making a face, he swallowed hard. Carrying the can, he walked out to the deck and poured what beer remained in the can into the water. God, he hated beer. When he'd told Spence to get some cold drinks for the boat, he'd expected soft drinks. But it was his own fault. Spence always liked to relax with a brewski.

He thought of the ice tea Jillian had brought out to him, and wished he had an icy glass of it now. He'd poured it down so fast this afternoon that he'd barely tasted it, and with her standing there looking so good in that sundress, the last thing on his mind had been the flavor of the tea.

The quiet warble of his cellular phone interrupted his thoughts. Crushing the empty beer can with one hand, he reached into the pocket of his tool belt, pushing past the Glock, and answered the phone.

"I told you cold drinks," he said without greeting into the phone. There was only one person it could be on the other end of the line. "Not beer."

"They're cold, aren't they?" Spence asked innocently. "And you drink them, don't you? I rest my case." He sighed heavily and gave a little laugh. "What I'd give for a nice brewski right about now."

"Okay, forget the beer for a moment. Did you get what I needed?" Cain asked irritably.

"Right here." For the next half hour or so, Spence explained the inner workings of the make and model air conditioner that was installed in the window of Jillian's house. Closing his eyes, Cain made mental note of the information Spence gave him, asking a few questions here and there, and creating pictures in his mind.

"So the fuses should be checked out first," Cain concluded. "Right?"

"That's what they tell me. From what she told the shopkeeper, the thing runs—just doesn't cool. Our repair guy says it sounds like a fuse. I'd check those babies out first before screwing around with anything else."

"Will do. You got the fuses for me?"

"Right here in my hot little hands. I can slip them in the boat while you're inside the house checking things out." He chuckled again. "Maybe I'll just help myself to one of those brewskis while I'm at it."

"Just make sure those fuses are there when I need them," Cain warned him, but there was no real anger in his tone. "And forget your miserable beer."

He punched the small button to end the call, then slipped the phone back into the pocket of his belt. Turning around, he glanced back at the house. He could see Jillian through the small kitchen window. It was nearly seven, and the sun sent shadows running long across the lawn. There was no sense putting it off any longer. He might as well go and get it over with.

Reaching for his gun from inside his tool belt, Cain picked up a small tool chest from a storage compartment beneath the bench seat and slipped it inside. Closing the lid, he picked up the chest and stepped out onto the dock. In his mind he went over again the information Spence had given him about the air conditioner. Jillian Hughes may be jumpy, but she was no dummy. He'd better sure as hell look like he knew what he was doing. The success of this mission depended on him being able to stay close to her; it wouldn't help their cause if he were to do something to make her suspicious of him.

Climbing down from the levee, he stepped purposefully up the walk and the back stairs and rapped gently on the screen door. Jillian peeked around the corner, a dish towel flung over one shoulder.

"Hello," she said, with a demure smile.

"Is this a bad time?" he asked uneasily, a little taken aback at how comfortable she looked in the domestic setting. Standing barefoot in the small kitchen of the modest little house, in the simple, narrow cotton dress, drying her dinner dishes, she looked nothing like a high-powered federal prosecutor or one of the privileged Hugheses. Damn the woman, he swore to himself, trying to ignore the tight constricting in his chest. Was there anyplace she wouldn't look good? Anyplace she wouldn't fit in?

"No, this is fine," she said, gesturing with her hand. "Come on in." Pulling the dish towel from her shoulder, she twisted it nervously as he opened the squeaky door and stepped inside the screened porch. "I thought you might be too tired after the day you put in today. Are you sure you wouldn't rather make this another time?"

"No, I feel great," he lied.

She walked back to the sink, slipping the towel through the ring on the cupboard door. "This is awfully nice of you, Cain. I really appreciate it. Thank you."

"Well, don't go thanking me yet," he warned, stepping through the open doorway into the kitchen. "I might not be able to do anything to help."

"Oh, I know. But I appreciate you offering to take a look, anyway." She clasped her hands together in front of her. "Could I get you something? A beer, maybe?"

Cain, still tasting the rotten banana-peel flavor of the beer he'd had earlier, shook his head. "No thanks."

"A glass of wine, then? Some tea?"

"The tea from this afternoon?" he asked hopefully.

"Is that all right?"

"It sounds great." He peered through the kitchen into the living room. "Okay if I go ahead and take a look?"

"Absolutely." She nodded, pulling a glass down from the shelf. "Go on in, I'll just get our drinks and be right there."

At the threshold between the kitchen and dining room, Cain paused and stared across the room at the old air conditioner in the window. Its plastic grate was yellowed and its knobs worn. He regarded it as he would a nemesis—cautiously and with a sense of dread.

Moving slowly across the room, Cain set his toolbox down and pulled out a screwdriver. He felt a little like a surgeon about to perform his duties for the very first time. In his head, he replayed the information Spence had given to him, carefully removing screws and gingerly pulling off the grate.

Gazing down at the dizzying array of shapes and textures, he slowly shook his head. He sure hoped Spence's expert knew what the hell he was talking about.

Chapter 6

"It works!" Jillian marveled, standing in the cool draft billowing out of the unbecoming grate. "It's really working. You're a miracle worker." She bent down and put her face in the full blast of the cold current. "I can't believe it."

"I can hardly believe it myself," Cain mumbled to himself as he slipped the screwdriver back into the toolbox and flipped the lid closed. Glancing back at her, he shrugged modestly. "There really wasn't much wrong with it."

He turned and watched as Jillian lifted her hair and cooled the back of her neck. She basked in the feel of the cool air against her skin much the same way she had enjoyed the water from the hose the other day on the lawn—unrestrained and uninhibited. There was something decidedly sensual in the pleasure she derived, something impulsive and hedonistic. It was as though she lost herself in the sensations, as though feeling and response captivated and absorbed her.

Cain felt the pressure in his chest start to build again, and his mind instantly became alive with images and imaginings. Would she lose herself as completely to other perceptions—to passion, desire, need?

"I swear, this is the coolest I've been since I got here," she commented casually, glancing over at him. Only then did she realize he stood watching her, and immediately her face flushed with color. Releasing her hair, she awkwardly straightened up. "It was really lucky you had some of those fuses in your boat."

He watched her heavy hair tumble down her back as she stood up, and he felt his mouth go dry. "You pick up all kinds of stuff here and there in my line of work."

"Thank you," she said, turning to him. Despite the cool stream blowing out from the air conditioner, she suddenly felt unaccountably warm. The room seemed so small, so cramped, and Cain had a way of swallowing up all the space, all the air. "Are you sure I couldn't pay you something? For the fuses at least?"

"Forget it," he said with a dismissive wave of his hand.

"At least let me give you another glass of tea," she said, starting quickly for the kitchen.

"No thanks, really," he said. Without thinking, he reached out and took her by the arm, stopping her.

They both froze in place, neither able to move. They stood rigid, staring down at the spot where he touched her. Cain marveled at how soft and smooth she felt beneath his hand, and he couldn't stop his thumb from slowly stroking the silky feel of her skin. The small movement created a delicious friction, but it only served as an appetizer, making him hungry for more.

Taking a deep breath, Cain pulled his hand away and reached for his toolbox. He had to get out of there. He needed a break from the woman, a breather, a chance to gather his forces and strengthen his resolve. He was exhausted from the long day spent working beneath the hot sun, and fatigue had his defenses down. Being around her now was dangerous—especially when the quiet little house lost in the delta made him feel as though they were a million miles from everyone else, and the rest of the world simply didn't matter.

But the fact was, the rest of the world did matter, and so did the job he had to do—a job that had nothing to do with touching Jillian. He lifted the tool chest off the floor and shot a glance in her direction, carefully avoiding any eye contact.

"I'll get out of your hair now," he said, starting toward the kitchen. "Let me know if it starts giving you any trouble."

"Oh, I will," Jillian said, quickly following along behind him. At the back door, she stopped. "And, Cain?"

He was already down the steps and on the walk, but hearing her say his name, he stopped and turned around. "Yes?"

"Thank you."

He shrugged. "No big deal—"

"No," she insisted, cutting him off. "I mean it. Thanks a lot. It was really very generous of you. Especially... well, especially since I haven't been very pleasant to be around lately."

He agreed wholeheartedly with that, but not for the reasons she meant. It hadn't been pleasant because every minute he spent with the woman was like walking a tightrope. He had to be on his guard constantly, always mindful not to fall.

"You're welcome," he said, relaxing a little now that there was space between them. "Go back inside and cool off. It's going to be a hot night."

Jillian leaned back against the doorframe and folded her arms across her chest. A curious smile played across her face as she stood looking across the yard at him. "You still think I'm a nut case, Cain?"

"I never said you were a nut case."

"But you thought it, right?"

"No, I never thought you were a nut case," he denied with a careless shrug. He turned and started walking again. "I just figured you were having a bad hair day, or PMS—something like that."

Jillian laughed as she watched him make his way down the walk to the levee and up to the dock. "Good night, Cain."

He stopped and turned back to her. "Good night, Jillian."

Cain stood on the dock until he saw Jillian turn and go inside, closing the door behind her. What was it about her? he wondered as he stood there looking back at the house. The way she acted, so grateful for such a small favor, you'd think no one had ever been nice to her before.

But he thought back to Washington, and all the phonies, hangers-on and wanna-bes he'd seen during his years with the Secret Service. A family like the Hugheses, with their political power and influence, no doubt had their share of those types. Maybe he'd been the one who'd jumped the gun, who'd overreacted about the episode this morning. She'd grown up with people wanting something from her; it only made sense she'd be suspicious of him, too.

Cain turned and started down the dock. Jillian had a right to be suspicious of him. He wanted something from her, all right. But it had nothing to do with her last name or her family connections. It had to do with that satiny skin of hers, and the soft, delicate feel of her.

His mind was still on her when he stepped off the dock and onto the boat. He was still thinking of how soft her skin had felt and how dark her eyes had been. But in an instant, all that changed. All his senses went to full alert, and years of professional training overrode all other thoughts.

Something wasn't right. Something was different. Glancing down, he saw something lying on the deck near his foot, and immediately he recognized it as the pair of wet shorts he'd draped over the side of the boat earlier. Seeing them now lying in a heap at his feet, he felt the hair at the back of his neck start to tingle. Someone was on his boat.

Nonchalantly, he set the tool chest down and casually opened the lid. Reaching inside, his hand silently slipped around the butt of his Glock, and in one smooth motion, it was up and leveled at the intruder.

"Wanna beer?"

The sound of Spence's voice in the darkness had his body sagging in relief and his temper rising. Tilting the nose of his pistol up and away from its deadly aim at Spence's forehead, Cain lowered his arms.

"You jerk," he cursed. "I nearly blew your damn head off. What the hell do you think you're doing?"

"Sorry. I'm sorry," Spence apologized, reaching up to flip on a light in the small cabin. Spotting the gun in Cain's hand, his face paled noticeably. "There was a call from New York."

"Why didn't you just call me?" Cain demanded irritably, gesturing to the phone in his tool belt with an impatient jerk of his head. "That's what we have the damn phones for."

"I didn't know if you had it with you or not," Spence said in his defense. "I mean, that could have been a little sticky with the lady inside, couldn't it? Her river-rat handyman getting a call on his cellular phone?"

"All right, all right," Cain conceded, seeing his point. Climbing down into the small cabin, he sat down on the bunk. Reaching up, he pulled his holster out from beneath the pillow. "What's up with New York? And keep your damn head down or she'll see you in here."

Spence waited while Cain slipped the gun into its holster and laid it on the bunk beside him. "They're not one hundred percent on this, but it's looking like the shooting at the home of the jury foreman might not be tied to Donelli."

"How so?"

"Seems the guy's kid has been in some trouble—guns, drugs, stuff like that. They think the shooting had to do with trouble between rival gangs."

"So, okay then, we can back off," Cain said, thinking he wouldn't mind putting a little distance between himself and Jillian Hughes right now.

"Oh, I don't think so," Spence said ruefully. "The venerable senator isn't buying it. He still thinks Donelli is behind the attack in some way. Wants us to stick like glue to his charming niece." Spence turned and gazed out the small porthole to the house and watched as Jillian's shadow passed by one of the windows. Smiling, he rubbed his hands together and made a low, crude sound in his throat. "I have to say, I wouldn't mind sticking close to a little piece of that."

Cain glared at his partner. His reaction had been immediate and visceral—a sudden pang of jealousy, strong and thoroughly unexpected. "What the hell is that supposed to mean?"

"What have you got—ice water in your veins, man?" Spence asked with a snort, swinging his head around to look at Cain. "Those legs and that cute little butt could stir a corpse. And I suppose you haven't noticed that set of—"

Cain hurled Spence off his seat, the fierceness of his hold straining the material of his partner's shirt and surprising them both. "Shut your face, or I'll do it for you."

"What the hell's the matter with you?" Spence choked. He fell back against a wall and nearly onto the floor when Cain dropped his hold. Scrambling to his feet, Spence straightened his shirt and rubbed at the spot on his neck where the material had strangled him. "Have you lost your damn mind?"

Cain drew in a deep breath and ran a shaky hand through his long hair. What was the matter with him? How could he have turned on his own partner like that? Spence was just making the same lewd comments he always made, the same comments Cain had turned a deaf ear to a thousand times before. He'd never been crazy about Spence's obnoxious habit of making crude remarks about women, but it had never more than mildly annoyed him before. But listening while his partner made those same rude comments about Jillian had been like waving a flag in his face. He'd seen red, and for an instant there, he'd wanted to tear Spence apart.

Turning to Spence, he sighed deeply. "Look, I don't... I don't want you to talk about her like that."

"Okay, okay," Spence conceded, regarding Cain carefully. "Look, I didn't mean anything. I didn't know that you..." He stopped, realizing he was treading on very shaky ground. "I didn't know it mattered."

Cain stared down at his partner, his face drawn and serious. "Well, it does."

The two men looked at one another, a wealth of communication passing between them in that one, fleeting glance. After a moment, Spence cleared his throat.

"Well, I'm taking off," he said, stepping up out of the cabin and onto the deck. He turned back and looked at Cain. "I'll be on lookout, so get some rest, man. You look beat."

Cain watched as Spence started to leave and felt a stab of regret. They'd been partners for a long time, and he would have thought nothing could come between them. Clenching his fists tightly, he swore to himself, cursing Jillian Hughes again.

"Spence, look, I'm sorry," he stammered, contrite and miserable. "I didn't mean—"

"Hey, forget about it," Spence said, cutting Cain off with a wave of his hand. "I was out of line. It won't happen again."

"It's just . . . I mean, she's—"

"Hey," Spence said, stopping him again. "I understand."

And looking into Spence's familiar round face, Cain knew that he did. There was no need for explanations, no reason to justify anything between them. They were partners, they trusted one another, and that was all that was important.

Cain went back to his bunk and fell onto it, exhausted. Reaching up, he flipped off the light, lying back in the darkness and letting the gentle sway of the boat lull his aching body. He could relax now, it was safe. Spence was watching.

But when Cain closed his eyes, he wasn't thinking about surveillance or all night stakeouts. The only image in his mind was the one he'd been trying to forget for what seemed like forever. But he was too tired to fight tonight, and the image of Jillian was far too strong. He gave in to the dream, gave in to the longing. Cain thought about how she had looked standing in the kitchen this evening, about her bare feet, about the way the cool stream from the air conditioner had tossed and tangled her beautiful hair.

But mostly, as he lay alone in the darkness, where secrets could more easily be admitted and hopes dreamed about, he thought about the way her skin had felt beneath his hand.

He thought about how much he'd wanted to keep on touching her, and about just how much he wanted her.

Jillian sat in the quiet darkness of the living room, letting the breeze from the air conditioner cool and relax her. In the stillness, she closed her eyes and let her mind drift.

He'd called her Jillian. He'd never done that before. She'd never heard him actually say her name. Of course, she knew it didn't mean anything. How could it? It was her name, for heaven's sake. What else would he have called her? It would have been a little silly if he were to have said Ms. Hughes, or ma'am.

Still, resting her head back against the overstuffed chair, she couldn't help thinking how she had liked the sound of her name on his lips. It had caused a curious feeling to begin bubbling around inside of her, a feeling she'd never experienced before. It was as though he'd said something more than just her name, something secret, something private, something very close to intimate.

It had been one hell of a day. It had started with a bang, but now, sitting in the quiet darkness of the living room, it was ending in a whimper. She thought of the look in Cain's eyes when she'd confronted him at dawn on the boat dock. There had been such anger in his eyes then, such contempt. It had been nothing like what she had seen in them when he'd stood in this very room just a few hours ago.

As Jillian thought about him and the way he had looked at her, a curious weakness engulfed her. Her arms and legs had become languid and limp, as though she were feeling the effects of some powerful and potent narcotic. What was happening to her? She couldn't remember ever having reacted to a man like this before. She hardly knew Cain, and yet she found herself drawn to him. She had loved Ron, and she had cared very deeply for Jeff, but never had her responses to them been so purely salacious.

She remembered how Cain had touched her arm, how big his hand had been, and how dark it had looked against her skin. There was such strength in his hands, such power. She'd heard of women fantasizing about the rough hands of a workman, about the feel of rough hands moving over their bodies and the feel of rough hands against their smooth skin.

Was that what she was experiencing? Was she responding to Cain because he was so different from the men she had known, because he was a workman, a laborer? Was the attraction she felt all part of some female fantasy?

Jillian liked to think of herself as a modern woman. She certainly understood that a woman could be attracted to a man on a purely physical level. Certainly two consenting adults didn't have to be in love in order to enjoy one another. She'd just never been one to give in to random urges or frivolous attractions. It wasn't her style. And besides, in this modern world, sex could be deadly, and she found that carefree behavior completely irresponsible.

But even with all that aside, she was still a Hughes. She'd worked too hard avoiding the public eye to risk having something as seedy and reckless as a careless little fling come back to haunt her. She'd endured enough of that after Jeff had gone public. She wasn't about to do anything in her life she wasn't ready to account for.

But Cain... what would it be like with Cain? Was she willing to be held accountable for him?

Jillian stood up. She had to stop thinking of him. It wasn't right. And she had to make certain she did nothing to invite or encourage him in any way. He was from an entirely different world, a world she knew nothing about. A man like Cain wouldn't be polite, wouldn't be intimidated.

If there was something he wanted, he would reach out and take it, he wouldn't let decorum or status stand in his way.

She clenched her fists tightly at her side. A woman knew when a man looked at her if there was something there. And when Cain had looked down into her eyes tonight, there had definitely been sparks. The thought had both thrilled and terrified her. Still, she couldn't let an attraction that was not only unwise and unsafe, but probably reckless and dangerous as well, make her do something she would live to regret.

He was just someone to think about, she told herself as she walked through the house, locking up. Someone to think about during the long summer nights, someone to occupy her thoughts and fill her dreams until the whole business with Donelli was over and she could go back to New York, back to her real life again. Fantasy was all right as long as it stayed in the realm of dreams and imagination. She could fantasize about Cain's rough workman's hands all she wanted, as long as she remembered it stopped right there.

But as Jillian walked down the hallway and into the bedroom, she couldn't help remembering there had been nothing rough in the feel of his hand on her. His touch had been gentle, and surprisingly tender.

She pulled her grandmother's old-fashioned quilt back across the bed, folding it against the scrolled ironwork of the footboard. Sliding in between the cool sheets, she remembered something else about his touch, something that sent another wave of weakness closing in around her. Besides being gentle, besides being tender, his touch had also been decidedly possessive.

Closing her eyes, she listened to the quiet hum of the air conditioner blowing its cooling breeze down the hallway and into her room. No one had ever looked at her the way Cain had looked at her tonight; no one had ever wanted her enough to forget about who she was, or where she'd come from. No one until Cain.

Jillian stepped back from the window, her hand covering her open mouth and the air stalling in her lungs.

She'd been aware that the pounding on the roof had stopped, so it hadn't surprised her when she looked out the kitchen window to see Cain walking across the lawn, heading for his boat. But what she hadn't expected was to see him toss his tool belt and work boots down onto the dock, pull off his red bandanna and dive headfirst into the river.

Over the last several days, she had stood at the very same window and watched him cool himself off with the river water more times than she cared to admit, but he'd only splashed the water onto himself then. To see him dive in completely—shorts and all—had surprised her. But only moments later—after she'd watched him swim to the far bank of the slough and back again, after he'd pulled himself up out of the water and onto the dock in one powerful thrust, after she'd noticed how the water had poured down his body and made his wet shorts cling tight—only then did her surprise turn to shock, and her shock to total wonder.

After a careless glance in the direction of the house, Cain nonchalantly reached to the waistband of his wet shorts, slipped them down his wet, tanned body and draped them over the side of the boat.

Jillian stood galvanized by the sight of him. The male form didn't get much more perfect than him—tall, lean, strong and powerful. He looked like something she'd seen in an art book, or in a museum somewhere—a statue, a painting, a work of art.

She stared, hearing the funny strangling sounds in her throat and the roar of her own heart pounding in her ears. He had stood there for only an instant, and then had disappeared into the cabin of the boat. But the image of Cain standing in the late afternoon sun, his black hair slicked back from his face, his huge body wet and perfect, was something she knew she would never forget.

Stepping back away from the window, Jillian wiped a hand across her forehead. Despite the coolness of the kitchen, a fine sheen of sweat had dotted her brow. She felt oddly weak, and her breath came in huge, heavy gasps. She leaned back against the tile counter, dazed and stunned, and tried to slow the rhythm of her heart.

The day had been a long and exhausting one for her. She had risen soon after dawn, when she'd heard Cain begin to work on the roof, and went directly to the garden. She'd worked through the morning and through most of the afternoon, stopping only long enough for a quick lunch around noon and an occasional glass of sun tea to replenish the moisture that seemed to pour so freely from her. But her hard work had paid off. She'd cleared the garden of the remainder of the brush and overgrowth, and had weeded two of the three main flower beds. She'd even had time to call Tess at the market and order several flats of bedding plants and seedlings.

Of course, she had been aware of Cain's presence on the roof constantly. But even though there had been time for little more than a brief hello or an occasional smile between them, there was none of the tension and stony silence of the day before. Jillian couldn't believe the difference this peaceful coexistence between them made, or how comfortable it felt. She seemed able to work longer and work harder, content in the knowledge that when she did look up, when their gazes did meet, she would be rewarded with a smile from him.

It was well after three by the time the heat, the humidity and the back-breaking work finally drove Jillian inside.

She'd showered and relaxed, finishing off a few jobs inside the house, but had come into the kitchen to prepare a light dinner. She'd toyed with the idea of perhaps asking Cain to join her, but that had been before—before she'd seen him, before she'd looked out her window and saw him standing there, before she'd known just how perfect he was.

Jillian closed her eyes, remembering the sight of him, how the water had trickled down his broad chest, how golden his wet skin had looked in the rays of the afternoon sun. A pressure began building in her chest, making it difficult to breathe and setting her heart to race again.

No, the dinner suggestion had been a bad idea, she decided in a flutter of nervous energy. She busily moved about the kitchen, putting the finishing touches to the pasta salad she had made for her meal. Besides, hadn't she decided last night not to do anything to encourage him, not to send any mixed messages? Things were pleasant the way they were. Better not to push it.

At least, not until the image of him standing there faded from her mind.

Jillian set a place for herself at her grandmother's dining room table and sat down to her quiet meal. But delicious as the salad was, she found she had no appetite for it. She felt too restless to eat, too agitated. She tried her best, but after a few bites, she cleared away dishes and put the rest of the salad away.

But with her dinner over and the small kitchen cleaned up, the evening stretched out long and colorless before her. The restlessness seemed worse than ever. Avoiding the backyard, and therefore any chance of seeing Cain, Jillian wandered out to the small front porch.

The shadows stretched long across the lawn, and the huge yellow sun hung low in the sky. The temperature had shifted dramatically since the afternoon, and the breeze off the delta felt surprisingly cool and brisk against her bare arms and legs. But Jillian didn't mind. The break from the oppressive heat felt wonderful, and the evening seemed perfect for a walk.

She quickly ran back inside to change out of the shorts and polo shirt she'd put on after her shower and into something a little warmer. She pulled out a long, deep V-neck cotton jersey tunic and a pair of matching cotton stretch pants, slipped them on and headed out the front door.

Cain climbed out of the boat's cabin and stretched out on the front deck. The weather had cooled considerably in the past several hours, and he propped himself against the boat's windshield and let the breeze cool his hot skin. From where he lay he could rest and watch the house—and Jillian—at the same time. Although it seemed he needed nothing more mundane than visual contact to be aware of the woman.

It seemed that when it came to Jillian Hughes, Cain possessed a special sort of radar that managed to keep him aware of her at all times. The entire day, whether he was actually in eyeshot of her or not, he felt her presence, her proximity. The heat and the work had been nothing to cope with compared to the effort he'd expended trying not to think about her, trying to get her out of his mind.

Cain closed his tired eyes for a moment, rubbing them with his hand. He was grateful the day was over, grateful that she'd gone into the house, grateful he could rest. He'd needed a break, needed time away from her, time to put the image of her out of his head. With her safely inside the house for the night, it was easier to do that. He laid his head back against the glass, grateful for the quiet moment and the cool evening breeze.

If he hadn't been so attuned to its sound, he might never have heard the quiet warble of his cellular phone inside the cabin. It had to be Spence, and Cain knew he wouldn't call unless it was important. He leapt to his feet and ran into the cabin. Grabbing the phone from the pocket of his tool belt, he flipped it on.

"What is it?" he asked without preamble.

"She's walking along the levee to the north of you—you better go after her."

"What?"

"Get off your butt and go after her," Spence said again, his voice urgent and impatient. "If she keeps going she'll be right on top of me."

Cain turned off the phone and tossed it back into his belt. Muttering something coarse and decidedly guttural to himself, Cain reached for his gun and positioned it in the waist of his jeans at the small of his back, then grabbed a faded sweatshirt and a battered pair of deck shoes.

He didn't want to follow the woman; he didn't even want to see her right now. Couldn't she just have stayed put? Couldn't she have stayed in her house and out of harm's way and just this once made it easy on him?

Swearing to himself, he climbed out onto the dock and headed down the levee at a run.

Chapter 7

Jillian could hardly believe her eyes. When she'd heard the sound of someone coming up behind her, her panicked mind immediately thought of one of Donelli's goons with a gun. The last person she'd expected to see was Cain.

"Hi," she said, stopping to watch as he jogged up to where she stood. He looked casual and relaxed in the jeans and sweatshirt, but she couldn't help thinking how he'd looked standing naked on the deck of his boat.

"Hi," he puffed, winded a little from his run. "I saw you walking from the dock. Mind if I tag along?" He hoped like hell it wouldn't sound as ludicrous to her as it did to him that he'd "jogged" over a quarter mile to catch up with her in order to walk.

"Uh...no, not at all," she stammered, almost as surprised by the offer as she was to see him there.

"It's a nice evening for a walk," he said as they started down the levee together. He'd never been very good at making small talk. "Looks like another storm might be blowing in, though."

"You think so?" she asked, looking at the cloud-streaked twilight sky. "Do you think that will cause a problem with the roof?"

"I wouldn't worry about it," he said nonchalantly, not entirely sure what condition the roof was in after his handiwork.

"I guess I'd forgotten how sudden these summer storms could move through here," she said causally, wrapping her arms about herself.

"I take it you're not around too often," he said conversationally.

"Not very," she explained. "After my grandmother died, it just didn't feel the same. But when I was a kid we used to visit. I guess there were thunderstorms back then, but mostly I remember the long, hot nights."

"Well, we still get those," Cain attested, noticing how her dark, shiny hair caught the deep golden rays of the sun. "You visited a lot as a kid?"

"Almost every summer." Jillian nodded, looking up at him. "I used to love it. Grandma Wells would let me sleep in the backyard when it got so hot in the house." She laughed, shaking her head. "Of course, I always woke up with tons of mosquito bites."

"We still have those, too," Cain added darkly, suddenly remembering the annoying bite on his arm. "I must have left a flap open last night on the canvas. One chewed on me pretty good." He slowed his pace just a little, noticing her long jersey sweater and pants for the first time. "What do you call that color?"

"What color?" Jillian asked, following his gaze to the front of her. Pulling at the material of her sweater, she looked up at him. "This?"

"Yeah," he said, gesturing with his hand to take in the length of her. "I don't know what women call their stuff—shirt? Sweater? What color is that?"

Jillian looked down at herself again. "Sea breeze or mist, I guess. I don't really remember. It's more of a pale aqua, or maybe blue-green..." She stopped, figuring he was hardly interested in precise shades or descriptions. Glancing back up at him, she shrugged. "Why?"

"It's the same as yesterday."

"I beg your pardon?"

"Yeah, you know, the dress," he clarified, actually feeling his mouth start to water just thinking how the rich, creamy color looked against her smooth, flawless skin. "From yesterday. You had on a dress. It was the same color, wasn't it?"

Jillian remembered the long, straight sundress she'd worn the day before and, glancing down at herself again, realized that, indeed, the tunic and pants were the same color as the dress. She looked back up at Cain, dazed and off balance to think he'd noticed. "You're right, I...I guess I didn't realize."

A gust of wind blew up from the water, sending a chilly breeze swirling about them. He looked down at her, his lids squinting into the wind. "I like it," he said in a thick voice. "It looks good on you."

Jillian didn't feel dazed any longer, or off balance. She was downright flabbergasted. He was hardly the suave, debonair type who casually tossed around compliments like kisses on the hand. It had been a shock to realize he'd actually noticed what she'd worn the other day, but a compliment, too? It was too much. She literally felt her jaw drop in reaction, and consciously had to bring it closed again.

"Th-thank you," she mumbled, feeling her face grow hot despite the coolness of the breeze. Unsure how to react, and desperate not to let him see how affected she was by his compliment, Jillian scrambled quickly to change the subject. "So, are you from Virginia originally, or were you just there when you were in the marines?"

Cain's world jarred violently and he came to a full stop. How the hell had she figured that out?

"What makes you think I was in the marines?" Cain asked as casually as he could, but every nerve in his huge body came to full alert. His mind reeled. Had she stumbled on the truth? What had tipped her off? What had he done to give it away? He began thinking of ways he would report this new development and how this would change the surveillance.

"Your sweatshirt," she said simply, pointing to the USMC logo and Quantico printed beneath it in large letters. "Quantico's in Virginia, isn't it?"

Cain looked down at the faded marine insignia on his shirt and swore to himself. He hadn't even thought when he'd reached for the sweatshirt about the printing on the front. It had been a stupid mistake, the kind of irresponsible, reckless oversight that blew covers and threatened entire assignments.

"Oh, no," he said, laughing foolishly, doing his best to keep the tone light and casual. "No, no." He pulled at the sweatshirt material nonchalantly. "This belongs to a buddy of mine. I don't know how I ended up with it."

"Oh, I see." Jillian nodded. "So you grew up around here, then?"

"Sort of," he said evasively. "You know, here and there."

It was obvious he didn't like talking about his past, and that only made her more curious. "Is your family in the area?"

"Not really." He shrugged. "They're pretty much scattered all over the place."

"I see," she said. Apparently his family background was off-limits, too, but she would back off from that. She wasn't exactly anxious to start swapping stories about families, either. "So, do you travel much on your boat?"

"Sometimes," he said, wondering if he'd made it clear enough to her yet that he wasn't interested in talking about himself. Even though it was necessary to protect his cover, he didn't like lying to her.

"It's a beautiful boat," she said, her curiosity getting the better of her. "It looks expensive."

He looked down at her. "For someone like me, you mean?"

She saw the flash of anger in his eyes, the flare of defensiveness. "That's not what I meant."

He smiled, glancing down the levee to where the boat was moored. Yes, it was, but that was okay. She was curious, and he probably couldn't blame her for that. "It's all I've got."

Jillian had questioned enough witnesses to know she'd gotten all the information she was going to from Cain. It was obvious he was a private person, and there was no crime in that. Still, she couldn't help but be curious. What kind of life had he led? Where had he come from, and where was his family? Was there a woman in his life, or maybe more than one? What had he done before he'd come into her life, and where would he head next?

They walked in silence for a while, both lost in their own thoughts. The wind buffeted around them, stirring the dusty levee path. The sun had begun to sink low beneath the horizon, and the sky glowed pink and supple.

In the soft light, she looked even more beautiful, and Cain could hardly keep his eyes off her. Her full lips and faultless features had every cell in his body humming and coming to life. He was no kid. He'd been around a long time and he'd learned the hard way that life wasn't always fair. But the injustice of it all had never seemed more apparent than at this moment. They were from two different worlds. She represented everything he'd come to despise about the power brokers and money-makers who peddled for a price the freedom people like him had worked so hard to achieve. She wasn't the woman for him, and he sure as hell wasn't the man for her. There could never be any real feeling between them—they were too different, their lives too diverse. But, seeing her beside him in the soft light of the setting sun, he couldn't remember having wanted a woman more.

"What was that?"

It was the tone of her voice more than the words themselves that had Cain reacting immediately. She was no little mouse who jumped at any small sound, and yet her voice had been full of fear. Automatically his hand moved to a position that would enable him to reach for his gun easily. "Where?"

"Right there," she told him, stepping slightly behind him and pointing to the tall tule grass growing along the levee. "I saw something over there." She looked up at him, her eyes wide and frightened. "There's someone out there."

"Stay here," he ordered, pushing her farther behind him. Carefully he made his way down the levee and into the dense foliage.

Jillian stood holding her breath as Cain disappeared into the tall grass. The glimpse of color and flash of light had frightened her, but seeing him vanish into the thick vegetation had her too scared to breathe. What if something really was out there? What if it was one of Donelli's goons? What if they hurt Cain? What if—

But her panic and wild fears were abruptly halted when Cain climbed up out of the undergrowth a moment later and onto the levee again.

"What was it?" she asked, rushing to him, her legs weak and rubbery in relief. "Did you see anyone?"

"Nothing." He shrugged, taking her elbow and gently urging her in the direction of the house. "Couple of kids fishing. But we better head back. It looks like that storm's moving in."

Jillian allowed him to lead her back, aware at all times of his arm at her elbow. The touch was light and casual, but it was enough to start her mind wandering. She remembered the look in his eyes when he'd reached out and touched her arm last night, and again how they had looked when he'd complimented her earlier. But it wasn't that innocent touch or the intensity of his eyes that had the ante upping and the stakes soaring. It was the image of him standing on the dock this afternoon—bronze, bare and breathtakingly beautiful.

"I'm going to give the roof a check," he said hurriedly when they'd reached the back door of her house. It was growing dark quickly, and drops of rain were already pelting them. Rushing away, he gave her a quick wave. "Good night."

"Good night," she called after him, wishing he would have stayed a while longer, maybe said her name one more time. "Thanks for the walk."

After checking the shingles and slipping a tarp over those areas left exposed, Cain climbed down the ladder and pulled it away from the roof. Securing it under the eaves, he headed back for his boat.

He could hear the quiet warble of the cellular phone even before he'd reached the vessel. Rushing down the dock and onto the deck, he took it from his tool belt and flipped it on.

"What the hell was that all about?" Spence's angry voice demanded before he'd had a chance to speak.

"Look . . . I'm sorry."

"Sorry? Where was your head, man? You practically walked her into my lap."

"I know, I know," Cain conceded, swearing to himself and knowing there was no excuse for what he'd done. Nothing could excuse the fact that he'd acted more like some kind of star-struck sap than a seasoned field agent. He'd allowed himself to become so caught up with how the sun had looked in her hair that he'd forgotten all about his partner's stakeout. Coupled with the blunder with the sweatshirt, he couldn't blame Spence for being angry. "Look, it was a mistake. I admit it. It won't happen again."

"Make damn sure it doesn't, pal," Spence warned, but his tone had softened considerably. He hesitated a moment, then sighed heavily. "You... okay?"

Okay. Cain knew it was his partner's polite way of asking if he knew what the hell he was doing. "Yeah, man, I'm fine."

Cain switched off the phone and tossed it down onto the bunk beside him. Spence was no idiot. He knew exactly what was happening. There wasn't a field agent working undercover who hadn't at one time or another blown it, who hadn't stepped over the line at least once, who hadn't dropped his guard and gotten personal at the wrong time and with the wrong person. No one liked it, especially a partner. It made you helpless. There was nothing to do but sit back and watch it happen. But there was an unwritten law between partners. You didn't censure, you didn't make judgments. You just went about your business and covered your partner's ass when you could. And one last thing: You stuck around to help pick up the pieces when it all came crashing down.

Spence knew what was happening, all right, and Cain knew his partner would make no judgments, no condemnations. All he'd wanted to know was if Cain was... okay.

Cain closed his eyes, rubbing at the dull throb coming from behind them. Yeah, he was...*okay.* The only problem was, he wasn't sure after all this was over if anything would ever be okay again.

Jillian shoved the trowel down into the soft ground, digging out a small, uniform hole precisely six inches from the last one she'd dug. Slipping the small bundle of alyssum from the plastic pot, she transplanted the cluster of tiny white blossoms into the hole and pushed the loose dirt in around it.

Stopping, she pulled off the visor and wiped her sweaty brow with the sleeve of her shirt. She turned and looked behind her to the neat row of pink-and-white alyssum clumps in her wake. The toiled flower bed looked rich and dark, and the rose and azalea bushes were neatly trimmed and shaped. Refurbishing Grandma Wells's garden had been a bigger undertaking than she'd anticipated, but it was finally taking shape.

She'd made remarkable progress in the last ten days, and she attributed much of that to the milder weather. It was still warm and the humidity was higher than normal, but since the summer storm a week and a half ago, the overcast skies had kept the unmerciful sun at bay and allowed her to spend longer days working in the garden.

Jillian thought back to the night of the storm, of Cain and the walk they'd taken along the levee. He'd been so attentive to her that night—talking with her, looking at her with those cryptic blue eyes, complimenting her on what she'd had on. It had been so unexpected—*he* was so unexpected. He'd looked at her that night as though he thought her beautiful, as though she were special, as though something were about to happen. She had gone to bed and lain awake

long into the night, listening to the rain and thinking...
remembering...fantasizing.

Turning toward the house, she glanced up at him as he
worked at sanding the chipped and peeling paint along the
wooden trim. The milder days had allowed him to get more
done, as well. He'd finished the repairs on the roof and had
begun to prepare the house for painting. But it wasn't just
his work that had changed. *He* had changed, too.

In ten long days, there had been no evening walks, no
comfortable conversations, no unexpected compliments. It
wasn't as though he was unfriendly exactly, or angry. There
was none of the strained silence, none of the tension between them, that had followed that embarrassing confron-
tation on the dock all those many days ago, but there also
was none of the warmth or the familiarity there had been on
their walk the night of the storm. He spoke to her occasionally, greeting her in the mornings and waving good-night
in the evening. But she felt a little as though she'd awakened on that morning after the storm to a distorted and different world.

Jillian slipped her visor back on and scooted down the
flower bed a bit, starting on another hole. Of course, she
had told herself over and over again that it was better this
way. She'd lectured herself on the dangers of getting involved with someone like him, even for just a harmless
summer fling. They were little more than strangers, they had
nothing in common, they lived different lives, and after the
summer, she doubted if she'd ever see him again.

She reached for another pot of alyssum, pink this time,
and transplanted the flowery ground cover into the small
hollow she'd dug. Yes, she decided again, it was better this
way. Maybe he'd sensed it, too. Maybe that was why he'd
pulled back. She preferred to think he felt that way rather
than admit he might simply have lost interest in her.

But whatever Cain's motivation was, she knew she should be grateful. At least he was thinking of the consequences—something she seemed unwilling to do.

She knew she'd conceded there was nothing wrong with a little fantasy, but it wasn't her fantasies that bothered her. It was remembering how he had looked at her, or the way he made her feel. It was the image of him standing on that dock—naked and beautiful in the fading sunlight. If only she could just purge that vision from her brain, make herself forget. But it seemed impossible to do.

Jillian moved farther down the flower bed again, squeezing her eyes tight in an effort to block the picture of him. She hadn't understood until she'd seen him standing on that dock just how beautiful and how perfect the male body could be. But the image haunted her constantly—in the quiet heat of the garden, during the long, lonely evenings, and especially during the endless summer nights.

Reaching for the trowel, she shoved it down hard into the earth to start on another shallow hole. Only this time, with her mind preoccupied with thoughts of how Cain looked naked, she'd miscalculated her aim, bringing the sharp, pointed edge of the spade down through the sturdy material of her garden glove and through to the flesh of her finger.

Pain was slow in coming, but sensation was immediate. She screamed. When she pulled off her glove, the gash near the first knuckle of her forefinger sent blood spraying in all directions.

Cain's instincts were automatic and immediate when he heard her scream. His hand went to his gun inside his tool belt the moment he heard her cry out. Across the yard he saw her—blood on her hand, her clothes, her face, and his heart momentarily halted in his chest. He moved, maintaining a cautious, crouched position as he ran across the yard. His eyes scanned in all directions, adrenaline turning his senses razor sharp, and his shrewd sapphire gaze searched for any sign of movement. In his mind, all he pictured was her blood. He had no way of knowing if she'd been shot, if she was wounded or dying.

He reached her within seconds, seeing the fear in her eyes and feeling himself die just a little inside. But when Cain saw the deep, ugly gash on her finger, his huge body almost went weak with relief. Slowly, he released his hand on the Glock inside his tool belt, and drew a deep breath into his lungs.

"It doesn't look too bad," he told her in a quiet voice, but she neither answered nor acknowledged him. She merely stood there, her eyes fixated on the blood streaming down the side of her hand. "Jillian," he said, taking her by the shoulders and giving her a gentle shake. "Jillian, it's okay. Did you hear me? It's just a cut. It'll be all right."

But his assurance did nothing to affect her. It was as if she hadn't heard, as if she wasn't even aware that he was there. She only stared down at the blood, her cries becoming more hysterical and more violent with each heavy sob she took.

Cain stared down at her. It didn't take a genius to figure out that something more was going on than a simple cut on the hand. But he felt powerless, unable to help. This wasn't something his specialized training or his expertise with a gun had prepared him for. Desperate, he swept her up in his arms and carried her across the yard into the house.

"It'll be okay," he said, talking to her in a low, soothing voice that belied his own anxiety. He sat her on the kitchen counter beside the sink, like a parent would a small child. Quickly slipping the clumsy tool belt from around his waist, he let it drop aimlessly to the floor. Turning on the faucet, he took her hand and held it beneath the cool stream of water.

The hysteria had subsided a little, leaving Jillian sobbing quietly. Tears flowed down her cheeks, dripping down on to her shirt, and an occasional shudder racked her body with a tremor. She stared, her eyes fixed on the sink, watching as the water, tinged pink with her own blood, swirled and flowed swiftly down the drain.

"I think it will be okay," he assured her after examining the wound carefully and wrapping it with a clean dish towel. "But if you like, I can drive you into Walnut Grove. There's a clinic there and we could have a doctor take a look."

But she didn't answer. He wasn't even sure she'd heard him. Another shudder caused her whole body to quake, and her gaze remained focused on the sink where the water now flowed clear.

Cain regarded her carefully, uncomfortably aware of the blank stare. Slowly reaching over and turning the faucet off, his mind moved fast and furiously. The injury to her finger had been superficial, but he had half a mind to bundle her up and drive her in to the clinic, anyway. At least then he'd be doing something. He felt so useless just standing there, so helpless—and it wasn't a feeling he was comfortable with. He wasn't the kind of man who had felt helpless many times in his life.

But how was he supposed to deal with this? Killers and bad guys he could handle, he could protect her from them. But this…this was a whole different ball of wax. She wasn't a weepy, overly emotional type of woman, someone to come all undone because of a simple little cut on the finger. He'd never seen her like this before, and he wasn't sure what he could do to comfort her.

Cain searched the cupboards until he found a small first-aid box, and after applying a healthy dose of antiseptic spray, he bandaged the finger carefully.

"It's okay," he said again, crumpling the wrappers from the bandages in his hand. But she had no response. She merely sat there on the counter, sobbing quietly to herself, still staring blankly into the empty sink. He reached out, placed a finger on her chin and turned her to face him. "Jillian, it's okay now. I've taken care of it."

At the sound of his voice, Jillian blinked. Her large, dark eyes shifted, finding his clear gaze and fixing on it. Little tears fell to her cheeks and a sob sent a shudder quivering through her. "Th-the blood."

"It's gone. The blood's all gone," he told her gently, lifting up her hand and pointing to the bandaged finger. "See? There's no more blood."

She followed his gaze to her finger, only to catch sight of her blood-splattered shirt. "Oh God, it's on my shirt," she cried, looking up at him helplessly. "It's all over me."

"No, no, it's okay," he said quickly, surprised by the sudden fury of her reaction. "Calm down, it's just a little dried blood. We can wash it out."

But she was beyond listening. She lunged back, her eyes filling with terror and her voice bordering on a scream. "Oh God, get it off me, get it away."

Cain felt himself panicking again. Desperate, he reached for the T-shirt, slipping it up and quickly pulling it over her head. There was no room for modesty or embarrassment in the emotional state she was in. Still, somewhere in his male subconscious he'd noted her beauty and felt the air catch in his throat.

"It's gone now," he murmured in a hoarse whisper, tossing the shirt to the floor. "The blood—it's gone."

She shuddered again, staring at the crumpled shirt on the floor as though it were some slain monster from a dream. Turning, she looked up at him, her eyes wide and her breath coming in huge, heavy gasps. "I'm sorry, I'm . . . I'm . . ."

"Hey, it's okay now," he assured her when her words drifted off. "Everything's all right."

"When I was little," she said in a low, dull voice, her gaze shifting back to her shirt on the floor, "my father was...my father..."

It suddenly hit him then, like a slap in the face. The image captured by that famous newspaper photo suddenly focused with crystal clarity in his mind. An eleven-year-old Jillian cradled her dead father's head in her lap, his blood splattering her dress and his sightless eyes staring blankly at her. What kid could come away from that unscathed?

"Oh God," he groaned, feeling her pain as though it were his own. With her still sitting on the counter, he gathered her up and pulled her to him. "Jillian, I understand now. I understand."

"Th-there was blood everywhere," she stammered, sobbing quietly against his shoulder. Her arms nestled between them, clutching at the thin, worn fabric of his faded chambray work shirt.

"Shhh, it's okay," he said in a soothing voice. "Don't think about it."

"A-and ever since then," she continued, closing her eyes tight to block out the image that had haunted her since that awful day when her father died, "ever since that day—"

"Don't, Jillian," he pleaded, feeling the pain in every tense muscle of her body and wanting nothing more than to put a stop to it. "That's all over now. Don't think about it."

But she couldn't stop thinking about it, she'd been haunted by it for as long as she could remember. "Ever since th-they...they killed him, the sight of...of..." Just thinking of the word made her shudder. "The sight of...*blood*—"

"No," he said, shaking his head.

"It has terrified me and—"

"Stop," he insisted.

"A-and it makes me—"

"I said stop!" he demanded, grabbing her by the arms and giving her a rough shake.

His voice boomed loudly in the small kitchen, and she stared up at him, stunned and speechless. The fear and the horror in her eyes clawed at him, and he pulled her back into his arms.

"It's over," he whispered, rocking her head against his shoulder. "There's no more blood, nothing more to be frightened of. It's over."

Then she felt him pull away, felt the touch of his finger on her chin. Opening her eyes, she offered no protest when he tilted her head back. She gazed up into his fiery flame-blue eyes, and it was only then that awareness began to sink in. Jillian realized for the first time that her shirt was off and that nothing was between them save the lacy material of her bra, and for the first time she felt the awful images of that terrible day from her past begin to fade.

"Over," she whispered, feeling the air thick and hot in her throat. It was over. She was no longer thinking of the haunting memories from that day, no longer thinking about the blood and the panic. She was only thinking about being in Cain's arms, and that was all that mattered. "It's over."

"Think of me, Jillian," he whispered, lowering his head slowly and pressing a gentle kiss along her cheek. "Think of this."

"Yes," she sighed, feeling her body grow weak.

"Think of me holding you," he murmured, his brilliant blue gaze holding hers captive as he bent to kiss the other cheek.

"Yes."

"Think of me touching you."

"Yes."

"Nothing else matters," he breathed, running a feathery kiss along her forehead. "Nothing, and no one else."

"No one," she repeated in a murmur, mesmerized by the sound of his voice and the touch of his lips.

He brought his mouth to within a breath of hers, the ache of desire so strong in him he could all but taste it. "Kiss me, Jillian. Please."

"Yes," she murmured dizzily, slipping her eyes closed and holding her breath.

The telephone sprang to life with a sudden vengeance, its ring shattering the silence of the kitchen as violently and unexpectedly as a terrorist's attack. Jillian's eyes sprung open, blinking in surprise and astonishment. Gasping for breath, she stared at Cain, confused and uncertain.

Cain held her close, reluctant for the spell to be broken, but one shrill ring after the other had it crashing into a million pieces. Maybe he should have been grateful that fate had stepped in and prevented what he clearly seemed unable to stop, but his aching body and raw emotions made that difficult to do.

He had no business kissing her, no business touching her, no business starting something he'd never be able to finish. She was frightened, vulnerable, and she'd reached out to him for comfort. But he wasn't who she thought he was, and there was no doubt in his mind that if she knew, she never would allow him to touch her.

"No," she protested when he released his hold on her.

"You'd better answer it," he said.

"Let it ring."

"Jillian—" He struggled, desperately searching for the strength to walk away.

"It can wait," she insisted, cutting him off and clutching at his shirt.

He looked down at her, into those eyes that had haunted him so many long nights. He was only trying to do the right thing. God, didn't she know how difficult it was for him when she looked at him like that? "It might be important."

"*This* is important," she insisted, feeling as though she were arguing the most important case of her life.

"But it might be ... your family."

Chapter 8

Jillian recoiled as though he'd struck her. "What do you know about my family?"

Her sudden withdrawal surprised him. "What do you mean?"

The telephone rang one last time, then fell silent, the stillness in the small kitchen almost deafening. She fumbled about on the counter for a dish towel and clutched at it to cover herself. "What do you know about me?"

"What are you talking about?"

"Tell me," she demanded. "Do you know who I am?"

"Jillian—"

"Tell me! Do you know?"

"Of course I know who you are," he said, forgetting all about his own struggle. "You're Jillian Hughes, for God's sake. What's the big deal?"

Jillian felt a cold, empty feeling in the pit of her stomach. Pushing past him, she jumped down from the counter. "And you know about...about my father?"

"Jillian, it's in history books. Who hasn't heard of Collin Hughes?"

"A-and about my family?"

Her eyes were filled with such betrayal, such hurt that he forgot about good intentions, he forgot about all the reasons he should stay away and not get involved. "Jillian, what is it? What's wrong?"

He reached out for her, but she shoved his hand roughly aside. She didn't want him to touch her, didn't even want him to look at her. He knew who she was. He knew all about her. She didn't know why, but it made a difference. It made all the difference.

She had thought she was far enough away. She had thought in the remote beauty of the delta, in this one little corner of the world, she had finally escaped her family's name and reputation. Here it had just been Jillian and Cain—just a woman and a man.

Only, he knew. He knew, and that changed everything.

"Go," she said, wanting neither his sympathy nor his understanding. "Leave me alone."

He looked down at her. If he hadn't known better, he would have thought that was regret in her voice. But what did she really regret? Her background, or the fact that he wasn't part of it?

"Just tell me one thing," he said, feeling his anger starting to build. "Tell me what difference my knowing about you and your family could make."

"Oh, it makes a difference," she assured him solemnly. "Believe me, it always does."

"That's ridiculous," he said, feeling the old doubts and suspicions about privileged backgrounds and class consciousness roaring to life. He took a step forward and reached for her again.

"Don't touch me," she warned, jerking her arm away. "Don't ever touch me again."

Her haughty tone and reproachful look had his anger flaring. He grabbed her by the arm. "Don't touch you? A moment ago you didn't want me to stop touching you."

"A moment ago I thought I was just another woman to you."

"Oh no, not you," he snarled, grabbing the towel she clutched to herself and snatching it away. "You're not just any other woman." He pulled her to him, crushing his mouth to hers. His lips were hard and demanding on hers, tolerating no debate, no resistance.

But Jillian offered no resistance. She was too overwhelmed, too inundated by the storm of emotion pounding away inside of her to think of resisting or fighting him off. She no longer felt the punishing grip he had on her arms, no longer was aware that the breath had stalled in her lungs and the blood had turned hot in her veins. There was only Cain—the touch, the texture, the feel and the taste of him.

His mouth pressed against hers, forcing her lips apart and forging a path to gain entry inside. His tongue plunged deep—tasting and exploring, drawing from her more than she was willing to give, more than she was aware she possessed.

Never in her life had she been treated like that. Never in her life had she been kissed with such boldness, such determination, such assurance. It was as though he'd made his declaration, pronounced his possession of her as though she had no choice in the matter. And never had she found herself so hungry for more.

In one swift motion, he pulled his mouth away and pushed her from him. "If you think that had anything to do with family name or background, you're a fool."

Jillian stood there, breathless and bewildered, as he turned and stalked across the kitchen and out the squeaky screen door. She sagged against the counter, having to steady herself with a hand along the tile. She was disoriented, confused. Hours passed, or maybe it had only been seconds. She felt dizzy and weak, and she gasped to pull more air into her depleted lungs.

"Cain," she murmured, liking the sound of his name on her lips even as she tasted him in her mouth. She said his name again as she moved on shaky, unfeeling legs, walking the short hallway to the bathroom, stripping off her soiled clothing and stepping into the spray of the shower. Leaning back against the cool tiles, she let the water stream over her. "Cain," she said again, her voice echoing against the walls and surrounding her with the sound of his name. "Cain, Cain, Cain."

Cain heard the loud slam of the screen door behind him as he stalked across the yard and around the corner to where the ladder stood propped against the house. Energy seethed through his body, pent up and restless. The way he felt, he could have finished sanding and scraping the rest of the house and have it ready to paint in a matter of hours.

But he didn't climb the ladder. He didn't reach for the sandpaper or steel brush. He merely stood staring at the ladder, energy coursing through his body, his fists clenching and unclenching.

Had she really believed it would make a difference to him? Did she really think that her family's name or influence made a whit of difference to him? Didn't she know the kind of power she had over him? Couldn't she see how much he wanted her?

But instead she'd looked at him with such anger in her eyes, such betrayal. He'd wanted to grab her and shake her, he'd wanted to shout and scream, he'd wanted to wring her neck until he could make her understand. But he hadn't done any of those things.

He'd kissed her.

Cain closed his eyes to the sudden surge of emotion that pulsated through his veins like a fever. His anger and frustration had caused him to be too rough, had caused him to hurt her. She wasn't the kind of woman a man wanted to be rough with. She was the kind of woman who demanded respect and consideration. The kind of woman a man would sell his soul to have.

He'd thought he'd wanted her when he believed her to be perfect, when she'd flitted in and out of her uncle's campaign offices, never giving him so much as the time of day. But he knew her better now. He knew she was far from perfect. He knew her secrets; he'd seen the flaws and discovered the imperfections. She'd become real to him—not a princess in a fairy tale, but a woman, flesh and blood. Fifteen years ago he had been awed by who she was and where she'd come from. But it was the woman he'd held in his arms who awed him now—the woman with all her frailties, all her foibles, all her needs.

He was a man, and he'd known many women in his life, but the taste and the feel of Jillian against him had obliterated all memory of anyone else. Never had he known a woman like her, and never had he wanted one more than he wanted her now.

Taking a deep breath, he started up the ladder. Needing the sandpaper, he reached for his tool belt.

His tool belt.

It was only then that he realized he didn't have it. He swore fiercely under his breath, remembering how he'd stormed from the house without giving it so much as a passing thought. That had been another dangerous slip.

Even though he didn't relish the thought of having to go back inside the house to retrieve the belt, he had little choice in the matter. He couldn't be without his gun, and he couldn't risk her finding it.

Slamming his fist down hard on the rung of the ladder, he climbed down. Muttering curses under his breath, he turned and hiked back across the yard to the porch.

At the steps he paused, not sure how he should proceed. His hand formed a fist, poised to knock at the door, but that traditional procedure seemed a little inappropriate given the dramatic method with which he'd exited just a short moment before.

Lowering his hand, he reached for the handle on the screen. He couldn't even envision what kind of greeting he might expect from her, what kind of reaction she would have at seeing him again. But gratefully it was quiet inside, no sign of Jillian anywhere.

He hardly expected her to still be in the throes of her childhood trauma, still vulnerable and frightened. She would have recovered from that by now. But he couldn't help wondering just how she would react. He had been rather surly, had intentionally been rough in order to make his point. Would she forbid him to touch her now? Would she order him out and away in that haughty tone he had such contempt for?

Glancing down, he spotted his tool belt on the floor in front of the sink. Walking across the kitchen to retrieve it, he picked it up. He had just turned and started back for the door when he heard the sounds of the shower running.

His body froze and he stood motionless, listening. Immediately his mind shifted, and he imagined her standing beneath the splattering spray, the cool, clear water pouring down her perfect skin, her perfect body. He remembered how delicate and beautiful her breasts had looked spilling out from the thin, lacy bra. He remembered the afternoon in the backyard when she'd cooled herself off with the garden hose. And he remembered the feel of her in his arms.

His body surged to life, and needs seemed to spring from out of nowhere. He gripped the tool belt until the hold became almost painful, fighting the rush of emotion swelling up from inside him, but nothing could stop the flow.

He had to get out. He had to walk out that door and never look back. If he stayed a moment longer, he knew he would never get away, there would be no stopping him. He took a few determined steps toward the porch door, but his course was halted suddenly by the sound of her voice.

She had said his name. Over the din of the water and his own thundering heart, he had heard her voice, he had heard his name on her lips. He turned, staring down the short hallway to the door at the end. Consciously or unconsciously, he wasn't sure which, he took a step toward the hall.

Again he heard her voice. Again she said his name. She said it over and over again.

There was no moment of hesitation, no instant of indecision or consideration. In that one amazing moment, he knew his path had been set, his course charted and his fate sealed. It was as though he'd only now recognized the divination, only now seen he was fulfilling what had all been decided upon years before. As if by some prophecy of old foretelling tales of young knights and beautiful princesses, he'd been guided down a predetermined passage. The struggles, the hostilities, the anger and contempt—all had been part of the natural progression, part of that predestined course to endure. A journey that had been leading all along to this one precise moment in time.

He didn't remember moving, didn't remember taking the dozen or so steps it took to propel him down the short hallway. All he knew was that he was at the door, and destiny awaited him on the other side.

Jillian held the bar of soap in her hand, working and kneading it beneath the spray of the water until a lush, rich lather emerged. She spread the luxurious foam up her arms and over her shoulders, along her abdomen and down her legs, savoring its smooth, creamy texture, its sleek, glossy feel.

She'd never felt this way before. It was as though every nerve ending in her body had suddenly been made more sensitive, as though perception and sensation had been intensified and magnified. She felt tingly, almost giddy, and all because Cain had kissed her.

She wouldn't allow herself to think of implications, of ramifications, of all the reasons why she shouldn't want him or how unwise an involvement would be. She no longer cared. She'd spent too many years of her life concerned with the consequences, trying to calculate and regulate impact and aftermath. She merely wanted to close her eyes and imagine his hands on her, caressing and massaging as the fragrant suds were doing now. In her mind she envisioned him coming to her, visualized him reaching out and taking her into his arms.

But unlike her dazed reaction to his kiss in the kitchen, in her vision she was no passive participant in the embrace. She imagined herself seeking and exploring. Imagined herself learning about him with both hands and mouth, discovering secrets and satisfying curiosities.

His name pounded through her brain—*Cain, Cain*—just as the water pounded against her—*Cain, Cain*. If she were ever given another opportunity—*Cain, Cain*—she wouldn't be timid or uncertain—*Cain, Cain*. She knew what she wanted—*Cain, Cain*. She wanted Cain.

She heard the sound of the shower door open. Felt the gust of cool air against her wet body. She turned, aware in that moment how quickly the line between fantasy and reality could blur and fade. There in the door of the shower stood Cain.

He stared at her, as though summoned by some ancient spell or incantation. She was afraid to move, almost afraid to breathe. She didn't want to do anything that might cause this vision to alter or disappear. At that moment, she didn't care if he was real or a dream, she didn't care if what she felt was reasonable or irrational. If this was a vision, she hoped it was a revelation of what was to come; if this was merely a dream, she hoped it was one she would never awaken from.

For a moment there was nothing, just the resplendent clash of realization as the flaming blue of his gaze assailed the midnight fire in her eyes. But then, with a flicker of lids his gaze shifted, dropping to look at the rest of her.

Cain felt a strangling sensation in his throat at the sight of her. She was beautiful—flawless to the point of perfection. Her long, wet hair fell to the tops of her breasts, whose supple, round centers were dark and hard. Her slender torso curved narrow at the waist, her hips round and firm, and her long legs smooth and tanned. He knew then that if he were to do without her, it would only be a half life for him.

She made no attempt to hide, took no effort to cover herself. She wanted him to look. She wanted him to see what she offered to him as she had to no other man.

The tool belt slipped heedlessly to the floor as he swung the narrow shower door wide. Unmindful of boots, disregarding jeans or shirt or bandanna, forgetting everyone and everything else, he stepped into the shower, into the spray and into her arms.

He pulled her to him, devouring her mouth with his mouth, grinding his body to her body. His hands roamed

over her smooth, wet flesh—touching, caressing. The feel of
her naked body was almost more than he could bear, and his
heart roared like thunder in his ears. The flavor of her
coursed through his system like a strong, intoxicating narcotic until he felt her in his blood, in his heart, and pulsing
through his brain. He couldn't get enough of her, wanting
more and more of what he felt he'd waited his whole life to
have.

His mouth was no less fierce on hers than before, but this
time she confronted him with her own harsh demands, her
own set of needs, and with a force that bordered on brutal-
ity. She opened her mouth to him, but her tongue challenged and did battle—tasting and exploring, searching and
enjoying. She wasn't vulnerable, nor was she shy. She was
a woman who knew what she wanted, and who would tolerate nothing keeping her from it.

None of the long, hot summer nights spent wondering,
none of the daydreams or fantasies, none of the glimpses or
voyeurism had prepared Jillian for the reality of him. He
was larger than life, more than she'd ever dreamed and all
she'd ever hoped for. The sensation of his clothing, the
roughness of the denim, the wet slickness of the chambray
along her naked body aroused and incited her senses. All
those constraints, all those latent needs, all those dormant
desires she'd suppressed for so long stirred and burst to life.

The nagging concerns, the rigid considerations that had
been placed on her from the moment of her birth fell vic-
tim to the melee of emotions. She wasn't thinking of her
family, of her reputation, of what was expected of her. For
the first time in her life there was no place for doubt and
uncertainty, for reservation or reserve. She was with Cain,
and there was nothing more important than that. She was
too desperate, too hungry, and she needed him too much to

think about such mundane things as consequences or repercussions. All she knew was that she wanted him—now.

Cain's hands moved over her, urgent and intent. Her skin was like wet satin, and he couldn't seem to satisfy his need to touch and feel all of it. It was as though he'd endured a lifetime of cold and darkness only to discover the sweet warmth of heaven and light at the end. He was desperate, rendered almost inanimate by the force of his emotions, and yet compelled into action by her bold actions and urgent moves. He had no time to think, to plan, to reason. It was all he could do to keep up, to simply feel and experience all there was of her.

His hands slid down the curve of her bottom, raising her leg, lifting her and pressing her into that part of him that ached for her the most. He heard a soft groan from deep in her throat, tasted it in his mouth and felt his body surge with desire. For as long as he could remember, he'd lived with the fact that he'd wanted her, but to realize she wanted him too was almost enough to push him over the edge. Almost.

Tearing his lips away, he pressed his mouth to her neck, tasting her flesh with lips and tongue. His hands traveled the slippery contours of her body, finding her breasts and caressing their beauty. Hard, dark nipples filled his hands, causing his body to grow harder and the breath to falter in his lungs. He moved his lips down, making a journey over the silky wet flesh from her neck to her breasts to pay homage to their taut, ripe fullness.

Her hands clutched his hair tightly, bracing against the torrent of emotions surging through her system. There was nothing shy in her reactions, nothing reserved. His actions were too decisive, too determined, too boldly explicit to allow for any of that. He swept her up in his passion, carried her along with his desire. He took no time for clever enticements or suave persuasions. He ravished rather than seduced, took rather than tempted. No one had ever wanted her like that before, and his frank, dauntless actions had her responding as she never had before. Pure, pristine pleasure coursed through her veins like lava from a fiery volcano, making the need in her almost unbearable.

The water turned Cain's hair to black silk, and her fingers tangled in its sleek threads. They found the red bandanna, pulling it from him and tossing it to the tiled floor. Only then did the craving for his flesh become urgent. She reached down, past the collar of his shirt, finding the buttoned placket front, and grabbed it tight.

Cain straightened, lifting his head and letting her have free rein. She tore at his shirt, ripping the material free and sending buttons flying in all directions. Pulling the shirt from him, she tossed it aside and moved her hands down his massive chest to the front of his jeans.

Jillian didn't even hesitate, slipping open the first button of his fly. Beneath her touch, she felt the pressure of him against the denim tighten and increase. Looking up, she challenged him with a look, slipping another button free, and then another.

Cain closed his eyes to the torrent of sensation, desire pounding furiously through him. The feel of her hands on him threatened what precious little control he had left. Reaching down, he grabbed for her, lifting her to him and pressing her back against the hard, cold tiled wall. Whatever plans she might have had to liberate him from his jeans and boots would have to wait. It was too late, and the craving too strong. He wanted to be inside of her.

Jillian wrapped her arms around his neck, pulling him to her. His massive chest crushed against her, making it difficult for her to breathe, but she no longer cared about such mundane needs. There were other, more urgent demands that commanded her attention. The fury within her was desperate, wild and out of control. What she wanted, what she needed, what she had to have was him inside her.

"Jillian," he growled, lifting her higher and pushing her legs apart. She looked up at him, her eyes dark and wide. He had seen those eyes in his dreams, had cursed them in his nightmares. But never had he ever thought they would be looking at him the way they were now—full of need, full of desire. Bracing himself, he brought his mouth to hers and whispered her name against her lips. "Jillian."

And then, covering her mouth with his, he pushed into her deeply, letting the warmth of her capture and surround all there was of him.

Jillian's eyes closed, her heart faltering in her chest from the pleasure and the impact. Nothing had prepared her for this. For a moment all she could do was tarry on the edge, feeling the force of his possession and allow her own body to accept and accommodate. But the fire within was savage, and the feel of him inside of her had it flaring up and raging out of control.

Her legs wrapped around him, holding him, feeling the potency in his strong, muscular form. Everywhere he touched, every place their bodies made contact, sent a wall of flame ravaging through her—mouth, breasts, arms, legs. His strong arms anchored her to him, and with every motion, every thought, every breath, she was transported nearer and nearer to madness.

The sounds of pleasure echoed through the shower—gasps, cries, moans. Jillian wasn't sure if they came from him or herself, nor did she care. They became a carnal symphony in her ears, and his decisiveness and tenacity conspired to make her a master musician. A force was building inside her, like a fireball building in the belly of a dragon. Every powerful move, each unrelenting thrust of his torso, every brush of his hand or flicker of his tongue brought her closer to the vent, closer to eruption, closer to that moment when she would burst open and explode into pure bliss.

Cain tore his mouth from her, burying his face in the soft, fragrant confluence of her neck and shoulder. They might have been strangers, they might have come from different worlds, different backgrounds, but none of that mattered now. There was no outside world, no altered state, no other reality. They had found a window in time, a black hole in the cosmos. A place where nothing existed beyond the tiny confines of that shower. The world outside had somehow dropped out of sight, had vanished and withered away, leaving only one man and one woman. For now, for this one glorious moment in time, she belonged to him—heart, mind, body and soul.

Then it was there for her—flash point, the point of no return. In a savage tempest of muscle and form, her body suddenly convulsed, her head flying back, her hands on his shoulders clutching into fists, and her legs constricting like steel bands around his waist. He held her, pushing deeply into her as she rode one wave after another. He heard her groans, felt her excitement, tasted her euphoria. He took pleasure in experiencing hers until he could stand it no longer, until the hunger and the fury in him had become too great.

Clutching her tight, he followed her into the abyss, the explosion inside of him fierce and ballistic. Never had it been like that, never had pleasure bordered so close to delirium, so close to madness. He surged into her—his heart forgetting its purpose, his lungs disregarding their objective. His legs felt weak, and he staggered forward, pressing deeper and deeper on his journey into that glorious void.

"Jillian," he cried out in little more than an anguished whisper. Then, covering her lips with his own, he be-

queathed to her all that he had, and let it carry them over the
edge and into the rapture together.

The water ran in an incessant, endless stream. It had long
ago turned cold, and one small fork sent a frigid current
cascading down Cain's back. His jeans were soaked black,
and his work boots had become saturated, but he was neither aware, nor concerned. It was all he could do to simply
remember to breathe again, to try and constrain his heart to
a uniform cadence rather than a violent thunder. To say the
experience had been profound for him might have been an
understatement; to say it had been life-altering, or mind-
blowing, or apocalyptic would not.

Cain lowered his head, kissing Jillian's shoulder, her neck,
slowly making his way to her lips. He kissed her on the
mouth, long and deep. It was a different kind of kiss—different from the brutal, angry way he'd kissed her in the
kitchen, different from the hungry, desperate way he'd
kissed her when they were in the frenzy of making love. This
kiss was deliberate, gentle and fraught with meaning.

Jillian closed her eyes, surrendering to the emotions in the
kiss even more completely than she had to the physical demands of their lovemaking. The cool tile at her back should
have been hard and uncomfortable, but she felt none of its
harshness. For her there was only Cain. The man had inundated her with the breadth of his desire; now he overwhelmed her with the depth of his passion.

This hadn't been the first time for either of them, but it
was as though they both somehow instinctively knew this
had been something different, something unique. It wasn't
exactly the kind of experience one blithely stepped away
from. Something extraordinary had just happened, something remarkable, and it was going to require time to recover, to recuperate and absorb.

"You're cold," he murmured against her lips, feeling the fine rash of goose flesh along her arms. Reaching over, he turned off the icy spray, and with her still in his arms, he carried her out of the shower.

Without the constant drone of the water, the stillness of the house seemed eerily silent. Jillian wasn't sure what to do, or what to say. She felt as though, along with her, the whole world was holding its breath, waiting to see what happened next.

But Cain seemed anything but uncomfortable. He was natural, at ease, as though they had been lovers for years and turbulent lovemaking was something they had engaged in many times. He reached for a long, fluffy bath towel, wrapped it about her and gently eased her down onto the narrow counter beside the sink.

Jillian sat looking up at him, while Cain gently dried the water droplets from her nose and cheeks. Finishing, he stepped back, slipping off his wet boots and discarding the soaked jeans.

Jillian clutched the towel about herself, her mouth going dry at the sight of him. She remembered how she had watched him that night on the dock, when he'd risen from the river like an ancient Greek god. But she knew he was no deity, no mythical creature from a dream or fantasy she'd created. He was a man—more man than she'd ever dreamed of.

"I'll get you a towel," she said, starting to slide down from the vanity counter.

"No," Cain said, stopping her with hands on her shoulders. He slipped the towel down, pulling it from her and leaving her bare. "I'm not finished with you yet."

Chapter 9

Jillian thought she had been drained of everything, thought she'd depleted all stores of energy, all reserves of strength. But he'd only had to look at her, he'd only had to say those few, direct words, and the embers of potency and zeal roared to life. She reached for him, accepting his kiss and sinking her hands into his long, slick, wet hair, but when she went to wrap her legs around him to pull him close, he stopped her.

"No," he said, lifting his mouth from hers and shaking his head. He caught one ankle as she lowered her leg, then reached for the other. "There wasn't time before," he murmured, kneeling down to place a kiss on the inside of her calf. "I didn't get a chance," he whispered, lifting one leg, and then the other, to rest on his shoulders. "And I need all of you," he breathed, pressing wet kisses along the inside of one thigh, and then the other, each kiss drawing him nearer and nearer the very core of her.

Jillian's world spun violently and careened out of control. Cain allowed her no time for protest, no time to balk or shy away. He was totally uninhibited, his actions bold and explicit, and he would tolerate nothing short of complete surrender.

And surrender she did, to a maelstrom of emotions that took her to the very brink of the void. Before Cain, there had only been existence, a barren, empty landscape of form and motion. But no longer. Now she had life. He bombarded her with emotions and sensations that breathed fire and creation. He inflamed her sensibilities, torched her perceptions, moved her beyond yearning, beyond arousal, beyond desire. She'd been cautious for so long, but she was cautious no longer. She relinquished all control, all authority to his skill and ability, trusting him as she had trusted no one ever before.

He did not let her down. His hunger for her was immense, and he gloried in her, worshiped her with every move, every touch. He felt the tension building within her, felt the hold on his own constraints begin to slip. She was wildly responsive, like no woman he'd ever known. She was beyond any dream, exceeding perfection, and he couldn't have wanted her more. No greater desire, no greater emotion existed. Rising to stand, he pulled her desperate body to his, thrusting deeply.

Jillian gasped loudly, her eyes opening wide at the extent of Cain's possession. She looked up, seeing the intensity, the ardor in his clear blue gaze and feeling her heart stumble in her chest. The feel of him inside of her took her breath, but the emotion in his eyes pushed her over the edge. Reaching out, she brought his mouth to hers and together they slipped into the chasm.

* * *

Jillian stared up at the ceiling, watching the shadows perform their crazy dance across it. With the sash of the window open, the breeze through the screen made the shadows of the lace curtains cavort wildly and furiously.

She had no idea how long they had lain there, but the way she felt at that moment, she only wished they could remain forever. She barely remembered Cain carrying her from the bathroom, barely remembered him gently depositing her onto the bed and gathering her into his arms. She'd been too spent, too overwhelmed to be aware of much of anything, except that he held her close.

Cain.

Glancing down, she looked at the strong arm around her middle, felt the warm length of his body pressed behind her and felt his gentle breath against her back. He'd held her then, and he'd been holding her ever since.

She was exhausted—the most delicious, amazing, wonderful weariness she'd ever felt in her life. But despite her remarkable fatigue, despite the quiet and the tranquility, she hadn't been able to sleep. She didn't want to.

She knew this whole afternoon hadn't been a dream. She knew that he was really beside her, that he had really held her and kissed her and done all those unbelievable things to her. She knew falling asleep wouldn't change that, wouldn't make him disappear…but she didn't want to take a chance.

It was getting late. The shadows on the ceiling grew long as the sun moved farther toward the horizon, and the breeze through the window had turned cool. Jillian lifted her hand, examining her bandaged finger, remembering the old nightmares that small cut had triggered.

It was strange, but those tormenting images from her past didn't seem so frightening now. Lying in the warm security of Cain's embrace, she felt as though nothing could hurt her—not the past, not those old memories, not even the faceless enemies that stalked her.

She wiggled her finger, twisting her hand about, noting how carefully and precisely the bandage had been placed around the wound. She remembered Cain's careful nurturing, remembered the expression on his face, the things he had said. She wasn't used to anyone fussing over her, attending to her. Her mother had never taken the time. A cold, distant woman who had been far too concerned about appearances, had not always been the most understanding mother to a sensitive little girl. She never would have tolerated a public display of emotion, would never have rushed to give aid and comfort as Cain had done.

Jillian remembered how upset she'd been when she'd discovered he'd known who she was—about her family, her past. It seemed so silly now. She had been afraid it would make a difference between them, but now she knew better. It had been foolish to think any of that would have mattered to him.

Closing her eyes, she thought back to that moment in the shower. That moment when she'd turned to find Cain standing there. Desire had erupted between them with an unexpected intensity. She had long known she'd wanted him, but she'd been unprepared to discover just how much he'd wanted her.

Just then she felt his large hand drift to the narrow indentation of her waist, sliding down her hip and around her bottom. Lifting up on an elbow behind her, he placed a kiss along her shoulder.

"I thought you were asleep," she said.

"I feel too good to sleep," he murmured. Turning her in his arms, he rolled onto his back and pulled her across him.

"I feel good, too," she said, smiling down at him, her fingers tickling the dark, curly hair on his chest.

"Besides," Cain said, sliding his hands down the length of her torso, as he pressed her close, grinding himself against her, "my mind keeps drifting to other things."

Jillian smiled against his lips. "I know what you mean." Drawing back, she looked down at him. "I can hardly believe this is happening."

"What? You and me?"

She nodded her head. "Yes. I mean, we hardly know each other."

He lifted up, giving her a quick peck on the mouth, then falling back against the pillow. "I think after this afternoon you'd have a hard time making a jury buy that one, Counselor."

She laughed and grimaced a little. "You know what I mean."

The smile faded slowly from his lips. "Yeah." Reaching up, he pushed her long hair back from her face. "Second thoughts?"

"Oh God, no," she insisted, reaching to caress his cheek with her hand. "Never."

"Then, what is it?" he asked, turning and pressing a kiss into the palm of her hand.

"Nothing really," she insisted, shaking her head a little. "It's just all happening so fast."

"Sometimes things happen like that," he said. How could he explain to her he'd waited fifteen long years for this afternoon to happen.

"I guess," she smiled. She ran a finger along his strong, firm chin. "It's just that nothing like this has ever happened to me. I know so little about you." She shook her head again when he gave her a deliberate look. "That's not what I mean. You know something about me—my father, my family. I don't know anything about you."

He tensed at just how true her observation was, and silently cursed the circumstances that had him living a lie. "You know the most important thing," he murmured, pulling her close. "I'm here with you. And nothing like this has ever happened to me before, either."

Jillian accepted his long, slow kiss, her heart filled with emotion. Pulling back, she gazed down at him, feeling a little giddy. "I just thought of something."

"What's that?"

"Do you realize I don't even know your name?"

"Of course you do," he scoffed.

"Cain. I know Cain," she conceded. "But that's it. I don't even know if that's your first name or your last."

"Oh God," he groaned. "Does this mean you're going to pull your gun again?"

She laughed. "Well, I don't know," she said thoughtfully. "That all depends."

"Oh? On what?"

She leaned close, grabbing him by his long hair and shaking a warning finger at him. "On just how cooperative you are."

"Oh, I always cooperate with a woman who carries a SIG," he murmured, lifting his head off the pillow and giving her a kiss.

"Well, that's a relief," she said, slowly straightening up. "I'd hate to have to get rough."

His eyebrow raised and lowered wickedly, and his hand slipped from her shoulder, down her arm, to the soft swell of her breast. "Well, gosh, when you put it that way..."

"That's enough," she warned, batting his hand away. "Now, getting back to what we were talking about..."

"Yes, what were we talking about?" he asked innocently.

"What is it?" she demanded.

"What's what?" he replied.

"Your name?"

"My name?"

Her eyes narrowed and her brow arched. "Don't make me get nasty now."

"Okay, okay," he groused, propping himself up on one elbow. He'd never used anything but the name Cain while working undercover, and with the kinds of people he was used to dealing with, the need for first names rarely came up. But this was different, this was personal. He wanted her to know his name. Smiling he gave a little bow. "Please, let me introduce myself. Ash Cain, at your service, ma'am. And I can't tell you what a—dare I say—pleasure it's been meeting you."

"Ash?" Jillian blinked, a flutter of recognition drifting out from somewhere deep in her memory. "For heaven's sake."

The distant expression on her face had him forgetting all about their teasing. There was no way she would have recognized his name. She'd never known it. "What is it?" he asked guardedly, but it was as though she hadn't heard. "Jillian? Answer me, what is it?"

"Hmm—what? Oh! I'm sorry," she said, shaking her head and dispelling the deep thoughts. "It's nothing, really. Just . . . I knew someone named Ash once."

"Oh?" Every muscle in his massive body tensed.

"Yes, and he had blue eyes like yours." But she stopped then and shook her head. "No," she said, changing her mind. "No, that's not right."

"He didn't have blue eyes?"

"Oh, he had blue eyes all right," she said, running a finger down his cheek. "But no one has eyes quite like yours." She waved her hand, dismissing the thought. "Besides, that was a long time ago, anyway."

"Tell me," he prodded against his better judgement.

"No, it wasn't important," she said with a small laugh. "It's just a funny kind of a coincidence, that's all. It's an unusual name, you know? Ash. You don't hear it very often. I guess that's why I remembered it."

"What happened?" he urged, curious for reasons that had nothing to do with the job. "Tell me about this other Ash you knew."

She paused, reluctant to tell the story. It was about growing up, about schoolgirl dreams and rites of passage and things she couldn't imagine him understanding. But there was something so intense in his eyes, something so emotional, she found herself thinking back, remembering.

"I was pretty young—eighteen, nineteen maybe, and it was during one of my uncle's campaigns. My cousins and I were on break from school and we used to spend a lot of time at his campaign headquarters—you know, answering phones, stuffing envelopes, stuff like that. Anyway, there was this young Secret Service agent assigned to my uncle. I had the worst crush on him. My cousin Hilary and I used to watch him and make up stories about him. Hilary found out from one of the campaign secretaries that his name was Ash." She looked up at him and smiled foolishly. "See? Just kind of a kookie fluke."

For a moment Cain couldn't say anything; it was all he could do to keep breathing. "You knew this guy, then? This...Ash?"

"Oh, heavens no," she laughed, rolling her eyes. "It was just a crush—real innocent, you know. I don't think I ever even knew his last name. He was older, and didn't even know I was alive. Well, except..."

"Except?"

She smiled as she remembered. "Well, there was this one time in an elevator. A reporter—a real creep—had started to bother me, grabbing and getting fresh. Well, Ash—my hero—showed up and got rid of the guy. I was pretty shook up, though, so he walked me down to the limo and... well..."

"Go on."

"Well, he... he kissed me." She turned to Cain and giggled a little. "I remember it so well because it was... well, it was my first kiss."

Cain felt as though he'd been hit very hard in the stomach. The room swayed around him and the ringing in his ears grew deafening. He thought back to that night in the parking garage.

That kiss. That kiss he'd never been able to forget had been her first.

"Jillian," he whispered, his voice rough and strained. "Jillian, I want you," he growled, pushing her down onto the mattress and pushing her legs wide apart. "I want you now."

Jillian had no idea where the urgency had come from, or the fury, but none of that mattered. His desperation had picked her up and swept her along with him, making her desperate, too. She arched up to him, accepting all of him that she could.

The demon inside of him was wild, and he pushed into her with a single-minded purpose that tolerated no distractions, no delays. She could only cling to him, riding the crest of his violent storm, feeling the feral, savage force within him propelling them forward and driving them on. Rapture came to her in a blinding paroxysm of light, sound and sensation. Within seconds he had followed, his huge body convulsing inside her—brash, reckless and commanding.

"You're mine now, Jillian," he murmured with his last bit of strength. "Mine."

"Yes," she murmured dreamily just before slipping into the welcoming darkness that blocked out everything else.

"I knew you were inside, I just figured..." Spence hedged, his voice trailing off. "Well, you know."

"Yeah," Cain murmured into the phone. It had been well after midnight when he'd awakened in Jillian's bed—hours past his check-in time. While Jillian slept peacefully, he'd slipped from the bedroom and retrieved his tool belt from the bathroom floor—along with his gun and cellular phone. Standing in the dark, empty kitchen now, he gazed out the window to the full moon outside and tried to ignore the concern in his partner's voice. "Anyway, I just wanted to touch base. I'll give you a call in the morning."

"I'll be here, buddy," Spence assured him good-naturedly. There was a brief hesitation, and Spence cleared his throat quietly. "Oh and, uh, Cain?"

"Yeah?"

"Stay cool, man."

"Got it," Cain said, switching off the phone. *Stay cool.* Didn't he wish that he could. Unfortunately, when it came to the woman in the bedroom, that seemed impossible. He'd been playing it anything *but* cool since the whole thing began.

Spence knew the tightrope Cain was walking, knew emotions ran high, ran hot. Still, it was important for them both that they keep up the facade. *Stay loose, man. Stay cool.*

Slipping the phone back into the deep pocket of the leather belt, he silently moved back through the house to the bedroom. On the bed, Jillian slept peacefully, the moonlight streaming through the open window, pouring over her like cream over a rich dessert. The white sheet silhouetted her beautiful body, and Cain felt the muscles in his chest constrict tightly.

Nothing could have prepared him for what had happened between them today—nothing. He felt a little as though he'd realized a dream, that he'd achieved his goal, found his cache of gold, his stockpile of diamonds. He owned her first kiss—what a treasure she'd bestowed upon him. Was it just fate that had brought them together again? Something had started with that one innocent kiss, something that had come full circle in this little house fifteen years later. Was it just coincidence, or was it part of some grand scheme, some predetermined design?

There had been something about her, something from the very first. And even though he felt something very different for the woman she was today than he had for the young coed she'd been back then, he couldn't deny the significance of that first encounter. He'd been young back then, dazzled by who she was and what she represented. None of that mattered to him now. It was *her*—Jillian—he wanted. The woman who had melted in his arms, whose taste invaded and incited him, and whose bed he never wanted to leave.

Walking silently to the bed, he soundlessly slid the tool belt beneath it. He remembered how she had looked when he had opened that shower door, when he had stood there devouring her with his gaze. There had been no outrage in her eyes, no indignation. There had only been desire. The need in her had seemed almost as great as his own, and joining with her had been like two souls fusing.

"Cain?" she mumbled sleepily when he slipped into the bed beside her.

"Shh, go back to sleep," he whispered, his lips brushing a kiss along her neck.

"Where've you been?"

"Locking up the house," he said, gathering her close. At least it had been partly the truth.

She smiled dreamily, snuggling into his embrace. "I guess we forgot."

Yes, he thought darkly, just like he'd managed to forget everything else when he was with her—like his partner, his responsibilities and the job he had to do. He couldn't let that happen again. "Go to sleep."

He held her close, feeling the slow, rhythmic pattern of her breathing. Lying in the darkness with his arms around her, he felt that there was nothing he couldn't protect her from. But he knew how deceptive those feelings were. There was so much that could happen, so much she could still be hurt by.

Cain remembered the terror in Jillian's eyes when the cut on her hand had triggered those painful memories from her childhood. He couldn't shield her from a painful past, but he would do everything he could to make sure nothing hurt her again.

He wasn't about to let any of Donelli's hired guns get to her, even if it meant taking a bullet himself. He could protect her from a hit man, but how could he protect her from the truth?

Sooner or later she would have to know—he would have to tell her who he was and why he'd really come. He knew her, knew how angry and betrayed she was going to feel. How was he supposed to safeguard her against that? How did he prepare her for the truth?

He felt her stir, felt the easy, unconscious movement of her body next to his. Would she understand in time? Would he ever be able to convince her how much this meant to him, how much he'd come to care? Would a summer filled with nights like tonight be enough? Would a lifetime? Surely she would see that being with her had nothing to do with a job and duty, and everything to do with love.

"Cain?" she murmured after a long moment.

Her quiet whisper scattered his troubling thoughts, but he was grateful for the distraction. That word *love* had just slipped in there so easily, it had taken him by surprise. "I thought you were asleep."

"One evening on the dock..."

"Yes."

"...you'd been swimming..."

"I remember."

"...and you climbed out and dried off with a towel..."

"Right."

"You didn't have anything on."

"I guess I didn't."

She raised up on an elbow and looked down at him. "I was watching."

He brought a hand up, letting it tangle in her hair, and pulled her close. "I know."

Chapter 10

Jillian blinked away the beads of perspiration stinging her eyes and tossed one last shovelful of potting soil around a newly planted cluster of Shasta daisies. Straightening, she stretched the tightening muscles in her back and squinted up at the unrelenting sun. The hot weather had returned with a vengeance, and even though she had four more pots of daises waiting to be transplanted, she wasn't sure she had the strength to get to them.

Pushing the shovel down into the dry ground, she rested her hands on the handle. She couldn't see Cain from where she stood, but she could hear the occasional grate of his sander or scrape of his wire brush at the front of the house. She pictured him perched on the ladder, scraping away the chipped and peeling paint, his chest bare and burnished and his huge muscles glistening in the sun.

A pleasant warmth radiated through her as she thought of him, a warmth that was nothing like the harsh, blistering rays of the sun burning her arms and legs. It was a pleasing heat, a very enjoyable, very satisfying feeling.

Last night had been a first, but not in the traditional sense. At thirty-four, she was far from being a virgin. After all, she and Ron had been lovers, and she had been married to Jeff for nearly a decade. She firmly believed comparisons had no place in the intimacies between men and women, and she was hardly interested in making them now. But it was impossible not to recognize and acknowledge that being with Ash Cain had been like no other experience she'd ever had in her life.

Shaking her head, Jillian closed her eyes to the rush of emotion that bubbled within her. Who was Ash Cain? What had he done to her? When had she begun to care? Where would it end? And why had it happened?

She had no idea how to answer any of those questions. Normally she would have tortured and tormented herself until she could, but she hadn't been behaving normally since she'd met him. The amazing part of this whole crazy thing was that for the first time in her life it didn't matter. It didn't matter that she had no answers, that she couldn't rationalize or justify. It was enough for now just to have him, to be with him, and to experience all there was of him that she could.

Turning, she glanced at the pots of daisies lined neatly along the garden's edge like dutiful soldiers silently awaiting orders. The sun felt ruthless against her skin, and she drew in a long, hot breath. The daisies looked so beautiful, and she was so close to being done. Wiping at her wet forehead, she grasped the shovel with both hands. Maybe she had just enough energy to finish up. Maybe.

"I'll just wait to hear from you, then," Spence said, yawning loudly into the receiver. "No sense making the lady suspicious with an inconvenient call."

"No sense in that," Cain mumbled back, wondering just how long it would be before she really got suspicious.

"Have you thought about..." Spence's voice trailed off, and there was a brief pause. "About after. About, you know, how you're going to... tell her?"

Cain closed his eyes, counting the times he'd asked himself that same question during the night. "Not really."

"Don't you think you should?"

"Yes, of course I do," he snapped, then paused and took a deep breath. "I... I guess I'll just cross that bridge when the time comes."

"How do you think she'll take it?"

"I don't know," Cain said honestly, having imagined scenarios of her reaction a dozen different ways. "She's a little hard to predict."

Spence hesitated for a moment. "This woman has really gotten under your skin, hasn't she?"

"Maybe," he hedged.

"The senator could be a problem. You know, if it doesn't work out."

"I can handle it," Cain grunted, thinking he could handle Graham Hughes a lot better than he could his niece.

"Well, I'll be here, man, if you need me," Spence assured him.

Cain smiled. "Thanks, buddy. Why don't you try and get some sleep now. You sound beat."

"I am," Spence grumbled, yawning again. "Man, I tell you, I'm getting too old for this crap. Stale doughnuts, cold coffee. This all-night stuff sucks."

Cain immediately felt guilty, remembering the wonderfully long and glorious night he'd spent in bed with Jillian. "Hey, weren't you the one who used to say it was the best part of the job? Like a camp-out?"

"Yeah? Well, I used to think nobody could beat Tyson and the Raiders would be in Oakland forever," Spence groused. "So what does that tell you?"

"Get some sleep," Cain chuckled, rubbing his scratchy eyes. "I'll check in later."

"Be cool, man."

"Right," Cain said, ending the connection and slipping the phone back into his tool belt.

Cool. Looking up, he squinted toward the sun, feeling the burning heat against his face. He had about as much chance of staying cool beneath that sun as he had of playing it cool around Jillian. It simply couldn't be done. It was a physical impossibility.

Reaching for the steel brush and sandpaper, he went to work on the crumbling paint around a rusted spout. But even as the sun beat down against his back, he remembered how cool and smooth Jillian's skin had felt—as cool and smooth as the river water flowing along the levee out back.

He thought of her confession last night. She'd seen him on the dock, she'd watched him, and the thought of her watching made the heat in him burn hotter than the blazing sun above. Spence had said the woman had gotten under his skin. He'd only guessed the half of it. She was more than just under his skin. She was in his head, and in his heart. He couldn't seem to get enough of her, and he suspected he never would.

Jillian reached down and halfheartedly finished digging the shallow hole. Reaching for the one remaining bunch of the daisies, she lifted them from their vinyl pot and settled them into place in the cavity. With an aching back, she crouched down, pushing the dirt haphazardly around them, patting it down.

Nearly finished, she thought in her feverish brain. Just a few handfuls of potting soil from the large plastic bag beside her, and that would be it. It had almost become a cause with her, a quest to finish before her strength gave out. But when she turned to reach into the bag of soil one last time, she was rudely grabbed from behind and hurled up to her feet.

She made contact with the hard muscle of Cain's chest with a jolt. Before she could react, his arms were around her waist and his lips nuzzled her neck.

"You should have your visor on," he scolded, feeling the heat of her skin against his lips, tasting the salt of her sweat. "You'll get sunburned."

"You don't like tan lines?" she teased, turning in his arms and reaching to embrace him despite her hot, sweaty body.

"I don't like to think of anything marring that gorgeous skin of yours," he murmured, running a hand down the flesh of her arm and pulling her up to his mouth for a quick kiss. Easing her back down to her feet, he glanced up at the sun. "I mean it, it's really heating up. Why don't you go inside and cool off? I turned the air conditioner on."

"Why don't you come with me?" she suggested, giving him a deliberate smile and sliding her hands down his imposing frame and giving his buns a playful squeeze.

He looked down at her with a slow, satisfied grin. There was so much about his involvement with her that was unwise, that remained uncertain, but there was one thing he knew without a doubt. He could please her. He had the ability to bring her pure, absolute pleasure, and he derived immense satisfaction in that fact.

"You forget," he said, pretending to scold by giving her hips a playful twist. "I'm working."

"Can't you take a day off?" she asked, twirling a long strand of his hair around her finger. "It's Saturday."

He shook his head. "Nope. My boss is a tyrant. She'd fire me—maybe even threaten to shoot me."

Jillian smiled. "Sounds like a lousy job. You ought to quit."

"Oh, I can't do that. I need it," he murmured, running a hand up her back. Would she still be smiling if she knew just how much he needed her? "Besides, it has its benefits."

Lifting up on tiptoe, Jillian gave him a long, sexy kiss. "Cain?"

"Hmm?"

"You're fired."

"I am?"

"Now get inside the house."

He looked down at her for a moment, wondering how it was possible to want her any more than he did right now. "I've got a better idea," he said suddenly, boosting her off her feet and flinging her over his huge shoulder like a rag doll.

"Cain, are you crazy? Stop," Jillian screamed, trying her best to wriggle free. "Stop! What are you doing? Cain!"

But he ignored her pleas, just as he ignored her struggles, and doggedly climbed the levee and sprinted out onto the dock. As he passed the boat, he slid off his tool belt and tossed it onto the deck. When he reached the end of the dock, he paused just long enough for her to realize his intent.

"Oh no," she said suddenly, shaking her head. She twisted and kicked, swatting at him feebly. "No you don't. No, Cain. Don't you dare. Don't you da—"

But it was too late. With a powerful thrust, he hurled them both off the end of the dock and into the cold, lazy flow of the river.

Jillian reached for the surface, gasping for air, her wet hair plastered to her face. "Oooh, you just wait," she warned, feeling about blindly, her hair like a mask over her eyes. The cold water felt brisk and refreshing against her skin. Spotting him through a break in the wet strands, she shook her finger. "You wait. You're in for it now."

But Cain was ready for her. He tackled her again, taking her under once more. They splashed and played like two kids, but they were far from being children, and games didn't occupy them for long. Quickly the play turned passionate. Beneath the water, Cain reached for her. And as the laughter stilled and the water swirled around them, he pulled her close for a kiss.

"You're just lucky I'm not in the mood to get really mad," she breathed against his lips, breathless and a little unsteady from the kiss.

"Oh yeah, boss lady," he murmured, tightening his hold on her. "What are you in the mood for?"

"You," she whispered, the smile fading from her lips.

In the haze of emotions that followed, Jillian could think of nothing but the touch, the taste and the feel of him. Clothing seemed to miraculously disappear—one piece after the other. She wasn't sure how it was done, or where they had gone, nor did she care. All that was important was that he was bare against her, and he wanted her.

They had drifted to the dock, and with one simple push, he had lifted her onto the deck of the boat. He must have carried her into the small cabin and onto his bunk. Either that, or she'd floated, for she had no recollection of having made it there on her own. All she remembered were his kisses on her mouth, her neck and her breasts.

"Cain," she murmured dizzily when he pressed her back onto the narrow bed. She wanted to feel him everywhere, even his name on her lips. "Cain."

At the sound of his name, Cain paused, pulling back and looking down at her. Never had she looked more beautiful, and he knew he would remember how she looked at this moment until his dying breath. Her eyes were half-closed, her breasts rose and fell with the urgency of her breath, and her lips were red and full. She was the picture of a woman on the verge, a woman ripe with desire, full of wants, full of needs and ready for her man.

Her man. That was him. At least for now, at least until the real world found them again. Until then, he was her man. She was his dream come true, his wish upon a star.

Positioning himself between her legs, he sunk into her slowly, knowing even as he possessed her with this intimate act, it was he who was the possession. Like that night so long ago in the back seat of her uncle's limousine, her eyes spoke volumes to him, and he realized now that it was his destiny to answer.

Their lovemaking began slow, deliberate, sure. For the moment, urgency wasn't an issue and desperation had long since been satisfied. There was a quiet window of calm that allowed them time to touch, to savor, to enjoy. Sensation didn't rain down like bombs in an air raid, overwhelming and uncontrolled, but rather drifted and floated through the air around them. It was possible to relish each sensation, explore and define every single one, and commit them to heart.

But inevitably, as emotion built on emotion, need on need, serenity gave way to necessity, and the calm ended in a storm. Clinging, they rode the tidal wave together to that magic place where hearts soared and souls collided.

"Take me for a ride?"

"Hmm?" Cain mumbled drowsily. He wasn't sure how long they had been lying on his narrow cot, but the way his body felt, it wasn't long enough. "A ride?"

"Yeah, on the boat," Jillian goaded, sitting up and giving him a shake. "Come on."

Cain rolled over onto his back and looked up at her, shaking his head in disbelief. "You aren't even a little bit tired?"

Jillian smiled. For some reason their intense lovemaking had left her feeling deliciously fulfilled and renewed, rather than exhausted. She felt ready to burst with energy. "Not even a little."

He groaned, rubbing his eyes. "A ride?"

"Yeah," she said eagerly, tugging on his arm. "Doesn't that sound fun?"

"Fun," he grumbled in a low voice, slowly sitting up. Looking into her bright eyes and lively face, he shook his head again. "You wear me out, lady, you know that?"

"Well, if you're really too tired . . ." she said wryly, sliding her arms over his shoulders and leaning down to give him a kiss on the nose. *"Gramps."*

In a move that had the breath catching in her throat, Cain had grabbed her and effortlessly brought her down onto the bunk beneath him. "I think the old man might still have a few moves left in him."

"I believe you, I believe you," she conceded, lifting her arms up to encircle his neck.

Cain lowered his head as though he meant to kiss her. He saw Jillian's eyes slide closed and her lips part in preparation. But with his lips hovering just a breath above hers, he suddenly stopped.

"Okay, let's go," he said abruptly, giving her a playful swat on the bottom.

He leapt to his feet, ducking just in time to avoid the pillow that came hurtling across the cabin at him.

* * *

"It wasn't my fault."

Cain put his hands on his hips and gave her a deliberate look.

"Well," she lamented defensively, making a face, "you said go faster."

"I said, speed up *a little*," he corrected, a small smile tugging at the corners of his mouth. "There's a difference."

"How was I supposed to know? Who'd have thought you could get going that fast in such a short distance?" She scowled, twisting her mouth. "It was just a stupid little bump. For heaven's sake, you'd think they'd build things a little sturdier than that." She paused, some of the defensiveness leaving her in a long sigh. "Can you fix it?"

Cain surveyed the two ugly dents in the hull of the boat. As long as the thing remained floating, he didn't care how pretty it looked. "Maybe, but that whole end of the dock is going to have to be rebuilt. I wouldn't trust it the way it is now. It could collapse."

Jillian stood up and cringed. The end of the dock drooped precariously, tilting badly to one side. Closing her eyes, she shook her head sadly. "Oh God, look at that."

Cain had to smile at the contrition in her voice. She had probably sounded very much the same way as a dark-eyed little girl having been caught doing something she shouldn't. What a charmer she would have been with those big eyes and pouting mouth. No wonder she was spoiled. Who could deny her anything? He'd actually been enjoying ribbing her about the "little mishap," but she looked so miserable, he didn't have the heart to continue.

Slowly, Cain rose to his feet. Sliding a comforting arm around her shoulders, he gave her a little squeeze. "You know, it's really not that big a deal."

She crumpled then, turning her head into his chest. "I feel so stupid."

"It was just an accident," he pointed out, stroking her long, dark hair and thinking she was about as far from stupid as you could get. "Besides, that dock didn't have too many years left in it, anyway."

"But your boat," she said, glancing up and looking down at the damaged hull again. "Look what I did to it."

"It's just a couple of scrapes," he told her. "I'll take care of it."

"But just look at it," she said again, turning and gesturing at the damage. "Your boat, Cain. Your beautiful boat. I am so sorry."

It wasn't until then that he realized just how very seriously she was taking it. She really felt badly. And they'd had such a great afternoon. After having changed into fresh clothes earlier, they'd taken a long, lazy cruise through the delta. They'd sat and talked. He'd told her how devastated he'd been when his older brother had been killed in Vietnam, and she'd told him about losing Ron, and how miserably her marriage had failed, and why. But that had been the only serious part of the day. They'd stopped for deliciously greasy burgers at Wimpy's Marina, cruised through the lush beauty of the Meadows, refueled at Owl Harbor and idly sailed back along the Mokelumne River. They'd joked and teased one another all the way home, and when she'd stubbornly insisted on piloting the boat back to the dock, he'd let her do it. It wasn't as though she'd banged into the dock on purpose; it had been an accident. He'd found it a comical, almost endearing comeuppance for her stubbornness.

But it suddenly hit him that she had no way of knowing that the boat really wasn't his, that it held no special meaning to him beyond the time he'd spent on it with her. All she knew was what he had told her—that it was all that he had, his prize possession, and she had wrecked it.

"Oh, sweetheart," he sighed, pulling her close. He understood how important it was to keep his cover intact, but he couldn't stand there and allow her to beat herself up over this. "Jillian, look at me," he insisted, pulling back and holding her firmly at arm's length. "Look at me. It's a couple of scratches. It can be fixed. It's not that important. Not important enough for you to feel bad."

"You aren't mad, then?"

"Mad at you?" he laughed, pulling her into his arms. "Don't you understand? I'm more concerned about how you feel than that damn boat."

I'm more concerned about how you feel... The words echoed through Jillian's head, bouncing back and forth, repeating over and over again. She looked up at him, her face full of emotion. There was so much she wanted to say, so much in her heart, but her throat was too tight to let the words pass. She could only stare up into his face and let her eyes communicate what she could never say.

"Come on," he said in a gruff voice, desire twisting in his gut. He purposefully set her away from him and automatically reached into the boat for his tool belt. "Let's go inside."

"Yes," she breathed out in a long sigh. She actually felt herself smiling, felt life coming back into her again. But when she glanced down at the tool belt in his hand, she cocked her head to one side. "What do you need that for?"

Cain followed the line of her gaze. He stared down at the tool belt in his hand like it was some kind of foreign object. How did he explain his need for it? After all, he hardly expected her to believe he planned on doing any work, and he certainly couldn't tell her the truth.

"Uh, I...I guess I don't," he shrugged, reluctantly setting the belt back down on the deck of the boat. He looked up at her foolishly and shrugged. "Habit, I guess."

His tired mind raced as they climbed down the levee and started toward the house. Finally, inspiration came to him. Snapping his fingers, he stopped abruptly. "Damn, I forgot to lock the hatch."

"The what?"

"The—uh—the hatch, you know," he said vaguely, turning around and quickly sprinting back up the levee. "I'll be right back."

He gave her no time to protest, bolting back to the boat and retrieving the tool belt. Moving quickly, he reached behind and slipped the gun into the waistband of his shorts and pulled his T-shirt over the top. Glancing down at the cellular phone, his mind raced for a place he might hide it. Deciding it was impossible, he slipped it back into the tool belt.

Leaping out of the boat, he started down the levee toward Jillian again. There was always the phone in the house. At least he had the Glock. That was what was important.

Jillian watched as he walked toward her, her heart swelling in her chest. She remembered those words again, those beautiful words he'd said. Like the refrain from a song that had suddenly become her favorite, she replayed them again and again in her mind. He'd been concerned about her, about how she felt. He cared about her, he had to. He'd all but said it, and she believed him.

She'd felt terrible about the accident. Growing up in a family where mistakes weren't tolerated, where one's first allegiance was appearances, and then perfection, any mistake, however accidental, was looked upon as an unforgivable error.

But not with Cain. Everything he had was in that boat, everything of importance. And yet he hadn't chided or chastised her. He hadn't scolded or reprimanded. He'd been more concerned about how she'd felt. She was a long way from understanding a man who placed her above all else that he had. No one had ever done that for her—not Jeff, not even Ron.

Yes, he cared about her, and the song played on in her head.

"I thought I'd better call while I had a chance," Cain whispered into the telephone receiver. Except for the steady drone of the air conditioner in the living room window, the house was quiet. After dinner, and after carefully stashing the Glock beneath the mattress of the bed, he and Jillian had sat on the front porch in the old fashioned swing and watched the sun set and the moon rise. Exhausted, Jillian had fallen asleep in his arms. She hadn't even awakened when he'd carried her into the bedroom and laid her gently on the bed. Taking advantage of the time alone, he'd slipped through the dark house and into the kitchen to quickly check in with Spence. "When did the call come in?"

"About an hour ago," Spence explained. "Apparently the senator's been pulling a few strings again. They're expecting to make the move sometime tonight." There was a pause, and then Spence's low chuckling. "Yup, by tomorrow morning our old buddy Donelli will be receiving all his messages through the warden at Marion."

It seemed almost too good to be true, Cain thought, turning the information over in his head. Alfred Donelli would be behind the walls of Marion Federal Penitentiary by sunrise. Not even Donelli's power and muscle could penetrate that maximum-security prison. By morning, he'd no longer be a threat to anyone.

"Anything for us?" he asked, greeting the prospect that their assignment was nearing an end with mixed emotions.

"Just that we're to maintain the status quo," Spence said. "Donelli's had plenty of time since his trial to arrange a hit, and Hughes isn't taking any chances. Our assignment hasn't changed. We're supposed to keep a lookout for anything suspicious."

Cain rubbed at his tired eyes and breathed out a long sigh of relief. As much as he hated lying to Jillian, he wasn't ready to face her with the truth, either. Telling her could prove costly, and he wasn't sure he was ready to take the chance yet. He needed time to convince her, to make her understand what he felt and what they shared was real, something that had nothing to do with the job he'd been assigned to do.

"Hey, still with me, bud?"

The sound of Spence's voice over the line stirred Cain from his reverie. "Hmm? Oh, yeah, still here."

"Everything going . . . good?"

Cain knew Spence wasn't interested in everything, just the relationship with Jillian. "It's okay."

"Just . . . okay?"

Cain smiled in the darkness. "Maybe it's a little better than okay."

"That's one very seriously wonderful-looking woman, I hope you know," Spence said in such a sober tone Cain could hardly take offense.

"I've noticed that," he laughed quietly, wondering when his partner had developed such a silver tongue.

"Yeah, well, just thought I'd point that out," Spence continued. "Get some sleep. You know where to find me."

"Right."

"And, Cain?"

"Yeah?"

"She wouldn't just happen to have a sister or anything like that, does she?"

"I'm afraid not."

Spence paused, then chuckled quietly over the phone. "You always were the luckiest bastard I ever saw."

Cain smiled again. "Good night, Spence."

"Hang in there, bud."

Cain carefully returned the telephone receiver to its cradle, standing in the dark kitchen and listening to the quiet hum of the air conditioner. Walking to the window, he looked outside. The moon shone high in the sky, looking big, round and white. It bathed the night in a blanket of dim, gray light, giving everything a strange, foreboding look. Despite the late hour, it was still hot and humid outside, and Cain didn't envy Spence his long night. There wasn't so much as a hint of a breeze off the water, and sultry conditions could make a stakeout seem endless.

He turned, staring through the darkness toward the bedroom. He thought of Jillian asleep on the bed, thought of how soft she felt, how good she smelled. So much had happened in the last twenty-four hours—enough to make his head spin, enough to change his life forever.

It felt so right with her, so natural. He'd never experienced such an immediate affinity with a woman before, such immediate comfort. They seemed so attuned to one another, so joined. It hadn't even been a consideration that he would return to the boat for the night. It had just been understood that he would stay with her, that they would share a bed together.

He thought of the dinner they had shared earlier, how they'd both maneuvered in the small kitchen—talking and laughing as they chopped tomatoes and peppers for the sauce they'd concocted to pour over fresh pasta. It was as though they'd been together for years, as though they were already a couple. And yet passion could ignite so quickly between them, it was as though every time was the first.

Would it be like that if they were married? If they shared a home and built a future? Would there be the easy conversation, the comfortable companionship, the flaring passion?

He shook his head, walking to the refrigerator and reaching for the pitcher of sun tea inside. Pouring the tea into a glass, he smiled at his own folly. They were crazy thoughts—thoughts one only dared think late at night and in the dark. The possibility of the two of them getting married was impossible. But then, he had to admit that a day ago the possibility of him sharing a bed with her had seemed impossible, as well.

He finished the tea, returning the pitcher to the refrigerator and the glass to the sink. Still, he couldn't help thinking as he walked the short distance down the hall to the bedroom just what it might be like to be her husband, to sleep with her every night, to know she would belong to him forever.

Opening the door, he stopped, gazing through the thick, gray darkness at the shadowy outline of her on the bed. Just seeing her had his calm, even heart rate speeding up. He imagined them together, imagined holding her, kissing her, giving her his seed. In his mind he could picture her, round and full with his child, thoughtfully and lovingly caring for his son or his daughter.

Closing his eyes, he shook his head, shook away the images of mother and child. Impossible dreams, he decided. Hopeless, impossible dreams that served no purpose other than to torture him, to taunt and tease him with what he knew he could never have.

Already he'd had more with her than he'd ever hoped, than he'd ever thought possible. And it was up to him to make the most of every precious moment.

One day at a time, he told himself. That's all he could ever hope for. With Donelli incarcerated securely within the walls of Marion Federal Penitentiary, the threat to Jillian had been greatly diminished. His assignment could end at any moment.

One day at a time. All the more reason to concentrate on what he had, rather than mourn what never would be.

"Come to bed."

Her voice startled him, his gaze lifting to find her sitting up on the bed looking at him.

"I thought you were asleep."

"I don't want to sleep without you," she whispered, slipping her T-shirt over her head and tossing it to the floor.

He moved across the room, sliding down onto the bed beside her and helping free her of the rest of her clothes. "You're beautiful," he said, marveling at the sight of her.

"Come to bed, Cain," she murmured again, reaching for the fly of his shorts.

Chapter 11

It sounded deafening, reverberating through the dark silence like an explosion of catastrophic dimension. The gun was in Cain's hand before his feet ever hit the floor. The pounding continued, almost shaking the house in its foundation. Cain grabbed for a pair of jeans he'd tossed beside the bed, slipping them on in one smooth motion.

"What is it?" Jillian asked, sitting up. Confusion and fear had her voice hoarse and unsteady. "Cain, what is it? What's happened?"

"Stay there," he ordered in a quiet voice, stepping out of the room and moving soundlessly through the dark house toward the front door. Instinct had taken over, and senses were on full alert. The gun in his hand was poised and ready. Something was wrong, he could feel it in his gut. The house was dark—too dark—and, except for the incessant pounding on the front door, too quiet. Glancing across the room, he looked at the air conditioner resting silently in the window. Power to the house had been cut off.

Nearing the front door, Cain grew more cautious. With the air conditioner off, the little house felt stuffy and hot. Sweat began to drip down his temples, his back. At the front door, he lifted the gun up, poised and ready. Peering through the lace curtain, he saw Spence on the porch outside.

Something was very, very wrong.

Reaching for the door handle, he slipped the dead bolt back and cautiously opened the door. Spence fell through the doorway, Cain barely catching him before he hit the floor.

"Oh my God," Jillian gasped, running into the room.

"Get back," Cain ordered, motioning to her with a jerk of his chin as he dragged Spence inside. Pausing momentarily, he reached back and pulled the door shut, bolting it again.

But Jillian had been unable to move. Having hurriedly thrown on clothes, she stood in the shadows and watched in numb silence as Cain dragged the stranger inside and cradled him in his arms. She was confused by the scene, frightened by it even, but her fear was dampened by an unexplained feeling of dread.

"Spence," Cain whispered, looking down into the distorted face of his partner. He didn't need to see the blood to know his partner had been shot, he could *smell* it.

"Saw them," Spence whispered, wincing with pain.

"Don't try and talk," Cain said, working quickly, tearing at the bloodstained shirt. "Just hang in there buddy. Hang on."

"H-had to warn you," Spence stammered with great effort, clutching at Cain's arm. "Two of them. Bastards saw me. Saw m—"

But he never finished. The hand on Cain's arm clenched once, then fell. The air left Spence's body in a strangled gasp. He was dead.

Jillian stood in stunned horror, feeling the floor beneath her feet pitch and sway. Something was awfully wrong. Something was very, very wrong. This had to be some kind of awful mistake, some terrible misunderstanding. This man—this stranger—had just died in her living room. What was happening? It made no sense.

And it made no sense that Cain held a big, ugly gun in his hand.

Jillian shook her head, backing toward the bedroom. This couldn't be happening, couldn't be real. Somehow she'd mistakenly awakened in a nightmare, and she had to find her way back out. But the sick, sinking feeling in the pit of her stomach told her there had been no mistake, that this was no nightmare—it was all unbelievably real.

Her gaze shifted to Cain as he prowled through the house. The gun in his hand looked so comfortable, so natural, and his movements were too practiced, too controlled. He'd done this before. This wasn't the man she knew, the man who lived on the river, who sailed the lazy delta waterways, who had charmed and teased and held her. This man was a stranger.

Cain's eyes scanned the blackness outside, searching for any sign of movement, any sign of anything. Spence was dead, but there was no time to mourn. If they were lucky, there would be time for that later—maybe. He had to concentrate on protecting Jillian now, on keeping her alive. That's all that was important.

Moving cautiously through the dark living room, he tested the light switches and telephone lines. All dead. Not an encouraging sign. Crouching low, he looked out the window again. The moon had sunk low, its glow faded and dim now, and the darkness made it difficult to see. But something was out there, he could feel it. Someone had put a bullet in Spence, and it was the same person who wanted to put one in Jillian.

He wasn't about to let that happen. Cain's hand tightened around the butt of his gun.

"Who are you?"

Cain turned around slowly, finding himself looking down the barrel of her SIG again.

"What are you doing with that?" he asked irritably, stepping back from the window and slowly straightening up. He started across the room toward her.

"Stay where you are," she demanded, fixing the gun's sight to the spot on his chest that had pillowed her head only a short while ago.

Cain stopped. It was her voice rather than her threat he reacted to. It was cold, flat and completely without emotion. "Jillian, put the gun down."

"Who are you?"

The question came out more like an accusation, and Cain braced himself. The quiet night had gone from dark and safe to dangerous and deadly in a matter of moments. Spence was dead, and now she was demanding the truth.

"You know who I am," he told her simply, but even in the darkness he could see the doubt in her eyes.

Jillian stared him straight in the eye, never flinching. It was odd. She was terrified, more frightened than she could ever remember being in her life, but for some strange reason she was having difficulty feeling anything. It was as though some defense mechanism had kicked in, some natural guard which provided her with a cold, unfeeling sort of calm. It was this calm, this detached composure, that had her mind moving a million miles an hour, that had prompted her to slip back into the bedroom and retrieve the gun from her nightstand. She didn't know what was going on, but she knew she'd feel better with the SIG in her hand until she *did* know.

"All I know is you're not who you said you were," she said calmly. "You're no roofer, no handyman. And you don't live on that boat."

His voice softened. "I thought who we were and where we came from didn't matter with us."

"It does if you're working for Donelli."

His head came up. "Is that what you think?"

"I don't know what to think."

He took a step toward her. "You think last night would have happened if I'd been sent here to kill you?"

"I—I don't know," she admitted, feeling her legs begin to tremble.

"I'm no hired killer," he said deliberately, taking another step toward her. "And you know it."

"What were you doing with a gun, then?"

He glanced down at the Glock at his side, and then back to the SIG leveled at him. "I'm not the only one with a gun."

"No, you're not," she acknowledged.

"So what happens now?" he asked, taking several more steps in her direction.

"Stop. Don't come any closer," she advised as he came closer, but he ignored the warning. "I'm warning you. Stop!"

"Or what, Jillian? You'll shoot me?" He closed the distance between them and brazenly pressed his bare chest into the barrel of the bun. "Go ahead, then. Shoot."

Her dark gaze practically seared him, and there was a split second, a fleeting moment, when he thought she just might pull the trigger. He looked down at her, thinking how only a few short hours ago she had undressed him, kissed him and made him feel as though he was the most important man in the world. She was so close he could all but taste her, had only to reach out and pull her to him. But the fact that he stood within reach didn't change the fact that the distance between them at that moment could have spanned the cosmos.

"I hate you," she muttered, lowering the gun and turning away.

"That's beside the point," Cain said coolly, but her words had pierced his very soul. Steeling himself to the dull pain in his chest, he snatched the gun from her hand. "In the meantime, my partner's dead and we've got to find a way out of here."

Jillian glanced down at Spence's lifeless form on the floor and a shudder passed through her. She slowly backed away, crouching within the dark, secure protection of the hallway.

Holding her arms tightly around herself, she watched as Cain prowled restlessly through the dark house. He wasn't one of Donelli's lackeys, and intuitively she had known that even before she'd confronted him. Unfortunately that left only one other alternative. And in a way, that almost seemed worse.

"Graham sent you, didn't he?" she asked, as he knelt beneath a window and peered out along the side of the house. "What is it? FBI? Secret Service? Or are you freelance, part of some kind of private security force?"

He turned and looked back at her. "Nothing as dramatic as that. Just plain old FBI. Undercover."

Undercover, she thought to herself. She could understand why. He was very good at it. She'd never suspected a thing. "Graham should have told me."

Cain glanced back outside again. Those had been his sentiments all along. "You'll have to take that up with your uncle."

She hesitated just briefly. "*You* should have told me."

Cain nearly winced. The words were like a knife in the heart. "Maybe."

"Didn't you think I had a right to know? Didn't you think I—"

"Look," he said impatiently, cutting her off. "In case you haven't figured it out, there are some real badasses out there who just killed my partner and who would like nothing more than to put a bullet through that stubborn head of yours. Now I've got my hands a little full trying to figure out a way to convince them not to do that. Do you think maybe we could talk about this a little later?"

Jillian glared at him, but of course knew he was right. The situation was grave. A man had just died, for God's sake. This was no time to be thinking about a broken heart.

But she wasn't about to sit there and do nothing. After all, she wasn't exactly helpless. She had a gun, and she knew how to use it. Pushing herself up, she crossed the room to where Cain crouched beneath the window.

"I want my gun back," she demanded.

"Get down," he snapped, grabbing at her arm.

"Not until you give me my gun," she insisted, pulling free of him.

The only sound she heard was a faraway tingle of glass and a funny little whizzing sound by her ear. But from one heartbeat to the next, she'd been hurled to the floor, Cain's heavy body on top of her.

"What are you doing?" she demanded, struggling beneath him. "Let me up, do you hear me? Let me up!"

But the sounds of more glass breaking, and that quiet hissing sound, had her forgetting about getting up. A lamp beside the sofa cracked and collapsed into pieces, and several pictures on the mantel fell and broke. She heard no explosion, no loud blasts like there had been in her nightmares, but she instinctively knew they were the results of gunfire. Someone really was out there. And they wanted her dead.

There weren't many times in his life when Cain had been frightened, but seeing how close that bullet had come to entering her head had scared the hell out of him. He'd moved more from instinct than strategy, having grabbed her and pulled her beneath him before he'd actually thought about it. He could keep her safe for the moment as long as he kept her down and out of sight, but stranded in the dark house with no lights and no telephone made them sitting ducks. Those goons outside weren't just going to give up and go away. Sooner or later they would try to come in and get her, and Cain wanted to be long gone before that happened.

"Why can't we call for help?" Jillian asked, her shaky, uneven whisper betraying just how frightened she was.

"Lines are cut," he said absently, shifting his weight off her to one side. "Stay down," he ordered, lifting himself up onto his hands and knees.

"Where are you going?" she asked, rolling over onto her stomach.

"Don't move," he warned, ignoring her question and starting to crawl in the direction of the kitchen. "Just stay there."

"Cain."

He stopped and drew in a deep breath. "What is it?"

"My gun. I want it."

Reaching down, he slipped the SIG from the waist of his shorts and handed it to her. But when she reached to take it, he tightened his hold. "Stay put, Jillian. Please?"

Jillian nodded, the look in his eyes causing a hard knot of emotion to form in her stomach. For just that instant, he'd become her Cain again—the Cain she knew, the Cain she'd come to care for. But the moment passed, and he turned and disappeared into the darkness.

Jillian clutched the butt of the gun, as if the tighter she gripped the safer she would be. But the feeling was only an illusion, and something inside her understood that. The deadening calm had begun to wear off, and lying on the floor in the dark living room, she felt the first flickers of fear.

Turning, she looked at the lifeless body of the man on the floor just a few feet from her. She hadn't seen death—not since that day when her father had died in her arms.

Squeezing her eyes shut, she turned and looked the other way. The man had been Cain's partner.

Cain's partner. It seemed strange. The Cain she knew was a loner, someone who lived and worked as he pleased, not someone with a partner. She began to realize just how little he'd told her of himself. Of course she'd been curious, but she'd been so concerned about keeping her own background out of the conversation that she'd been content to steer clear of the entire subject. What they had done and who they had been before they met hadn't seemed important.

She'd been wrong. She realized just how distorted and unrealistic her image of him had been, how she had romanticized and fantasized and made him a rugged nonconformist in her mind. Someone who scorned custom and formality, who broke through barriers and despised convention.

She couldn't have been farther from the truth. He was a federal agent! You could hardly get more conforming than that. She'd been surrounded by men like that all her life.

Not only had they protected her as a child and watched over her as a teen, but she worked with them as a U.S. attorney. Dozens of agents, from a variety of federal agencies, assisted her on the cases she investigated, and she'd thought she could spot that type of cool character from a mile away. They were the proverbial "good soldiers" who unyieldingly toed the line, who held their sense of duty above all else, and who doggedly followed orders and completed their assignments.

Jillian closed her eyes, squeezing the butt of the SIG even tighter. The heat was oppressive, and the air in the house felt thick and stale. The darkness had begun to close in, and the silence roared in her ears. Fear twisted a degree tighter in her stomach as she glanced nervously about. She felt exposed, vulnerable lying in the middle of the room, and she wished Cain would return. Despite the hurt and betrayal, she still felt better with him than without him.

Glancing about, she silently crawled a few feet to where her grandmother's easy chair sat. Huddling next to its bulk, she felt better. But she couldn't help thinking about the times she'd sat with Grandma Wells in that chair, and a lump of emotion formed in her throat.

Glancing through the darkness, she saw Cain's dark mass move soundlessly through the kitchen. It seemed so obvious now—the silent moves, the careful actions, the quiet command of emotion—why hadn't she seen it before? She should have recognized the evidence of highly specialized training. Training that allowed him to blend into the background, to watch, to listen, and to lie in wait until the time came for action. All the signs were there, but she'd never suspected a thing.

But then, Cain had been different. Cain had been nice to her, friendly and interested. He'd gotten her to drop her guard, to forget about caution and concern, to reach out.

He'd been so believable. She'd actually believed him when he'd said all those things to her, actually believed that he cared. Of course, that had been before she'd known it was all part of his job, all in the line of duty.

She closed her eyes again, but it wasn't to block out the fear this time. It was to stop the sting of tears. What a fool she had been, how easy she had made it for him. He must have gotten a real kick watching her fawn all over him. What a laugh he must have had.

A tear dropped from her lash and began to slowly roll down her cheek. She knew the truth now, though, and that changed everything. There'd be no more mistakes, no more deceptions. She'd been taken in once, but never again.

"Jillian."

Cain's whispered startled her. "What is it?"

"Over here," he whispered, motioning to her from the doorway between the kitchen and dining room. "Come on. Hurry. And keep down."

She felt enormously awkward, but she scooted across the living room floor and into the dining room toward him. Suddenly, there was another barrage of gunfire coming from the direction of the living room, and instantly Cain was on top of her, shielding her again. The clamor of glass shattering sounded like small explosions, one after the other, and the pictures and bric-a-brac that shattered and fell added to the pandemonium. It stopped as suddenly as it started, and when it was over, Cain lifted himself off her.

"Are you all right?"

Jillian nodded. "F-fine."

"Let's go, then. We're getting out of here," he said, taking her by the arm and almost dragging her into the kitchen. "We'll head for the boat."

"What?" she demanded, pulling her arm free. "I'm not going out there."

He looked down into her fiery eyes, wishing just once she would do what he asked her without having to argue the case. "Jillian, we can't stay here."

"Well, we can't go out there," she said. "It's...it's crazy."

"It would be crazy to try and stay," he told her, biting back his impatience.

"Uh-uh," she said adamantly, shaking her head. "I'm not going out there."

"This isn't up for negotiation," he pointed out, taking her by the arm again. "I'm not going to argue with you."

"But wouldn't it be safer to just hole up in here? Stay down, out of fire?" she asked, resisting his hold. "It'll be daylight in a few hours. Surely someone will see there is something wrong and call the police."

"By morning we'll be dead," he snapped. His patience had finally reached its limit. He was angry and annoyed by her stubbornness, and he grabbed her roughly by the shoulders. But hauling her to him, bringing her close, his anger faded and his voice softened. "Those goons out there aren't going to wait forever. Eventually they'll come looking for us." His hold on her shoulders tightened, and her scent swirled around him, making him remember what it was like to really hold her. "Jillian, we're talking about staying alive here. There's no appeals process with a bullet. Trust me, please?"

Jillian dropped her gaze, pulling free of his hold. She didn't want him touching her, didn't even want him near her. It was too painful, too uncomfortable. But even though she knew she would never trust him again with her heart, instincts told her she could trust him with her life. Looking away, she silently nodded her head.

"Stay close," he said, taking her hand and heading for the back door. "And keep your head down."

They crawled through the kitchen to the back door and out onto the small, screened porch. The screen door stood in front of them like a silent, stoic centurion. Cain suddenly remembered the loud squeak it made each time the worn hinges were placed into action. Passing through it undetected would be impossible. They might as well announce their location through a loudspeaker.

"The back window," Cain whispered, pointing back in the direction they had come.

Retracing their steps, they crawled back through the kitchen and down the hall to a rear bedroom. The wood frame of the old-fashioned sash window had swelled over the years, and it moaned in protest at being asked to move. Cain was adamant, however, and ultimately the stubborn sash gave way to his considerable strength. Soundlessly Cain climbed out the window, then turned and lifted Jillian to the ground. Grabbing her by the hand, they stole across the lawn, jumping hedges and ducking behind shrubbery.

Jillian didn't think, didn't feel, she just ran—as hard and as fast as she could. She kept her eyes focused on the levee and the dock beyond, not even thinking about the fact that they were trampling through the soft dirt of her garden, or that they plodded through the newly planted ground cover and daisies she had worked so hard to transplant. None of that was important now when their lives hung in the balance.

They reached the levee, and Cain's strong arms propelled her up it. Their footsteps on the damaged, sagging dock sounded like eruptions in the dead silence, and the wooden planks swayed and moaned ominously.

"Get that back rope," Cain ordered in a rough whisper as he lifted her onto the deck of the boat. As Jillian freed the tow rope at the stern of the boat, he unfastened the remaining ropes and pushed them off. As the boat drifted away from the dock, catching the current, Cain grabbed Jillian by the arm. "Get inside," he whispered, pulling her toward the cabin. "And stay down."

They drifted silently, and the water lapping against the side of the boat was the only sound breaking the stillness. As they picked up speed, Cain maneuvered the wheel until they headed down river.

Jillian crouched in the hatch, her eyes scanning the blackness of the levee and dock behind them. It was only when reflex took over and had her gasping for air that she realized she'd been holding her breath. She'd just let out a long, deep sigh, when she thought she saw something moving in the darkness. Tension immediately filled the air of the small cabin like the darkness and a strange, eerie prickling sensation had the hair at the back of her neck standing on end.

"Cain," she whispered, reaching up and tugging on his arm.

"Shh, not now," he whispered, intent on steering the boat through the dark waterway.

"Cain," she said again, her voice more insistent.

When he looked down at her, she gestured wildly to the levee behind them. Glancing back, he immediately pulled out his gun. "Hang on."

But Jillian barely had time to breathe before sound and motion exploded. In two almost simultaneous actions, Cain turned the ignition key and opened the throttle full. The boat's powerful motors roared to life, raising them up and lunging them forward. But in that same instant, Jillian heard sounds from the dock. Bursts of popping and small, white explosions of light snapped as gunfire erupted.

She didn't have to think about ducking for safety—she'd been knocked flat when the boat lurched forward. Glass shattered and wood splintered, and the fiberglass paneling groaned as it endured the brutal assault. The cabin seemed to be filled with those horrible whizzing sounds as bullets filled the air above her, and she panicked, groping frantically for cover.

Scrambling, she took shelter in the relative security beneath a small counter beside the tiny refrigerator. From where she huddled, she could see Cain outside at the wheel, the wind buffeting his hair wildly about his face. His attention was focused on navigating the boat through the narrow slough, but occasionally he would glance behind them to return fire.

It was only as she crouched there, watching as he fired his gun, that she'd remembered the SIG. She'd slipped it into her pocket when she'd untied the boat, and in the pandemonium and confusion, she'd forgotten all about its heavy weight against her side. Remembering it now, though, she reached down and retrieved it from her pocket and clutched the cold, ruthless steel to her chest.

It seemed as though the panic and confusion might go on forever, but eventually Jillian heard the sounds of gunfire, and those horrible whistling noises made by the bullets through the air, begin to lessen, then stop. Cain maintained the boat's frantic speed, charting a wild, crazy path through the darkness, but he'd slipped the gun back into the waistband of his jeans.

Tentatively, Jillian inched away from her hiding place. Still holding her gun, she came unsteadily to her feet. She stood in the middle of the small hold, bracing herself against the counter, her body swaying with the erratic motion of the boat. She took a few hesitant steps, bumping from side to side, until she reached the hatch.

"D-did we make it?" she asked against the roar of the wind. "Is it safe?"

"For the moment," Cain said, glancing behind them. But when she started to step up onto the deck, he stopped her. "Better not. We're not out of the woods just yet."

She stepped back down, turning to sit on the small step. "What do we do now?"

"Well," he said, reaching inside the cabin to flip on a tiny overhead light, "if you'll reach into my tool belt over there next to the bunk and hand me the cellular phone, I'll call this in and get some help out here."

In the dim light, Jillian glanced about the tiny cabin and felt her heart lurch painfully in her chest. The bedding on the bunk was still rumpled and snarled from their lovemaking, and it glared at her now like a silent and bitter accusation. Had it only been the day before when they had swum in the water, when they had laughed and kissed and made love? How could so much have changed since then?

She found the tool belt, suddenly remembering now how Cain had wanted to take it with them into the house. She even remembered the odd expression on his face when she'd asked him about it.

Slipping her hand into the deep leather pocket, she pulled out the small, slim cellular phone. Staring down at it in her hand, she shook her head. Not exactly standard equipment for roofers and handymen, she thought darkly, but no doubt helpful to the undercover agent. Turning, she flipped the light switch off and handed the phone to Cain.

Cain's call was short but precise, and when he'd finished he tossed the phone onto the seat opposite him.

"So, what now?" Jillian asked, looking up at him expectantly.

"Now we beat it to Antioch," he told her, referring to the sizable community located where the delta waterways converged into the back bay of San Francisco. "We'll be met there."

Met there. Words that said nothing, revealed nothing and conveyed nothing. Jillian was well versed in those kinds of evasive, emotionless, no-comment sorts of phrases. She'd heard them all her life.

"Then what?" she asked, not bothering to push for specifics.

"Then hopefully we catch the bad guys."

Jillian squinted into the blackness behind them as Cain negotiated a turn, bringing them out of one quiet slough and into another. *Catch them.* Could this nightmare possibly end so easily? "Do you actually think they'll try and follow us?"

"You can bet on it, and that's why you need to stay down," he said, gesturing toward the cabin with a bob of his chin. "Those guys aren't the kind who pick up their toys and go home after one try." He suddenly breathed out a little laugh. "But at least you slowed them down."

"Me? Why? What did I do?"

He glanced down at her again, a little half smile softening the hard lines of his face. "Well, I'm afraid one of those ugly bastards walked a little too far out onto the dock." His smiled widened just a fraction when he saw realization light up her eyes, and he couldn't help another little laugh. "Sure would be a shame if he didn't know how to swim."

"He fell in?" she asked, her eyes wide with recognition.

"With a splash." He smiled down at her. "Nice job, Counselor."

Chapter 12

Cain charted a tangled path, weaving and winding a trail through twisting sloughs, past dark coves and by countless small marinas. The delta swallowed them up, its snarled maze providing protection. Cain stuck to the narrow, remote waterways, carefully avoiding when he could the wide, better-traveled ones where they might be spotted. Dawn was still hours off, and with the moon gone, the sky was brilliant with stars.

Jillian sat on the small step of the hatch, tightly hugging her knees to her chest. She couldn't bring herself to move deeper into the cabin. Just thinking about that narrow bunk plagued her with painful memories. She wanted to stay as far away from that bunk—and those memories—as she could, and for the time being, the steps were as far as she could go.

She stared up into the night sky. They had twisted and turned so many times she was hopelessly lost, all sense of direction gone, but it didn't bother her. Cain was in charge.

He knew where they were, and she trusted him to get them to where they were going.

Trusted him. How could she trust him? How could she trust the man who had lied to her? The man who had purposely deceived and misled her?

Jillian looked up at Cain as he piloted the boat through the dark waterways. Her heart twisted painfully, and a hard knot of emotion formed in her throat. She didn't know exactly why it was she trusted him—instinct, maybe, or intuition—she only knew that she could. Somehow she knew that no matter what, he would take care of her. But not because he cared for her, she quickly reminded herself, because it was his job.

She thought of the way he'd handled himself—the cool professionalism, the reserved confidence, the calm composure. A seasoned pro. There had been no panic, no moment of indecision—not even when his partner lay dead in his arms. His focus had been clear from the beginning, his purpose defined. He was a man comfortable with running risks and taking chances, a man accustomed to danger and threats, and a man all too familiar with guns and violence.

A man just like Ron.

She squeezed her eyes shut. What was it with her? Even without trying, she'd managed to get tangled up with the very kind of man she'd sworn she'd never get involved with again. Did she have a weakness for supermacho superheroes? Did she like the threat of danger, the whisper of excitement, the hint of uncertainty?

She opened her eyes and looked up at Cain again. No, she decided, feeling the emotion swell in her throat. There was no heavy psychological reasoning behind her attraction to him. Cain had simply been like no one else she'd ever known before—not Ron, not Jeff, not anyone else. And the same intuition or gut feeling that assured her she could trust him, also had her knowing she'd never meet anyone like him again.

A long black strand of hair blew across his face, and Cain turned his head just enough for the wind to blow it back. He steered the boat from the secluded confines of the slough and out into the broad expanse of the Sacramento River. The warm, balmy air against his face felt good, as did the speed of the powerful engines. Despite holding it at full throttle, he felt as though they were plodding through the water. He wanted her out of there, wanted her safe, and the taut, nagging tension along the back of his neck told him she wasn't yet.

He'd seen the kind of firepower those creeps at the house had. They'd come prepared. It wouldn't surprise him if they'd had their own boat, or even a helicopter stashed away somewhere to help them finish the job.

He glanced down at Jillian perched nervously on the step at the entrance of the cabin. Frankly he wished she would go inside the cabin and lie down. It would be safer, but he knew she wouldn't. He'd seen her face when she'd looked down at the bunk and he'd known all too well what she'd been thinking, what she'd remembered. Seeing the bunk had made him remember, too, but it had also made him understand just what he'd lost.

Cain's hand tightened on the wheel. Didn't Jillian know he'd never meant to hurt her? As long as he lived, he knew he wouldn't forget the look on her face when she'd realized the truth. The expression in her eyes had nearly killed him. The anger and the fury had been all over her face, but it was the pain in her eyes that had nearly done him in. He'd seen that look in her eyes before—on that long-ago night in her uncle's limo. Only, this time it was different. This time he was the one responsible for putting the pain there.

His hand formed a fist, and he slammed it down hard against the wheel. If he'd just had some warning, if he'd only been given some time. He could have broken it to her slowly, he could have explained things, justified and rationalized what he'd done. Maybe she still wouldn't have been able to forgive him, but at least she wouldn't have had the pain. He'd have given anything to have spared her from finding out the way she had. The truth had come flying at her like those damn bullets. And from the look in her eyes, it had been just as deadly.

Cain's mind shifted to Spence, and he thought of his partner's heroic efforts to warn them. To the very end, Spence had been there for him—keeping lookout, watching his back. Spence had saved their lives.

His gaze drifted over to the cellular phone lying in the seat across the small aisle. How was he going to live with the truth—the stark, brutal truth—that he was responsible for Spence's death? For he'd killed his own partner as surely as if he'd pulled the trigger himself. Whitewashing the facts wouldn't change them; trying to justify or vindicate himself in order to make things more palatable wouldn't let him off the hook. Spence had died trying to warn him, and if Cain had been on his boat where he should have been, instead of breaking every rule in the book by being with Jillian, he would have been there when Spence tried to call. Spence wouldn't have had to leave his stake-out, wouldn't have been spotted by those bastards. Spence wouldn't have died.

Cain's hand gripped the wheel tighter, and grief and remorse tasted bitter in his throat. He'd screwed up badly on this one—and the price of his mistakes had been big. He'd been sent there to do a job, but instead he'd let his personal feelings get in the way. Jillian had become more important to him than the job he'd had to do. Cain never should have

touched her; he never should have allowed himself one moment with her until it had all been over, until the job had
been completed and the danger past. He could have gone to
her then, he could have been honest, direct. There would
have been no need for deception, no need to lie. His care-
lessness had not only cost Spence his life, but it had also cost
him the woman he...

The woman he *what?*

He glanced down at her. Brutal honesty. If he was going
to talk honesty, he should at least be honest with himself.
She wasn't just a woman he remembered from the past, she
wasn't just a woman he wanted, a woman who attracted
him. She wasn't a job or assignment. Jillian Hughes was the
woman he loved.

Cain turned the wheel, sailing past a thick stand of tule
and bamboo that grew like a small island in the middle of
the river. The noise from the engines, along with the motion of the water, had a small flock of birds squawking
loudly and taking flight in the night sky.

"What was that?" Jillian asked anxiously, standing and
stepping up out of the cabin.

"Just some birds—don't worry about it," he assured her.
Catching her arm, he stopped her as she moved farther into
the open. "I really wish you'd stay below."

Jillian pulled her arm free and stepped back down. She
was restless, her nerves on edge. It seemed as though they'd
been on the boat for hours, and the tension was getting to
her. "How much longer?"

Cain glanced out over the bow into the distance. "Not too
much. We're on the river now. It won't be much longer."

Frustrated, Jillian sat back down on the step and pushed
her long hair to one side. Reaching up, she massaged the
tense muscles at the base of her neck. It would all be over
soon. It was time to get back to business, time she got back

to the old habits again, the old routines. She had to look ahead, had to begin weighing the consequences again and dealing with the ramifications.

It wouldn't be long before Cain delivered her to safety, before his job would be done, his assignment completed and his responsibilities at an end. Of course, she would be expected to show proper gratitude. She would be called upon to display the intrinsic Hughes dignity and reserve. After all, it would be the right thing to do. Forget that it would be painful, forget that she would be dying inside, and forget that it would be like putting a gun to her head. But even that wouldn't be the hardest part.

She'd never felt more alive in her life as she had in these few short weeks with Cain. And despite her anger and disappointment, despite the lies and dishonesty, walking away from him was going to be the most difficult of all.

But she would do it. She would do it because *it was the right thing to do,* and she always did the right thing. Well...at least she always had done the right thing until she'd met *him.* She'd thought she'd thrown caution to the wind when she met him, she thought she had been taking a chance, living life to the fullest for the first time. But her splendid burst of freedom, her grand attempt to break tradition, had all been a sham—something designed and manipulated by a seasoned federal agent with an eye for duty and a job to do.

But all that hardly mattered, because it was almost over now. She would go back to New York, back to work, graciously accept the FBI's offer of protection until the hit men were apprehended, then get back to normal.

Normal. She smiled sadly to herself. How dull that sounded. How dull her future sounded. How bleak and colorless it seemed going back and picking up where she'd left off, worrying about cases and files, investigations and trial dates again, as though nothing at all had happened. Was she just supposed to forget about Lighthouse Landing, forget about Cain, about the way he made her feel?

She jumped when she felt Cain's hand on her arm. Her head snapped up, and she resisted when he reached down with his free hand and pulled her up onto the small seat beside him.

"No," she protested, struggling. "Don't."

"Let me," he murmured, ignoring her protest and pushing her long hair aside. Slowly his large hand began to gently massage the area where she had been rubbing. "I want to help."

Help. This didn't help her. It only served to make it all the more difficult. She sat frozen, her senses sent spinning by the feel of his hand along her skin. What power was it that he had over her? She was humiliated, furious, outraged by the deception he'd perpetrated against her, and yet here she was, rendered immobile by his touch alone.

But she had to be strong. She had to start thinking again, she had to start doing the right thing again, making the right decisions, and there was no way she could do that as long as he was touching her.

"Don't," Jillian said firmly, shaking her head, but when she shifted to move, he stopped her.

"No," he whispered, slipping his arm around her waist and sliding her to him. From behind her, his lips brushed the back of her neck. "Nothing's changed, Jillian. Not you, not me."

He pressed a kiss into the back of her neck, and emotion surged up from the very depths of her soul. She cried out, tormented by what she was feeling and hating herself for that moment's hesitation when she wanted nothing more than to forget everything else, press into his warmth and follow her heart.

"No," she groaned, her voice not sounding nearly as determined this time. "Please, let me go."

"I can't," he whispered again. The hand he had on the steering wheel slipped to join his free hand at her waist, and he pulled her onto his lap. "Jillian, don't you know? I can't let you go."

It was a moment in time, a fleeting lull in a race against time. He kissed her shoulder, her neck, sliding his cool, hard lips along her chin to her lips. How could she want him? she wondered dizzily in a more lucid outpost of her brain. And yet she did. She wanted him even though she hated herself for it. But sometimes self-respect took precedence over need—especially when you'd been raised a Hughes.

"No," she said again. In a final burst of courage, desperation and pride, she pulled out of his grasp. "This has to stop," she professed, breathless and stumbling back onto the seat across the narrow aisle. "I don't want this. It's not right."

"Not right?" Cain asked skeptically, settling back in his seat and correcting their course through the water. Years of conditioning allowed him to maintain a cool, unaffected exterior, but beneath the surface his breathing was labored, and he nearly shook with the need to hold her again. "Why don't you tell me what's so wrong about it?"

"I don't have to tell you anything, and I don't want you to touch me again."

"So you mean it was all right to touch you as long as I was your handyman, your lackey—is that it?" he asked, his tightly suppressed emotions making his words sharp and harsh. "Sweaty bodies and dirty hands turn you on?"

She bristled at his sarcasm. "You're crude."

"I thought that's what you liked." His reflexes were far too quick for her, and he caught her hand before it made contact with his cheek. He hated the pain he saw in her eyes, hated himself for putting it there. The anger died inside of him, and his voice softened. "Why does it have to change, Jillian? We're still the same people."

"How can you say that?" she said, snatching her hand from his grasp and scooting back against the seat. "You lied to me, kept the truth from me."

"I had a job to do."

"Oh, that's right. Your job," she nodded. "Exactly what was your job, Cain? To be nice to me? Become my friend?"

"Stop it, Jillian."

"I mean, having to listen while I went on and on about my life, about Ron and my marriage. It must have been very boring for you."

"Stop it."

"And all that stuff about my family, my ranting and raving about you knowing who I was. How did you ever keep from laughing?"

"Stop."

"And tell me, Cain, did the bureau make the final decision about taking me to bed, or was that all your idea?"

"Damn it, Jillian," he exploded. She jumped as he pounded his fist down hard on the narrow dashboard, denting it. Reaching across, he grabbed her roughly by the arms and yanked her to him. "You little fool, you don't even have a clue, do you?"

"Cain, stop, you're hurting me." She struggled, but he ignored her.

"You have no idea what you've put me through, how long I've wanted you, how long I've waited."

"Let me go."

"I wanted you even when I told myself I didn't, when you'd looked right through me as if I wasn't even there, even when that punk reporter tried to maul you in that elevator and scared the hell out of you!"

Jillian stopped struggling and stared up at him. At first she was confused, wondering what it was he was talking about, but eventually realization began to sink in. A curious tingling sensation in her heart and in her head stirred memories—a look, an expression, a move, a stance. It wasn't possible. How could it be? Not Cain, not him. He couldn't have been Ash, the Secret Service agent who had filled her adolescent dreams all those years ago, her knight in shining armor who had saved her from danger and given her her first real kiss.

"But you know, I hardly blamed the creep," Cain went on, giving her no time to comprehend. "You didn't know back then. Those eyes. Damn you, you didn't know what you did to a man when you looked at him. You still don't." He pulled her close, digging his hands into the soft flesh of her arms. "I'd waited fifteen years for you, and nothing— no job, no lie, *nothing*—was going to get in my way."

"Cain—"

But he wouldn't let her finish. He brutalized her mouth with a kiss filled with all the power of his anger, his frustration and . . . his love. Time seemed to stop in a harsh moment of raw emotion and fierce reality. When he pulled his lips from hers, he and Jillian were both breathless, both shaking.

"If you think that had anything to do with a job or following orders, then you're a fool," he growled.

But not even the strength of the emotions between them was enough to stop a bullet. It propelled its way through the boat's windshield as easily as it lodged itself in Cain's chest.

"Get down," he shouted, pushing Jillian toward the hatch, but another bullet ripped through his shoulder, nearly spinning him around, and then another.

"Cain!" Jillian screamed, staring in horror as his clear eyes shadowed over. *"Cain."*

With what strength he had left, he pushed her down, shielding her body with his own. But three bullets were even more than he could fight, and he felt his strength slip away with the blood down his bare chest.

"No!" Jillian screamed again as he slid down to the deck. Tears streamed down her face as she reached for him, his blood drenching her hands, her clothes. "Cain, answer me. Cain."

But he couldn't answer her. There was only the sound of the huge engines idling as the boat drifted aimlessly in the water.

Just then she caught sight of movement beside them. Looking up, she saw another boat bearing down on them from the left. Dawn had not yet begun to break, but even in the darkness she could see the silhouettes of two men standing on the deck. Their coarse, ugly features were shadowed and dark, but she didn't need to see their faces to know who they were. They were the men Donelli had sent, and they were the men who had shot Cain.

Slipping her hand inside the pocket of her shorts, she reached for the SIG. Swatting away the tears in her eyes, she stepped up onto the deck and took careful aim.

"Bastards!" she screamed, leveling the sight at first one dark figure, and then the other. She took precise aim, thinking of Cain lying behind her in a pool of blood, and emptied the magazine.

For a moment she thought the heavens had opened up, for the brilliant light streaming down from up above flooded everything in a blanket of white. It wasn't until she heard the thunder of an engine and the heavy blast of wind from its huge rotary blades that she realized the light came from a helicopter hovering just above them with the letters *FBI* painted on its underbelly. The calvary had arrived.

But Jillian felt no relief, no joy. In fact, it was as though she had no emotion left within her. She calmly turned, slipping the SIG back into her pocket, and returned to Cain lying on the deck. Cradling his head in her lap, she talked to him in a low voice and pushed his long hair away from his face, remembering another time when she'd held the head of someone she loved.

Activity occurred around her—boats, helicopter, federal agents, coast guard. She was aware of it all, but it simply didn't interest her. She was content to let people and events happen around her, as she held Cain's head in her lap, stroking and soothing.

It was only when the Medi-Vac unit arrived that life seemed to enter her body once again. Somehow she'd gotten shoved to one side by the team of paramedics who began to work furiously on Cain. She stood in stunned horror and dread as equipment and personnel passed her, all intent on tending to Cain, who hadn't moved since he'd fallen. She stared down at his rugged face, his dark, tanned skin so wan and ashen now, and she felt more frightened than she had when the bullets had been flying.

"Are you injured?"

"Hmm...what?" Jillian jumped, surprised to see the young woman beside her.

"Were you hit at all?" the female paramedic asked, pointing to Jillian's shirt.

Jillian glanced down at herself for the first time, only to discover that she was covered with blood.

Cain's blood.

She gasped in surprise, but her shock had nothing to do with the aversion to blood that had plagued her since that awful day when her father had died. It had to do with seeing just how much blood Cain had lost.

"Why don't you come over here and sit down," the paramedic suggested, taking her by the arm.

"It—it's not my blood," Jillian explained, her voice quivering with emotion. "It's not my blood."

"Come on with me, anyway," the young woman said, leading Jillian to the back of the boat. "Let me check you out just to be sure, okay?"

Jillian sat down, turning to look at the team who continued to work on Cain just a few feet away. Looking back at the paramedic who was attending to her, she caught the woman's hand. "Is he going to die?"

The young woman glanced over to the others. "He's lost a lot of blood. But he's got the best unit in the program helping him." She patted Jillian on the hand. "They'll do everything they can."

"Miss Hughes?"

Jillian glanced up at the tall, middle-aged man standing above her. He wore a black Windbreaker jacket with FBI emblazoned on it in bright yellow. "Yes?"

"Special Agent Andrew MacArthur. Do you feel up to answering a few questions?"

Jillian glanced over to the crowd around Cain and silently nodded her head.

"Were you aware Special Agent Cain was working with a backup agent?"

Jillian thought of the man lying dead in the living room of her grandmother's house. "Spence."

"That's correct—Agent Spencer Anderson. We've been unable to make contact with Agent Anderson and—"

"He's dead," she said bluntly, cutting him off. "You'll find him in my house at Lighthouse Landing."

MacArthur signaled to another agent on one of the boats moored alongside them, then turned back to Jillian. "We've apprehended two suspects, Miss Hughes. Did you at any time see the faces of the men who pursued you? Do you think you could identify them?''

Jillian remembered the two ugly faces she had seen a split second before she'd opened fire. "I saw them. I can identify them.''

"That's good, good,'' MacArthur nodded, making a notation on a small notepad. "Just one last thing, Miss Hughes. The two suspects have several gunshot wounds to the chest and—''

"Did I kill them?''

MacArthur stopped writing and looked at her. "*You* shot them?''

"Yes.''

"With what? Cain's gun?''

Jillian shook her head, put a hand in her pocket and pulled out the SIG. MacArthur reached down and took the gun from her, pursing his lips together in a silent whistle.

"You didn't answer me,'' Jillian said, looking up at him. "Did I kill them?''

MacArthur shook his head, regarding her very carefully. He'd been around a long time, and he thought he'd seen it all. But Senator Hughes's niece had managed to surprise him. "No, but you managed to shoot them up pretty good.''

Just then, a gurney was lowered from the Medi-Vac helicopter to the team on the deck of the boat. They all watched as the medical team lifted Cain's motionless body onto the gurney.

"What is that?'' Jillian demanded, looking to the young woman beside her. "What's happening?''

"They're airlifting him to the trauma unit at Alameda General.''

Jillian stood up, grabbing MacArthur by the arm. "I want to go.''

"But, Miss Hughes, your uncle is waiting—''

"I don't give a damn. How do I get to that trauma unit?"

MacArthur looked down at her. She wasn't turning out to be at all what he'd expected. Signaling to another of his agents, he motioned to her. "Come on. I'll take you."

They waited until Cain and the medical team had been lifted aboard the hovering Medi-Vac helicopter, then MacArthur escorted Jillian to the FBI's own waiting chopper. The trip to the hospital was short and uneventful, and they landed on the helipad just after the Medi-Vac unit. While Cain was rushed into the emergency room and surgery, Jillian was escorted to a waiting room.

MacArthur stayed with her in the small, sterile-looking waiting room, and a steady stream of agents made their way in and out to speak with him—checking in, receiving orders, making reports. Occasionally one would come in with a few questions for her to answer, or request her to clarify a particular point, but other than that they left her pretty much alone. MacArthur, however, continued to hover around, and as one long hour slowly followed the other, Jillian began to realize it had more to do with design than courtesy. Special Agent MacArthur was Cain's replacement, the new agent assigned to watch over her and keep her safe.

Safe. Jillian thought of Cain's motionless body. She hadn't felt safe since three bullets had ripped ugly holes through his chest, since she'd seen his brilliant blue eyes glaze and shadow over, since he'd collapsed at her feet. And the way she felt now, she didn't think she'd ever feel safe again.

There was no future for her with Cain—there never had been. Still, she couldn't bring herself to leave, she couldn't bring herself to just walk away. Not until she knew he was all right, that he would live.

The picture of him lying there on the deck of the boat in a pool of his own blood haunted her. Nothing could have more efficiently shown her just how impossible the situation between them really was than three gunshot wounds to the chest. Even though there were lies that stood between them, it was the dark, dangerous world he lived in that she could never forgive.

Jillian had waited in a hospital once before, waited for a doctor to come in and tell her that Ron had died. She had sworn then that that would never happen to her again, and yet here she was, waiting again. But this time it was different, this time her life with Cain had already ended—whether he lived or died.

Only...she prayed with all her heart that he would live. She could face not having a future with him, but she wasn't sure she could face a world without him in it.

"Jilly? Jilly baby?"

There was only one person Jillian allowed to call her by that awful nickname. Graham Hughes was one of those rare individuals who looked confident, self-assured and comfortable in any situation, whether it was sitting at the negotiating table with representatives of the world's superpowers, or standing with arms open wide in a hygienic-looking hospital waiting room. It was his insistence and influence that had brought Cain and the FBI into her life in the first place, and she was furious with him for his interference and meddling. But at the moment she didn't have it in her heart to reprimand or lecture him. She was exhausted, alone and frightened. And seeing him standing there with his face full of emotion and looking endearingly familiar, she'd never been so glad to see anyone in her life. Standing slowly, Jillian hesitated only a moment before running across the room and into her uncle's embrace.

"I came as soon as I heard," he said, hugging her tight. Pulling back, he helped wipe away her tears, then spotted the dried blood splattered on her arms and clothes. "Oh my God, are you all right? They told me you hadn't been hurt."

"I wasn't," Jillian assured him, walking with him back to the hard, vinyl sofa where she'd been sitting. "I'm fine."

Before sitting down, Graham Hughes turned to Special Agent MacArthur hovering nearby and extended his hand.

"Senator," MacArthur said, shaking Graham's hand and giving a slight nod of his head.

"Any word of Cain?"

"Nothing yet, sir."

"And his partner?"

"Agent Anderson's body has been recovered from the house in the delta, sir."

Graham Hughes took a deep breath and slowly shook his head. "What about Donelli's men?"

"We have two suspects in custody in the prison ward, Senator," MacArthur explained. "Your niece has identified them both."

"Prison ward?"

"Uh…yes," MacArthur hedged, shooting a quick glance in Jillian's direction. "Both suspects were wounded during pursuit."

"I shot them," Jillian announced in an unemotional voice.

Graham whirled around and looked down at Jillian. "You?"

"I'd meant to kill them," she went on. "And I would have if the water hadn't been so rough." She glanced up at him and shrugged. "What kind of spin can your people put on that?"

Graham looked down at his niece, seeing the defiance, the strength and the determination in her eyes, and thinking how much like her father she was. Jillian had the same courage, the same temper and the same fire in her gut. Protecting her from a vengeful Mafia don was a hell of a lot easier than protecting her from herself. Sitting down beside her, he placed a comforting arm around her shoulders and let out a long sigh. "I don't suppose we'll need to worry about that."

Chapter 13

It seemed as though earth and the cosmos had conspired together to slow the passage of time. To Jillian it felt as though it had stopped altogether. The waiting seemed endless.

Dawn finally emerged, bringing faint light creeping through the windows at a painfully slow pace. MacArthur had brought in hot coffee and a few stale doughnuts from the hospital cafeteria, but Jillian hadn't been able to face either. She was too restless, too upset to eat, and she was fairly certain that if she didn't hear something about Cain soon, she would go stark raving mad from the waiting alone.

She was in limbo—torn between a desire to go and a need to stay. It made no sense. She couldn't explain the reasons why, but she just couldn't make herself leave until she heard something. Once she got word, it would be all right. She could go and resume her life again. But until then, she could only wait.

Graham looked at the dark circles beneath Jillian's large eyes and ran a weary hand over his own tired eyes. He'd tried his best to convince her to go to the hotel room he had arranged for. She was exhausted and needed rest badly. But even though he'd assured her he would notify her as soon as there was any word on Cain's condition, she had flatly refused. Because he knew all too well how willful she could be when she'd made up her mind about something, he'd let the matter drop. But he couldn't help thinking that maybe Cain had been right. Maybe she was just plain stubborn.

"Well, I don't know about you, but I need to stretch these old legs of mine," Graham said, slowly lifting himself off the narrow sofa. He took a few stiff steps toward the window, then stopped. "Jilly, come here," he said, motioning to her. "Look at this."

Jillian begrudgingly joined him at the window. Outside, a glorious sunrise had painted the sky with a magnificent display of pink, blue, yellow and red. Immediately she thought of all those sunrises she had watched on the mornings she had awakened to the sounds of Cain on the roof. Things had seemed so easy then, so safe and uncomplicated. The little house in the delta, the lazy summer days—and Cain.

But it had all been a lie, staged and performed for her benefit. There had been nothing slow and easy about it. It had been a carefully planned illusion, a mirage to mask the clandestine activities of an FBI stakeout. And all pretense of safety had shattered like glass after she'd been stalked by two hit men. Nothing had been what it seemed—nothing. Not the delta, not her safety, not even Cain.

"It's been a long night," Graham said, taking a deep breath and putting his arm around her.

Jillian nodded, pulling out of his hold. She was exhausted, and the fatigue made her restless and irritable. She wasn't in the mood for comfort or for conversation. She wanted to hear something about Cain. She wanted to hear Cain would be all right.

"This waiting," she said, taking a deep breath. "It's getting to me."

Graham turned his head and looked down at her. "You know, they probably won't let you in to see him right away. It could be a while before he's allowed visitors."

Jillian walked a few steps closer to the window and peered out at the deserted street below. "I know, I just..." Her words drifted off, and she leaned her forehead against the cool glass and closed her eyes. "I just want to see for myself that he's all right."

One of the senator's bushy gray eyebrows arched up just a fraction. "And then what?"

Jillian opened her eyes and turned around to face him. "And then it's over. Then I go back home, back to work. Get..." She took another deep breath and clenched her fists at her side, the words still wanting to stick in her throat. "Get back to... normal again, try and forget about all of this."

"I don't think any of us are going to be able to forget this. Not me, not you." He paused for a moment, shooting her a sideward glance. "Not Cain."

Her eyes narrowed, chin tilting back slightly too high to be anything but defiant. "You had no right to play with my life that way."

"I had every right," he scoffed. "You were in danger. You expected me to sit back and do nothing?"

"You went behind my back. How could you? You should have consulted with me. I had a right to know what was going on."

"Wait just one little minute here," Graham said, stopping her with a raised hand. He'd been around a long time, and despite his niece's considerable abilities to put people in the hot seat, she still was no match for him. "Let's just back up a little, shall we? You were the one hell-bent on refusing any protection, the one who refused to cooperate. You were the one who insisted on going it alone."

"And you should have trusted me to handle this myself," she maintained mulishly.

"It's a damn good thing I didn't, young woman," he said in the authoritative tone that made his opponents quake on the floor of the Senate. "Otherwise you'd have been dead by now."

Jillian glared at him, a wave of anger flaring to the surface. "Maybe I would have," she said in a low, tightly controlled voice. "But we'll never know, will we? I'm alive and it only left one agent dead, and another dying. Tell me, Graham—are we Hugheses really worth all of that?"

Graham regarded her for a long moment, then a slight smile softened the hard lines around his mouth. He snorted, shaking his head slowly. "By God, Cain was right when he called you stubborn. You are stubborn, just like your father. You go down slugging."

"But Cain's the one down now," Jillian pointed out, the anger leaving her as quickly as it had appeared. She turned and stared out the window again.

"You care about him." It was a statement, not a question. Graham knew his niece and knew she didn't give her heart easily.

"That was before I knew who he was."

"That makes a difference?"

She whirled back around. "How can you ask me that? You know what it was like for me after Ron."

"But Cain isn't Ron. They're two different people."

"But they have the same kind of job. I'm never going through what I went through after Ron died. Never again."

"And yet here you are."

She shrugged, conceding the point. "Here I am."

"Doesn't that mean something?"

"It means I want to make sure he's all right."

"That's it?"

"He saved my life. I owe him that much."

"It sounds as though you might have saved his life, too."

She squeezed her eyes shut. "Or, just maybe, I'm the one responsible for getting him killed."

"He'll pull through," Graham assured her. "Cain's tough. That's why I wanted him for the job."

The job. It's what had brought him into her life, and it's what would keep them apart. She turned back and looked at her uncle. "Well, the job's over now."

"Is there someone here from the FBI?"

Immediately all attention was drawn to the door of the waiting room. The doctor who stood just inside looked as haggard and worn-out as the surgical greens he was wearing.

"That's me," MacArthur said, rising to his feet.

"Your agent, uh, an..." He flipped through several pages in a chart. "Ash Cain?"

"Yes?" Jillian answered, pushing past Graham and MacArthur. "What about him?"

The doctor glanced up from the chart, his eyes widening at the sight of dried blood on her shirt and arms. "Are you all right? Has someone looked at you?"

"I'm fine," she insisted, brushing off his concern with a wave of her hand. "Please tell me, what about Cain? When can I see him?"

The doctor's eyes bounced to MacArthur, who nodded silently. "They're bringing him down from surgery. He got through it all right, but it was touch and go there for a while. He nearly bled to death, but we're pumping some back into him. With time, and barring anything unforeseen, he should be expected to recover. He'll be in recovery for at least . . .''

But Jillian heard none of the rest of it. She'd heard all she wanted. She stepped away from the others, walking back to the windows to watch the sun climb upward in the sky.

The waiting was over. Cain was alive; he was going to be all right. It was time to let go.

After some expert convincing by Graham, the doctor agreed to allow Jillian to see Cain for a moment. He led her into the intensive-care unit and to the small cubical where Cain lay surrounded by a mass of machinery and equipment.

Jillian stood in the doorway, her heart twisting tight in her chest. His long, black hair was slicked back, and a sheet covered most of the mammoth bandage on his chest. His eyes were closed, and his handsome face looked drawn and pale. She stepped gingerly through the menagerie of equipment, walking to the gurney and staring down at him.

This wasn't how it was supposed to be, she told herself, blinking back the tears that stung at her eyes. This wasn't the grand exit she had pictured in her head, the classy retreat she had planned. But looking down into his peaceful face, she realized she had to leave right now. It was cowardly, and it wasn't the way she'd planned it, but it couldn't be helped. Unless she left right now, when he was too weak, too powerless to stop her, she wasn't sure she would ever be able to walk away.

"Cain," she whispered, tears spilling over her lashes and down onto her cheeks. There was no response, but she hadn't expected one. There was only the quiet beeping and buzzing from the machines attached to him. Carefully she reached out, touching his hair, his cheek, his lips.

How had things gotten so complicated? When had it all changed? It had been so simple in the beginning, so easy...so right. It had just been the two of them—just Cain and Jillian. Two people, alone, happy and falling in love.

Love. No, she didn't love him. She couldn't. She didn't even know who he was. She'd fallen in love with a fantasy, a dream.

Just then another sob strangled her, and she swore to herself under her breath. Why couldn't the fantasy have been real? Why couldn't they have gotten on his boat and sailed off into the sunset? Just this once, couldn't there have been a happily ever after?

Bending close, Jillian brought her face down to his. Once, she decided, brushing her lips against his. She'd say it once—just to hear the words, just to test how they felt on her lips. For the sake of the fantasy, for the sake of the dream, she'd pretend for a moment that it all had been real.

"I love you Cain," she murmured against his lips. "I love you."

In her fantasy, he whispered back. In her dream, he loved her, too. But in reality, there was nothing else. Straightening up, she quickly turned and walked out.

It felt as though a truck had driven in and sat on his chest—an eighteen-wheeler, to be exact. Just the effort it took to breathe exhausted him, and he lay back against the pillow feeling weak and frustrated.

Cain glanced up at the tiny three-inch television mounted on the light stand attached to his hospital bed. He was just in time to catch a glimpse of Jillian's lovely face. An uncomfortable spasm tightened in his chest, but it had nothing to do with the three bullet holes that were healing there. Word of a member of the Hughes clan surviving an assassin's bullet was big news, and the media had been having a field day for days.

Seeing Jillian on the TV screen, he found himself holding his breath. She stood in the center of a horde of reporters on the steps of the federal courthouse in New York, fielding their questions and handling their comments like the pro that she was. She looked cool, confident and very beautiful in the precisely tailored three-piece suit, and a hard lump of emotion formed in his throat.

Releasing his breath in a long, slow sigh, he shook his head. Bracing himself, he lifted an arm and reached to the panel of buttons beside him and switched the set off. The slight movement sent a hot wave of pain rippling through his damaged chest, but it was worth it. He'd seen each of the numerous CNN reports several times already; he didn't need to see yet another one. He'd heard all the reports of the daring FBI rescue, of the arrests of two suspects, and of the confessions that had been obtained implicating Alfred Donelli. There had been plenty of reports on the charges that were being filed against Donelli for solicitation of murder, and on the high praise from all over Washington being heaped upon the FBI team who had foiled the hit. He wasn't interested in hearing any more about it.

There was only one thing that mattered in all the reports, anyway, one message that rang out loud and clear. Jillian was gone. She had gotten on a plane and gone back to her life in New York without so much as a glance back.

Of course, he told himself he should have known what to expect, he should have known it wouldn't be any different. But still, he had hoped. He had hoped it would be different because Jillian had been different. She wasn't part of that arrogant and indifferent money and power establishment he'd grown to hate during his years in D.C. What they had shared had been real. What they had found together had been special.

And yet, she had still walked away. But not because of social standing and arrogance. She'd left because she had it in her head that anything more between them was impossible. She was convinced there were too many problems, too much deception and too much history, and God knows he knew how stubborn she could be when she had her mind set on something. She had made up her mind that it was over between them. Done. Finished. And there was no convincing her otherwise. She'd made her decision and had left him little choice in the matter. All he could do was lie there and accept her conclusion.

The problem was Cain didn't accept it. He thought she was wrong—he *knew* she was. But making her see that was more than he could handle with three bullet wounds to the chest.

His mouth was dry. Actually it was beyond dry—it felt more like a desert. Carefully lifting his arm, he reached for the plastic glass filled with tepid water that sat on the table in front of him. He'd just managed to close his hand around it when a sudden stab of pain shot through his chest. He winced, dropping the glass and sending the water spilling and soaking his bed.

"Damn!" he cursed in frustration, slamming a fist down on the bed, only to have another hot knife pierce his chest cavity.

"Looks like you could use some help," a young nurse said as she rushed to help him. "We don't want those wounds to open up again."

"To hell with them," he grumbled irritably, falling back against the pillow, exhausted. "Let them bleed."

"Oh, we don't want to do that," the nurse said cheerily, ignoring his anger. Testy patients were just part of the job for her. "How are we ever going to get you better if that keeps happening?"

We? Cain thought cynically, having taken just about all he could of cheery hospital manners. Last time he looked he was alone in the bed. He opened his eyes and watched the nurse as she skillfully went about her work. She'd been his nurse since he'd transferred out of intensive care four days ago. She was young, and attractive enough with her short platinum-blond hair and large blue eyes. She always had a sweet smile for him, was attentive and almost never missed an opportunity to lean close or to touch. And even in his weakened condition, he'd managed to notice how very cute and sexy that curvy little figure of hers was.

Cain might have taken three bullets in the chest, but he wasn't dead. He could still tell when a woman signaled she was interested, and if he wasn't mistaken, this young woman had been signaling a lot in the last four days. It wasn't purely male ego that had him convinced if he were to make the right overtures, she would more than likely take him up on any invitation. The problem was, he knew it would be useless.

If only it was that simple. If forgetting Jillian was merely a matter of finding another woman, or of starting another relationship, he would do it in a New York minute. But the fact was, it was going to take a lot more than a few nights in the arms of another woman to get her out of his system. He'd wanted Jillian Hughes for longer than he cared to admit, but having her had satisfied nothing. It had only made Cain want her that much more. It didn't matter how hurt he felt, or how angry, or how frustrated he was by her stubbornness and unreasonableness. Forgetting her wouldn't be easy. It would be impossible.

"There," the nurse said. As she reached to fluff his pillow, her full bosom brushed the side of his arm. "Better?"

"Fine," he mumbled, remembering how soft and beautiful Jillian's breasts had felt against him. "Thanks."

"Would you like me to turn on your television?" she asked, reaching for his glass and refilling it with water. She stuck in a fresh straw and offered it to him. "You could probably find some news, or maybe a movie."

Cain shook his head, sipping the water through the straw. He appreciated her diligent attendance, but he just wished she'd leave him alone to brood in private.

"I could bring you some juice if you'd prefer," she offered.

"No," he mumbled as she returned the water glass to the table.

"How about something to read? The book cart is just down the hall. I'd be happy to read to you if you're too tired—"

"No, really," he insisted. "Nothing."

"Are you sure?"

"I'm sure." He looked into her bright eyes and felt a pang of guilt. "Honest, but thanks."

"Okay then," she said, obviously reluctant to leave. "Well, I guess I'll go. If you need anything—" she stopped and handed him the buzzer "—just give me a ring."

Cain nodded, but already he'd stopped listening. He'd closed his eyes, allowing his mind to drift. But actually it hadn't drifted at all; he had directed it to exactly where he wanted it be. With Jillian.

"How are you feeling?"

Cain opened his eyes, surprised to see Graham Hughes standing in the doorway to his room, holding a shopping bag and wearing a wide-brimmed straw hat. "Like I was shot at and hit."

"You look it, too," Graham smiled, stepping inside and letting the door close silently behind him. "But I'm glad to see you haven't lost your sense of humor." He paused a moment, scratching his head. "On the other hand, as I recall you had a rather lousy sense of humor. I'm happy to see it's improving."

"So tell me, Senator Hughes, to what do I owe this honor?" Cain asked drolly, pushing a button on the panel beside him to raise the head of his bed. "I would have thought you'd be back in Washington taking advantage of all of the free press. Hugheses are big news these days."

Graham tossed the bag down onto the bed beside Cain and shrugged. "I'm not up for reelection for another four years, and you know how fickle voters can be. They'll have forgotten all about this by the time I need their support again." He pulled up a chair and sat down beside the bed, tossing the hat onto the bed table between them. "I wanted to come by and see how you were doing, thank you personally as long as I was in the area." He stopped, pointing to the bag. "There are some magazines and a couple of books in there to keep you busy. Wouldn't want you to get bored."

Cain glanced down into the bag and nodded. "Thanks." Looking back up at Graham, his eyes narrowed. "Now, why don't you tell me why you're really here."

Graham smiled again, shaking his head. "Suspicious bastard, aren't you?"

"You forget, I was in Washington a long time," Cain shrugged, the careless gesture causing him to flinch suddenly. He gingerly shifted his weight to one side, trying to find a more comfortable position. "Besides, I know you."

Graham's faced sobered at seeing Cain's obvious discomfort. "Why don't I ring for the nurse," he suggested, reaching for the buzzer. "Maybe she could give you something—"

"No!" Cain groaned with such force that he winced again, and when he saw Graham's startled expression, he managed a small laugh. "Do me a favor, don't call the nurse."

Graham slowly sat back down. "Don't tell me you've managed to complicate another woman's life already."

Cain's smile faded. "What are you talking about?"

Graham leaned back in the chair and folded his arms across his chest. "Oh, you're a smart guy. I think you know."

Inwardly every muscle tensed, but outwardly Cain showed no sign of tension. "If this is your way of warning me away from your niece, I'm afraid you're too late. She's taken care of that herself."

"Oh, you don't have to tell me," he said, his hands coming up in surrender. "I was treated to quite a stern lecture downstairs the other night about interfering in her life."

"Downstairs?"

"In the waiting room."

Cain looked up. "When was this?"

"The night you were shot, of course."

"Jillian was here?"

"All night."

Cain was quiet for a moment, turning the revelation over in his head. "I thought she'd left immediately for New York."

"Oh, she did, she did," Graham assured him, carefully and expertly appraising Cain much the same way he'd appraised his political cronies over the years. "Just as soon as she'd gone back to the house and packed up, and..."

"And...?" Cain prompted, wondering how many times in his political career Graham Hughes had infuriated his opponents with that self-satisfied smirk of his.

"And once she found out you were going to pull through."

Cain flinched as another small missile of pain was launched in his chest, but this time the ache had nothing to do with the physical wounds. It was the pain of loss, one he understood would be there long after the bullet holes had healed.

Okay, he thought quickly, so maybe she'd taken time for one brief look back. It meant nothing. She'd still walked away. She'd still left him when he hadn't been able stop her.

"I didn't know," he said, glancing across to Graham. "No one told me she'd been here."

"They let her come in for a few minutes, after the surgery. She'd gotten it in her head she was responsible for you getting shot."

"What? That's crazy."

"Yes, well, I tried to tell her, but you know how that goes."

"Yeah," Cain grumbled. Didn't he ever.

"Willful," Graham sighed.

Cain shook his head. "Stubborn."

Graham conceded the point with a smile. He stood up, walked to the narrow window and gazed outside. "You know, she shot them—the two men."

"Yeah, I know. Mac told me," he mumbled, cursing to himself. It was a miracle she hadn't taken a bullet herself. "Which only goes to prove she has no business having a gun. She's dangerous. I'd told her to stay down, but would she listen?"

"I don't think her personal safety was uppermost in her mind at that moment."

"You mean, you've been able to figure out how that woman's mind works?"

"It's not that difficult."

"No? Then I wish you'd explain it to me."

Graham turned around and looked across the room at Cain. "She was merely doing what any woman in her position would do."

"Oh yeah? And what was that?"

"Protecting the man she loves."

Cain's head snapped up. "What are you talking about?"

"What part didn't you understand?"

"Jillian isn't in love with me."

"I happen to disagree."

"You're way off on this one, Senator," Cain scoffed. "If she's so in love with me, she's got a damn funny way of showing it. She couldn't get out of here fast enough."

"Maybe," Graham said, walking back to the bed and picking up his hat. "But *you* seem to forget I practically raised her after Collin died; her mother was no help to her. Losing her father had been difficult. She was a very sad, very frightened little girl after that." He picked up the chair and positioned it against the wall where he'd found it. "There's a lot of that frightened little girl still in her. More than she'd care to admit."

Cain remembered the cut finger, and her reaction to the blood. How many times had he seen her vulnerability, her sensitivity, her fear and her pain?

"Oh, and I know she's got a lot of good excuses. She can cite chapter and verse all kinds of reasons for leaving. The truth was kept from her, your job is too dangerous—on and on." He stopped and smiled smugly. "You have to remember, she's a Hughes, after all, and we Hugheses make damn good lawyers. That woman can put together one hell of a good case. But..." He paused, letting his hands slap the sides of his legs to make the point. "The truth of the matter is, she's lost a lot of people in her life. People she loved. I suppose it's not unreasonable to think she'd be reluctant to take another chance. The way she sees it, if she doesn't try, she doesn't get hurt." He quickly raised his hands up, as though Cain would argue the point. "I know, I know. It makes no sense. God knows I've tried to point that out to her, but you know how unyielding she can be."

"Stubborn," Cain whispered.

Graham smiled as he walked slowly to the door and pulled it open. "You're a good man, Cain. You saved her life, and I'm grateful."

"Just doing my job, Senator."

"Maybe," Graham said thoughtfully, slipping his hat on his head. "I owe you one."

Cain watched the door gently close, then slowly shook his head. "Score's even."

Chapter 14

Jillian stared out the window at the tangle of traffic around them. It was hot, and her flight in from New York had been over an hour late landing.

"Would you care for some coffee?"

The voice on the intercom made her jump.

"Uh, no. I'm fine," she said, glancing at the driver through the glass partition and giving him a little wave. "Thanks."

"It's in the panel to your right if you change your mind."

Jillian's gaze flickered momentarily to the mahogany cabinet he'd indicated, and then back. She nodded again, giving him a polite smile. "Got it. Thanks again."

She looked about the plush interior of the limousine and slowly shook her head. What could Graham have been thinking? She had hoped to slip into the federal courthouse in Sacramento as inconspicuously as possible, but that would be a little difficult in this thing. She might as well have hired a brass band.

She was nervous, and she twisted the small bit of fabric in her hand. Glancing down, she stared at the red bandanna in her grasp. Cain. He would be there. She would be seeing him again, and she wasn't entirely sure she was ready.

She squeezed the bandanna tight, its faded cotton soft and cool in her moist, trembling hands. It was still knotted, forming a circle exactly the way it had been when she'd slipped it off his head.

She had found it on the bathroom floor when she'd gone back to the house to pack the morning she'd left the hospital. It had been a torturous trip back to Lighthouse Landing, seeing her grandmother's comfortable little house scarred and damaged. There had been broken glass strewn all over, and blood on the carpet where Spence had died. But worst of all had been the garden—trampled and forlorn.

Everywhere Jillian had looked there had been reminders. When she'd reached down and picked up Cain's bandanna, it hadn't been her intention to keep it. She just hadn't been able to let it go. She wasn't sure what it was that made her slip it into her suitcase. It wasn't as though she felt she would need any tangible reminders to help her remember him. She just hadn't been able to leave it behind.

How many times had she seen him tie it around his forehead? How many times had she wanted to slip her fingers beneath it and pull it off? How many times had she done that very thing?

It had been eight weeks since that awful night in Lighthouse Landing, since their peaceful sleep had been shattered by a hail of bullets, and eight weeks since she'd waited in that awful hospital to see if Cain would live. Eight weeks. Two months. Sixty-one days. Such a short period of time really, and yet it seemed like a lifetime.

Her hands tightened around the bandanna as the car pulled into a secured underground entrance to the courthouse. It had probably been a mistake to keep something of his. After all, holding it and touching it had only made her memories more vivid, more difficult to forget. She had hoped that once she'd gotten back to work, gotten back into her regular routine with her regular friends in her regular locales, she would begin to feel better, but that hadn't happened yet. Instead she'd been miserable, tormented by memories and plagued by loneliness. Cain was on her mind constantly. Jillian wondered how he was, where he was, and how his recovery was coming. Did he ever think about her, or had he gone on to another job, another assignment without so much as a thought to what they had shared?

She glanced down at the bandanna again. If keeping it had been foolish, then sleeping with it each night would qualify as sheer lunacy. Unfortunately, that's exactly what she'd been doing.

"All set, Miss Hughes?" Mike Christopher, the young FBI agent who'd been her constant companion for the last eight weeks, asked her as he stood by the open back door of the limo.

Jillian had dutifully accepted the protection offered to her by the bureau, but after eight weeks of exhaustive investigation, it looked as though they were finally becoming convinced that the threat to her was no longer viable. Agent Christopher had been polite enough, and as unobtrusive as possible, but his constant presence had only served as a painful reminder, and Jillian looked forward to the day when she could truly put all this behind her.

"Thanks, Mike," she said, reaching for her briefcase and stepping out of the car. "Have they been waiting?"

"I've been told we're right on time."

She allowed him to escort her through the underground parking area toward the elevator. Their footsteps echoed hollow and loud off the bare concrete floors and walls.

As a lawyer, Jillian had tried to prepared herself for this day. Emotionally, she had wanted to just concentrate on putting all her feelings and memories of Cain behind her and forget about him. But she of all people knew that was impossible. There were legal procedures that had to be met, appearances that would have to be made. After all, a crime had been committed. Two men had been arrested. She had known that eventually both she and Cain would be called to testify. It was inevitable that they would be meeting again. But even though she'd known it, she still wasn't ready.

The elevator doors quietly opened, and she stepped inside. As they began to ascend, Jillian unzipped her purse and placed the red bandanna inside. What would he think if he saw her with it? Would he think her a fool? Would he remember? Would he laugh?

Stopping at the lobby, the elevator nearly filled with additional passengers. Jillian and Agent Christopher were jostled to the back, pressed against the paneled rear wall.

"Did they tell you when they thought I might be called?" she asked in a low voice, turning to her companion.

"No, I'm sorry, they didn't," he said with regret. "But hopefully it won't be long."

Not that it mattered, Jillian thought glumly. She just wanted it over with. There would no doubt be a room for the witnesses to wait in until such time as they were called to testify, and the thought of spending long hours confined in that room with Cain made her stomach knot tightly.

The elevator swished to a quiet stop, and Jillian glanced up at the lighted number display above the door. Third floor. Three more to go. Unfortunately no one got off the crowded elevator, but one more person did get on. As people shifted and squeezed to make room, Jillian felt all the air in her lungs depart in one long, strangled gasp. Over the crowded assembly of heads and shoulders, she saw Cain board the elevator.

Cain punched the button again, harder this time. What the hell was taking the damn elevator so long? He swore to himself, restlessly pacing back and forth in front of the doors. He wasn't nervous about testifying, just the opposite, actually. He was anxious to do what he could to put those two slimes behind bars, but still he was uneasy. He wanted to get started. He wanted to get things going.

He wanted to see Jillian again.

The doctors had assured him that he had made a remarkable recovery, but the long hospital stay and the weeks of recuperation had taken their toll. He wasn't a man used to being idle, but he'd been forced to tread water for eight weeks now. But all that was over. He was healed and ready for action.

The light above the elevator lit with a ping as the doors opened in one smooth, soundless motion. Just great, he thought darkly as he surveyed the interior of wall-to-wall people. He fit himself inside as best he could, and the doors slid closed behind him.

It wasn't that he actually saw her, because he hadn't—he couldn't, in fact. But there was just something he *felt* from the moment he'd stepped inside. Turning his head, he peered cautiously through the silent crowd, his gaze homing in on her as though she'd sent out a hidden signal.

"Jillian," he said, causing the entire population of the small enclosure to turn in his direction.

"H-hello," Jillian stammered, managing a meek smile. Unconsciously, she sagged back against the wall, praying her knees would hold and she wouldn't collapse in a heap on the floor.

He looked so different and yet so wonderfully familiar. He hardly resembled Cain—*her* Cain with the red bandanna and bare chest. Yet she recognized him as Ash Cain now. His hair was shorter, his face clean shaven, and the conservative dark gray wool suit fit him with precision and grace. No wonder she'd noticed him as a teenager. What woman wouldn't?

The elevator reached the sixth floor, and people slowly began to file out. Stepping to one side, Cain waited until Jillian and her bodyguard stepped into the corridor, then fell into step beside them.

"Just get in?" he asked, after introducing himself to Agent Christopher. He could see the tension in her tight expression even though she did her best to hide it.

"Yes." She nodded. "Just about a half hour ago." Bracing herself, she looked up. His rugged features and smooth skin looked tanned and handsome, but she couldn't help remembering how pale and weak he'd looked in that recovery room. "How is everything? You're feeling okay?"

"I feel fine," he said, dropping his gaze to her lips and thinking how much better he'd feel if he could taste them just once.

"Back to work?"

"Pretty much. How about you?"

"Pretty much."

"Miss Hughes?"

Jillian turned to see William Farrow, the federal prosecutor handling the case, coming out from one of the courtrooms. Stopping, she extended her hand.

"Bill, it's good to see you again."

"It's been a long time," he said, taking her hand. He turned to Cain and offered a hand. "Ash, you look a whole lot better than you did when I saw you in the hospital."

"I feel a lot better, too," Cain said dryly as they shook hands.

Farrow turned back to Jillian. "I didn't think you'd remember me."

"The National Bar Association Convention in Boston. What was it—three, four years ago? You did the workshop on . . . searches?"

"Search and seizures, right. Four years ago."

"I enjoyed it."

"Thank you," he beamed, obviously pleased. "Our entire office followed the Donelli prosecution. It was a brilliant piece of prosecution."

"Thanks," she mumbled, shifting a nervous glance in Cain's direction. She felt so stiff, so terribly self-conscious. How could she be standing there chitchatting inanely when Cain stood right beside her? She could barely breathe let alone carry on a conversation. Since he'd climbed onto the elevator he'd been staring at her, and she was convinced she could actually *feel* his eyes on her. This whole thing was turning out to be much more difficult than she'd even imagined.

After a few torturous minutes longer, Bill Farrow finally escorted them to the room where they could wait until they were called. As Agent Christopher waited outside in the hall, Jillian and Cain entered the small conference room.

There were several people in there—other witnesses Farrow intended to call—but Jillian was only aware of Cain. She headed toward the middle of the room for a table that had several chairs positioned around it.

"Coffee?" Cain asked, signaling to the large coffee urn and stack of cups on a cart in the corner.

Jillian thought of a cup of hot, bitter coffee and her stomach churned uneasily. "No, thanks."

She opened her briefcase and sat down, pulling out some of the files she'd brought with her from the office. It wasn't as though she actually expected to get any work done, but she was desperate for any diversion that would give her a respite, an opportunity to gather her composure, strengthen her reserve. She looked at the three empty chairs around her. What would she do if he were to come and sit down in one of them? What would they talk about? What would she say to him?

She glanced up at the large, round clock mounted on the wall. It was only a little after ten. It could be hours before she was called. How could she stand it? How was she ever going to make it?

Jillian was so wrapped up in her agonizing internal debate, it took her a while to realize that Cain had gotten a cup of coffee and had casually strolled to the large window at the end of the room and stood there staring out. He hadn't come anywhere near her.

She slowly closed the file and tossed it back into the briefcase. Leaning back in the chair, she rubbed at the tension building at her temple. What an idiot she was. She'd been so concerned about how she was going to discourage Cain, it hadn't occurred to her it might not be a problem.

She turned and glanced at his tall frame silhouetted against the light. She was such a hypocrite. She'd accused him more than once of paying attention to her only because of his job, and yet she hadn't really believed that—not really. Somewhere in the back of her mind, she believed he had cared for her on some level, to some degree. It's what had made their situation so tragic, so sad. There had been real feeling between them, and job and duty had gotten in the way.

Turning back around, she began to search through her briefcase again. Her head was pounding, and she reached for the small bottle of pain relievers she always kept in an inside pocket.

Empty.

Cursing under her breath, she grabbed for her purse and prayed by some miracle she'd find something for her headache in there. But when she unzipped the bag and looked inside, her gaze was immediately drawn to Cain's red bandanna.

"Souvenirs?"

"Hmm? Uh—what?" Jillian stammered with a start, dropping her purse to the ground. Scrambling quickly before he could reach it, she pulled the bag back onto her lap and looked up to find Cain's clear blue eyes watching her carefully. Giving him a flustered smile, she ran a nervous hand through her hair and hurriedly zipped her bag closed. "What was that?"

"The files," he said, nodding to the folders in her briefcase. He walked around her and pulled out a chair and sat down. "Souvenirs from the office?"

Jillian glanced to her briefcase, and then back to him, her heart racing a mile a minute. For one horrified moment, she thought he had seen the bandanna, and it took a moment for his meaning to sink in.

"Oh, souvenirs!" she laughed, her body nearly going weak with relief. "Right, I get it. Yes, I guess they are."

"Playing catch-up?"

"Most of the time."

He finished the rest of his coffee and set the white foam cup on the table. "You look good."

It was hardly a compliment. His eyes were narrow and hard, and the expression on his face was hardly one of admiration. Still, it surprised her to hear him say it.

"Thank you," she said, hoping her face didn't flush too much. "So do you." She gestured to the suit and tie. "Very different."

Cain looked down at himself and smiled that quirky little half smile. "I didn't think the judge would appreciate jeans and a bandanna."

She tensed immediately at the mention of the red bandanna and cleared her throat. "Yes, well, I suppose you're right."

He was quiet for a moment, staring at her from the far side of the table. "I like the other color better."

She looked puzzled. "I beg your pardon?"

"This one's nice, too," he quickly added, pointing to the pale pink linen suit she wore. "I just like that creamy green color better."

Jillian suddenly remembered his unexpected compliment that night on the levee about the color she wore. Memories came rushing back, and she remembered how handsome he had looked that night, how he had stared at her, and the sound of his voice. Emotion twisted tight and painfully in her chest.

"Ash Cain?"

Cain looked up at the bailiff standing in the doorway and signaled with his hand. "Right here."

"They're ready for you, Mr. Cain."

Cain turned his gaze to Jillian and shrugged. "I guess this is it."

"I guess," Jillian said tightly. It had come so quickly. She had dreaded the thought of having to wait long, painful hours with him, but now that it looked as though that wasn't going to happen, she felt oddly disappointed. She blinked quickly, hoping her eyes wouldn't appear too watery. "Good luck. It was . . . uh, nice to see you again."

"Yes," he said, rising to his feet and smiling down at her. "It was ... nice. Goodbye, Jillian."

"Goodbye," she whispered as he turned and started for the door.

Goodbye. Suddenly that had become the saddest-sounding word she'd ever heard.

Somehow she made it through the rest of the morning, but the long hours of the afternoon dragged on interminably. She kept thinking Cain might return, that he might be called again, that he might just want to see her again. But hour after hour came and went, and there was no further sign of him.

Restless and miserable, Jillian paced nervously up and down the room. This whole day was turning out to be one of the worst in her life, and she just wanted to get as far away from this tiny little room, this courthouse and this town as she possibly could. Finally, just a little before four o'clock, Bill Farrow came in.

"I'm really sorry about the wait," he apologized.

"What's the holdup?" she asked testily, even though she understood how unpredictable court timetables could be.

"We've hit a snag with one of our experts," he explained. "I'm afraid it's looking like we won't be getting to you until tomorrow."

Jillian sagged down onto a chair. That meant another day, a hotel room and more waiting.

"I really feel badly about this," Farrow insisted. "But I promise, you will be one of the first on the list to be called in the morning."

That wasn't much consolation, but Jillian knew she had little choice. She had wisely made reservations at a downtown Sacramento hotel before leaving New York, just in case something like this was to happen. After making a few quick phone calls, she opened the door and found Agent Christopher dutifully waiting for her.

"They're bringing the car around now," he informed her in his typically smooth, unruffled manner.

Jillian glared at the young agent. She was exhausted after the miserable day. Her suit was wrinkled, her blouse was limp, and her head pounded furiously. But Agent Michael Christopher looked as cool and collected as he had when they'd boarded the plane this morning.

Just like every federal agent she'd even known, she thought darkly. Ever vigilant, ever cool, ever ready.

She thought about Cain, about how handsome he had looked in his fastidiously tailored suit that seemed to be the standard uniform for all federal agents. She glanced up and down the corridors outside the courtrooms, wondering if, by chance, he might have waited around to see her again.

The corridors were deserted.

Struggling with another rush of despair, Jillian let the very capable Agent Christopher escort her into the elevator. The pushing crowds and the rushing hordes were gone and the elevator swiftly descended to the underground parking garage, making only one brief stop at the main lobby. Jillian stood and watched the brightly lit panel above the doors faithfully chart their course, thinking the sinking sensation caused by the elevator's descent characterized her spirits exactly.

At the parking garage, the doors opened soundlessly, and they walked toward the waiting limo. The driver courteously opened the door for her as they approached. She climbed inside, sinking back exhausted onto the soft cushioned seat. The driver and Agent Christopher had just climbed into the front driver's compartment when Jillian was startled by a knock on the window beside her.

"How about a lift?"

Even though the back windows were darkly tinted, she recognized Cain's dark, looming silhouette outside. For a moment she couldn't do anything—not even breathe. She forgot all about her headache, about her exhaustion and her limp and wrinkled clothes. She'd spent the last eight weeks telling herself she never wanted to see him again, and yet now she couldn't wait. With numb, almost lifeless hands, she reached for the handle and opened the door.

He stood looking down at her, one arm braced against the limo's roof, the other draped over the door. It was as if she'd been transported back fifteen years, to the time when she'd sat in the back of her uncle's limo, lost and afraid. She suddenly had a very clear, very real picture of him then—short hair, dark suit...and those eyes. How could she not have recognized those eyes?

"Wow," he said, with a silent whistle. "Déjà vu, right?"

"Right," she murmured, remembering how he had leaned down and kissed her fifteen years ago. A flicker of excitement raced through her, hot and dangerous. What if he were to kiss her now?

But he didn't. He merely opened the door wider and settled himself on the plush seat opposite her.

"Thanks for the lift."

"No problem," she whispered, shaking her head just a little to dislodge the old memories. "Where are you headed?"

"Just up the street," he said, pointing indifferently. "I'll tell the driver."

The limo pulled out of the garage and onto the street, slowly making its way into the crunch of late afternoon traffic.

"They kept you a long time," he said after a few moments.

"Yes," she said with a sigh. Her heart was beating so fast she was certain he'd be able to hear it in the quiet lushness of the limo. "And I didn't even get called. I have to come back tomorrow."

"So that means you have to stay the night?"

"Right." She sighed again, nodding. She hesitated for a moment, but silence with him made her uncomfortable. His gaze was too intense, and the limo's plush compartment too intimate to be anything but unnerving.

"Déjà vu," he said again, leaning back into the seat and gazing at her from across the narrow aisle.

Jillian managed a small smile across her trembling lips. It did seem ironic they'd end up together again in a limo after all these years. "What goes around comes around, I guess."

He cocked his head to one side. "Did you really mean it when you said you had a crush on me then?"

Her cheeks flamed, and she dropped her gaze to her lap. She'd told him that story after they'd made love, before she'd known who he was. "Yes."

He laughed, shaking his head slowly. "It's crazy how things turn out, isn't it? I mean, think about it—I was interested in you, and you were interested in me." He paused for a moment, long enough for her to look up. "I wonder what would have happened if things would have worked out for us—back then, I mean."

Jillian couldn't talk; her voice was gone. She could do little more than give him a quick shrug.

"Just think," he said, leaning back to relax and cradle his head in his hands. "We'd have been spared a lot. You wouldn't have lost the man you loved. Ron—was that it? And you wouldn't have married the wrong guy." He paused for a moment, studying her through narrowed lids. "And maybe I wouldn't have made my wife so miserable because she wasn't you."

"Your wife?" Jillian sat up suddenly. "Y-you're married?"

"Not anymore," he assured her casually. "It was over a long time ago. But it does make you think, doesn't it? If we'd have gotten together back then, it would have saved a lot of people from getting hurt."

Jillian turned and stared out the window. She didn't like thinking about all of that, didn't like theorizing about what might have been—not now, not when it was so late, so hopeless now. His breezy, nonchalant manner only made her more uncomfortable and served to demonstrate just how casually he took all of this. It wasn't casual to her, it was tragic. Anxious to change the subject, she cleared her throat again and turned back to him. "How did your testimony go?"

"Okay," he said. "Wasn't much I could tell them. Mostly about Spence."

Jillian noticed the line across his forehead deepen just a fraction. "I'm sorry about your partner."

He shrugged indifferently, but the pain in his eyes belied the careless gesture. "It's a chance you take with this job."

"I guess it is," she mumbled, glancing down at her tightly clenched hands again. Oh yes, she thought darkly, the job. Cain's job. She knew all about the risks and the dangers in a job like his. She'd gambled once with a job like that, and she couldn't face the thought of taking those same kinds of chances with Cain. The stakes were too high this time. It had taken her years to get over losing Ron, but there'd be no surviving a world without Cain.

"Well, you know how it is," he went on. "It's the same for you."

His comment pulled her from her disturbing thoughts. "Me?"

"Yes, in your job."

"My job? My job isn't dangerous."

"It isn't?" he asked guilelessly.

"No," she said adamantly. What could he be thinking? How could he even compare the two? "Whatever made you say that?"

He shrugged innocently. "I thought it was your job to send the bad guys to jail."

"Well, we do, of course," she conceded, accepting the overly simplistic explanation. "But that's hardly as dangerous as undercover work."

"Really? How so?"

"Cain, that's ridiculous," she said, sitting up in her seat. "I mean, you deal with drug dealers, murderers, desperate people. They have guns and laundered money and aren't afraid to use them to get what they want. That's hardly the same as a criminal court case."

"Oh? And you don't deal with drug dealers and murderers and desperate people in the courtroom? You never confiscate weapons and drugs?"

"Well, of course I do, but it's hardly the same thing."

"It's exactly the same thing."

"Cain, I don't face the kind of danger you do."

"Jillian, I'm in no more danger than you are on any given day. There isn't anyone who doesn't assume some risks every day of their lives. Crossing the street can be dangerous, but that doesn't stop us from doing it."

"But we all have to cross the street from time to time. Not all of us get shot at," she pointed out.

"Oh? Have you ever been shot at?"

"Well . . . yes, but—"

"Have you ever used a gun?"

"Well, that was differ—"

"Have you ever had a hit put out on you?"

"Cain, this is pointless."

"Answer the question. Have you?"

She took a deep breath. "You know that I have."

He leaned forward, his hands on his knees. "Well, you've got one on me there, Counselor. That's never happened to me."

She stared at him, his blue eyes challenging her with the truth. This whole thing was preposterous. He'd made it sound as though her job held every bit as much danger and risk as his did, and that simply wasn't the case.

"It's not going to work, Cain," she pointed out. "It's not the same thing, and you know it. What risk I assume as a prosecutor isn't anything like what you face every day. You're the one out there with nothing but your cover between you and a bullet. I can always have protection, go into hiding if need be."

"Nobody can hide that well. Are you forgetting Donelli's men found you?" He turned and rapped on the window of the driver's compartment, signaling for him to stop. As the car moved to the curb and eased to a stop, Cain reached for the door. But before opening it, he stopped suddenly and turned to her. In one smooth motion, he grabbed her around the neck and pulled her to him.

Jillian felt light-headed, dizzy, as though there had suddenly been a drop in the air supply. He was so close, so big, he seemed to take up all the space, all the oxygen in the small compartment. She could feel his hot breath in her hair, smell the spicy scent of his cologne. He was so handsome, so strong and determined. She thought for a moment he was going to kiss her, then realized it was just that she wanted him to.

"And understand, there is no place you could hide that I couldn't find you," he said in a coarse voice, bringing his lips to within a whisper of hers. "Think about what I've said, Counselor."

Then he was out of the car and down the street before she could even take another breath. When life finally came back to her, she stepped out of the car. She wasn't sure what her intention had been—to call out to him, stop him, run into his arms. But it didn't matter. It was too late. He had disappeared into a crowd of pedestrians.

Chapter 15

"I'm sorry," said the telephone receptionist in a nasal voice. "Agent MacArthur has left for the day. Would you care to leave a message?"

Jillian's hand clenched into a tight fist in frustration. "It's really important that I get in touch with him this evening. Do you have a home number where I can reach him?"

"I'm sorry, ma'am, we're not allowed to give out that information. Perhaps another agent could help you?"

Jillian sat up straight in the chair and squared her shoulders. She didn't like having to do this, but she was desperate. "Look, this is Jillian Hughes with the U.S. Attorney's office and I really have to talk with MacArthur. Couldn't you give me his number?"

"I'm sorry, Miss Hughes," the operator said stiffly. "But I'm afraid we're still not authorized to give out that kind of information. If you like, I could put you through to the supervisor on duty."

Jillian rubbed at the dull throbbing at the bridge of her nose. "No, never mind. Thank you."

She dropped the telephone back onto its cradle and tossed her pen down on the desk. Well, that idea had gone down in flames. What next?

She flipped through the names and numbers of those listed in the directory section of her Filo-fax. Surely someone listed in the thick log could help find Cain, because one way or another that was what she was going to do.

Think about what I've said, Counselor.

Cain's parting words to her as he'd stepped from the limo and disappeared into the crowd stayed with her. And that's all she'd been able to do for the last several hours. *Think.* His words buzzed around her head like bees around a hive. She heard them while she'd checked into her hotel, while she'd unpacked and while she'd sat alone in the hotel's restaurant and shoved food around her plate.

At first she'd thought he'd been way off base when he'd tried to make comparisons between their jobs, about the dangers and the risks they both faced. Any association between the two professions seemed ridiculous. They were completely different. What risks she assumed as prosecutor in any given case were simply part and parcel of the job she'd been hired to do. If there were hazards or potential for danger in her job, she hadn't considered them too great to risk.

But the lawyer in her had to admit he'd presented a pretty convincing argument. Was there more risk in what she did than she'd realized?

She suddenly remembered an episode with Jeff that had happened several years back. It had been before things had started to fall apart between them. She'd just begun work on the Donelli case, and a high-ranking Donelli associate had been arrested. He'd indicated he might be willing to talk a deal, but only if he could deal with her directly—just the two of them alone in his cell. She'd agreed, of course, anxious to get as much against Donelli as she could, but she remembered how nervous Jeff had been about the meeting. Somewhere, perhaps, she'd considered the potential risks involved in getting into a cell alone with a criminal. Of course it was dangerous, but for a chance to get the testimony she needed, it had been worth the risk. Perhaps, just as Jeff hadn't understood her need to take that risk, she herself hadn't really tried to understand that Cain also did what he had to do.

Jillian rubbed at her tired eyes, realizing just how narrow her focus had been. She'd been convinced she would be safe in Lighthouse Landing. No one had known about Grandma Wells's house, about the summers she had spent there and the memories it had held. She'd told no one about that private place, or about her plans to go there. And yet she hadn't been safe there at all. The danger posed by Donelli's threats had been greater than she'd realized. She hadn't been able to hide. They had found her, and she shuddered to think about what could have happened had she been there alone—without Cain, without help.

She flipped aimlessly through the lists of names and addresses. She wasn't sure yet what exactly it was she wanted to say to Cain—maybe just that she'd been a little hasty, a little too quick to judge. That maybe she'd only been looking at the argument from one side, and that maybe she had been a little . . . stubborn.

But Jillian knew it wasn't just stubbornness that had made her react the way she had. It had been fear. Cutting through all the excuses and reasons, all the causes and rationales, what had stopped her from rushing into Cain's arms the moment she'd seen him was fear. She was afraid—of trying again, of risking her heart, of losing again.

Just then, a name leapt from the page and into her line of vision. Of course, she thought as she reached for the phone again. She should have thought of this before. There was one person she knew for certain would be able to find Ash Cain in a hurry.

"Jilly, do you have any idea what time it is here?"

Jillian glanced at her watch, cringing just a little. Sometime after midnight in Washington. "This is important, Graham. I need your help."

"What is it? Has something happened? Are you all right?"

"Nothing's happened, Graham. I'm fine. Really, I'm fine," Jillian quickly assured him, hearing the alarm in his voice. "I need to find Cain—right now, tonight. Can you help me?"

There was a long pause on the end of the line. "What's so urgent?"

Jillian wasn't sure how to answer that. Where did she start? "I... Graham, I've been very stupid. I have to find him. I have to let him know..."

"Let me make a few calls," he said, not needing to hear her finish. "Give me the number where you're at—this may take me a while. I'll call you back."

"Thanks," Jillian said, a swell of emotion in her chest. "And, Graham?"

"Yes?"

"I love you."

"I love you, too, baby."

Jillian felt enormously better. Graham would come through for her, and for once she didn't mind at all his considerable influence and ability to pull strings—especially when it meant it would find Cain.

Jillian kicked off her shoes and reached up to begin un-
buttoning her blouse. The burst of nervous energy she'd
experienced after talking with Cain in the back of the limo
had made her forget the fatigue of a long day waiting at the
courthouse, but it had expended itself now. She just wanted
to get out of her rumpled suit and into a hot shower, then
spend what was left of the evening waiting for Graham to
call back. Of course, what she was going to say to Cain
when she found him was still a mystery, but she'd think of
something.

Opening the door to the shower stall, she turned on the
water, adjusting the temperature. Then, pulling off her
blouse—her skirt and lingerie quickly following—she
stepped beneath the warm, stinging spray.

The water felt good against her skin, and her stiff, tired
muscles began to ease and relax. She closed her eyes, letting the spray pour over her, and she thought back to that
afternoon when she'd cut her finger with the gardening
trowel and Cain had carried her into the kitchen and bandaged her wound. She'd taken a shower that afternoon, too,
and it was a shower that changed her life forever.

Cain had climbed into the shower with her that day—
bold, brazen and completely uninhibited. Water had
drenched his clothes, had soaked his boots, but he had been
unmindful to all of that. He had wanted her, and he'd focused all his attention on getting what he wanted.

Jillian closed her eyes to the surge of longing that washed
over her like the water from the shower. No one had wanted
her the way Cain had—no one. He had let nothing stand in
his way of having her—not her uncertainties, not her family name and not even the job he had to do. And yet she had
allowed everything to come between them—her anger, her
stubbornness and her fear. How could she have been so
stupid? Why had it taken her so long to see?

She loved him. She loved him and she'd been afraid of losing him. She'd been afraid to take a chance at happiness for fear of losing him to a bullet and a dangerous job. But walking away had solved nothing—she'd lost him, anyway. What kind of life had it been for her these last two months?

A shallow, empty one.

Jillian thought about what Cain had said this afternoon in the limo. The attraction between them had its beginnings during that political campaign years before, when a young Secret Service agent kissed a blushing debutante. They'd had a chance then, but they'd let it slip away. They'd gone their separate ways only to have fate bring them together again and offer them one last try.

She opened her eyes and glanced at the frosted shower door. What if, by some miracle, he was there? She wouldn't be the fool she'd been in the past. She would reach for him and never let him go.

But as she stood there letting the water stream over her, a hard knot of emotion swelled in her throat. There was no miracle, no new beginning, no Cain.

She turned off the faucet and stepped out of the shower, reaching for the fluffy bath towel. Wrapping it about herself, she looked in the mirror. She saw the sad eyes of a woman in love staring back at her, and felt the sting of tears. Fate had given her a second chance, and she'd let it slip away. But she wasn't going to wait around and see if she got a third chance. She was going to make that happen herself. One way or another she was going to find Cain. She wanted him and she was going to do whatever she had to to get him back.

Every muscle tensed as Cain thought of Jillian in the shower. He wasn't sure if slipping past her bodyguard and into her hotel room was the wisest thing he'd ever done in his life, but it was certainly one of the most reckless. He had no idea what her reaction would be, but with a woman as volatile and unpredictable as Jillian Hughes, it would be impossible to predict. Still, it was something he felt he had to do.

The illustrious Senator Hughes had left him with a lot to think about after their conversation in the hospital eight weeks ago. But even without Graham's insights, Cain knew the final chapter between him and Jillian was far from over. He'd invested too much time, and too much of himself was tied up with the woman, to be willing to just turn around and walk away.

She had a problem with what he did for a living, a problem that had started long before they had become involved. He understood that; he could appreciate her fears and concerns. But she wasn't a little girl anymore. They were adults, and adults worked out their problems. He wasn't going to let her just stamp her foot and stubbornly refuse to listen. He was going to make her listen, even if that meant he had to keep her prisoner in this hotel room until she began to see reason.

He listened to the sounds of her in the shower, and his body surged with need. He thought of that afternoon in Lighthouse Landing when they'd made love in the shower. If he were to go in there right now, would she turn him away?

Desire gnawed at him, and his whole body trembled. She thought he took too many risks. If she only knew what a coward he really was. He'd been on countless stakeouts, had been involved in countless raids and shoot-outs, but standing in the quiet darkness of this hotel room he'd never been more frightened. Never had there been so much at stake.

Suddenly the shower went silent, and Cain battled a burst of panic. Was he up for this? Was he willing to take the risk?

He loved her, but what if he wasn't able to make her love him back?

Jillian finished brushing her teeth, turned off the faucet and dropped her toothbrush back into her makeup case. She knotted the towel around her tighter, then flipped off the bathroom light. But when she turned to start for the bedroom, she collided full force against a wall of hard muscle and bone. With a strangled gasp, she was hoisted up and into Cain's powerful embrace.

"See?" he murmured, sinking his hands into her damp hair and bringing his mouth to within inches of hers. "Even with a bodyguard outside, I can get to you."

"Cain," she whispered, her heart thundering in her chest. She could hardly believe her eyes, hardly believed he was real. She wanted to tell him everything she'd been thinking, all the conclusions she'd drawn and the decisions she'd made, but her head was spinning and her mind had become a blank slate. Where were all her brilliant explanations, her eloquent closing arguments? There was so much she wanted to say, so much she wanted to tell him, and yet all she could do was stand there and stare up at him, feeling helpless and numb.

"We all take chances, Jillian," Cain said, knowing this was about the biggest one he'd ever taken. The sweet, spicy scent of shampoo and bath soap swirled around him, making him dizzy and a little light-headed. His hands roamed the soft folds of the towel in search of her. She felt soft, warm, and he'd been without her for so long. "That's what life is all about. There are no guarantees. I can't promise you I'm going to live forever, or that I'll never get shot at or have to use a gun again. I can't promise that I won't worry about you and be afraid when creeps like Donelli make threats."

"Oh, Cain, no..." She struggled with her words, wanting to tell him that it no longer made a difference to her, that it no longer mattered, but he stopped her.

"No, let me finish," he demanded, his hold on her tightening. "There are no guarantees, but I can tell you you're the only woman I've ever really wanted. You make me crazy and angry and frustrated and...very, very happy." He stopped, pulling her mouth to his, and kissed her deeply. "And I can promise you one thing—I'm always going to love you."

"Oh, Cain," Jillian whispered, tears brimming in her eyes as she brought her arms up around him. "Cain, I love you."

There was one instant—one fraction of a second when she saw the look of surprise on his face, when she realized she'd caught him completely off guard, and that look was one Jillian knew she would never forget. But it was there for only a moment. Because after that, he gave her no time to notice anything else.

Cain's mouth crushed hers, the deep growl in his throat signaling just how desperate and hungry he was. He pulled her tightly to him, molding her body to his and kissing her as though he never intended to stop.

Jillian couldn't breathe, she couldn't think, but it no longer mattered. She was with Cain, he was touching her, kissing her, loving her, and that was all that mattered. There was no longer form and shape to her world, only feeling and sensation, and they traveled through her like wild and violent storms. She had suddenly been transported to the bed, the towel had somehow disappeared, and she was frantically pulling at his clothes, freeing him from them and exposing his glorious body to her urgent hands.

She kissed him—lips, neck, shoulders, back, chest. She was ravenous for him, more desperate than she could ever recall being. Being with him was better than she remembered, better than she thought it could ever be. She wanted him so much that she didn't care if she ever found the real world again. If it were possible to exist on this magnificent plane of consciousness somewhere between hunger and fulfillment, needing and having, it would be all she could hope for. It was only when her lips grazed a hard, darkened scar left from where a bullet had ripped through his chest that she reached for reality.

"Oh God, Cain," she gasped, running a hand over the rehabilitated skin. Pulling back, she saw another, and then another, and tears filled her eyes again. "Oh, Cain," she said, looking up at him, tears spilling down her cheeks. "Look at this. Look what they did to you." She leaned down and touched each scar with her lips, kissing and soothing.

Cain braced himself against the onslaught of emotion caused by her lips on him. "I can't even remember it."

"But you must have suffered so much," she murmured, trailing a path of kisses up his chest, along his neck and to his lips.

The feel of her lips on him made him feel weaker than he had when he'd woken up in the hospital to find she had gone. Lifting her off him, he stared down into her eyes. "The only thing that hurt was being without you."

"You'll never be without me again," she whispered as her hold on the real world began to slip once again.

"Never again," he groaned, capturing her lips and pushing into her in one powerful thrust.

The telephone surprised them both. They hadn't been sleeping, but lying together, exhausted, enjoying the blissful aftermath of hours spent lovemaking.

"Who would be calling at this hour?" Cain asked, lifting his head just enough to place a light peck on the end of her nose.

Jillian jumped up. "Oh my God, I forgot. *Graham*."

"Graham," Cain repeated. "What does he want?"

But Jillian didn't take time to explain. She reached for the telephone. "Hello?"

"Well, I'm sorry it's taken me so long, but I was finally able to reach someone I know from the Bureau. He agreed to meet me down there, and we pulled Cain's file. Have you got a pencil and paper? I've got a couple of numbers you can try."

Jillian cringed, thinking of Graham and his friend meeting in the middle of the night. Dutifully, she grabbed for a pen and paper and jotted down the numbers, feeling guilty as hell.

"Graham," she said, swatting at Cain's hand that kept wanting to caress her breasts. "I'm sorry, I didn't mean for you to go to so much trouble. I can't tell you how much I appreciate it."

"If it helps Jilly, it's worth it," Graham said, then yawned noisily over the line. "Well, I have to be up in a couple of hours. Keep me posted."

"I will," Jillian said.

"Tell Graham I—" Cain started, but Jillian slapped her hand over his mouth so fast he forgot what he had been about to say.

"What was that?" Graham asked. "Is someone there with you?"

"No, no," Jillian insisted, putting a finger to her lips to hush Cain. "Just the television. Graham, thanks again. Now get some sleep. I love you."

She hung up the phone and covered her face with her hands. Her entire body shook with emotion.

"Jillian, what is it?" Cain asked, his voice suddenly concerned. "What's the matter?"

But when she turned to face him, he realized it wasn't sorrow she'd been overcome with, but laughter.

"I'm so embarrassed," she gasped, scooting back across the bed and into his arms. "Poor Graham."

"Why, what's happened?" Cain said, getting caught up in her laughter even though he had no idea what was responsible for it.

She told him about the favor she had asked of Graham, and of the trouble he'd gone to in order to help her. "I mean, he actually got someone to meet him in the middle of the night to open up your file," she said, grimacing and wrapping her arms around his neck. "I didn't have the heart to tell him I'd already found you."

Cain smiled and pulled her to him. "I thought I was the one who found *you.*"

She shrugged, moving her body along his. "I'd have found you, one way or the other."

"Think so?" he asked, sliding a hand down the length of her torso.

"Know so," she murmured, reaching to kiss him. But before her lips made contact, she pulled back. "Do me a favor? Promise me you'll never tell Graham."

"I promise," he whispered, lifting his head up from the pillow and kissing her first. "On second thought, I'm calling it in."

"You're calling what in?" Jillian sighed, feeling warm and loved and wonderful.

"The favor."

"Oh." She giggled. "You're calling it in already?"

"I'm calling it in."

She pulled out of his arms and scooted back against the headboard of the bed. Folding her arms across her chest, she gazed down at him. "Okay, what is it? What do you want?"

"I want you to marry me."

The teasing smile faded slowly from her face. "Are you serious? You're not joking, are you?"

"I'm not joking," he assured her, stroking her cheek with the back of one finger. "Marry me?"

"When?"

"Now, today. I don't care, as long as it's soon."

"Why?"

"Why? Because I don't want to wait. Because I've waited too long already."

"No," she said, sitting up. "Why do you want to get married?"

He regarded her for a moment. "Why do you think?"

"Cain, I love you so much."

"Does that mean you will?"

She turned and reached for her purse on the nightstand. Pulling out the red bandanna, she unknotted it and slipped it around her neck. "I'm always happy when I can do a friend a favor."

"I love you, Jillian." Cain smiled, pulling her into his arms.

"I love you too," Jillian whispered against his lips. "And the answer is yes."

* * * * *

HE'S AN

AMERICAN HERO

He's a man's man, and every woman's dream. Strong, sensitive and so irresistible—he's an American Hero.

For April: KEEPER, by Patricia Gardner Evans: From the moment Cleese Starrett encountered Laurel Drew fishing in his river, he was hooked. But reeling in this lovely lady might prove harder than he thought.

For May: MICHAEL'S FATHER, by Dallas Schulze: Kel Bryan needed a housekeeper—fast. And Megan Roarke did more than fit the bill; she fit snugly into his open arms. Then she told him her news....

For June: SIMPLE GIFTS, by Kathleen Korbel: For too long Rock O'Connor had fought the good fight to no avail. Then Lee Kendall entered his jaded world, her zest for life rekindling his former passion—as well as a new one.

AMERICAN HEROES: Men who give all they've got for their country, their work—the women they love.

Only from

IMHER08

MILLION DOLLAR SWEEPSTAKES (III)
AND
EXTRA BONUS PRIZE DRAWING

Three new stories celebrating
motherhood and love

Birds, Bees and Babies '94

NORA ROBERTS
ANN MAJOR
DALLAS SCHULZE

A collection of three stories, all by
award-winning authors, selected
especially to reflect the love all
families share. Silhouette's fifth annual
romantic tribute to mothers is sure
to touch your heart.

Available in May,
BIRDS, BEES AND BABIES 1994 is a
perfect gift for yourself or a loved one
to celebrate the joy of motherhood.

**Available at your favorite
retail outlet.**

Only from

 Silhouette®

—where passion lives.

ROMANTIC TRADITIONS continues in April with Carla Cassidy's sexy spin on the amnesia plot line in TRY TO REMEMBER (IM #560).

"Jane Smith's" memory had vanished, so when Frank Longford offered her a safe haven and a strong shoulder, she accepted. Then the nightmares began, with memory proving scarier than amnesia, as Jane began to fear losing the one man she truly loved.

As always, **ROMANTIC TRADITIONS** doesn't stop there! July will feature Barbara Faith's **DESERT MAN**, which spotlights the sheikh story line. And future months hold more exciting twists on classic plot lines from some of your favorite authors, so don't miss them— only in INTIMATE MOMENTS Silhouette®

And now for something completely different from Silhouette....

SPELLBOUND ROMANCE

In May, look for
MIRANDA'S VIKING (IM #568)
by Maggie Shayne

Yesterday, Rolf Magnusson had been frozen solid, his body perfectly preserved in the glacial cave where scientist Miranda O'Shea had discovered him. Today, the Viking warrior sat sipping coffee in her living room, all six feet seven inches of him hot to the touch. His heart, however, remained as ice-cold as the rest of him had been for nine hundred years. But Miranda knew a very unscientific way to thaw it out....

Don't miss MIRANDA'S VIKING by Maggie Shayne, available this May, only from

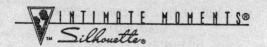

INTIMATE MOMENTS® Silhouette®

IT'S OUR 1000TH SILHOUETTE ROMANCE, AND WE'RE CELEBRATING!

JOIN US FOR A SPECIAL COLLECTION OF LOVE STORIES BY AUTHORS YOU'VE LOVED FOR YEARS, AND NEW FAVORITES YOU'VE JUST DISCOVERED. JOIN THE CELEBRATION...

April
REGAN'S PRIDE by Diana Palmer
MARRY ME AGAIN by Suzanne Carey

May
THE BEST IS YET TO BE by Tracy Sinclair
CAUTION: BABY AHEAD by Marie Ferrarella

June
THE BACHELOR PRINCE by Debbie Macomber
A ROGUE'S HEART by Laurie Paige

July
IMPROMPTU BRIDE by Annette Broadrick
THE FORGOTTEN HUSBAND by Elizabeth August

SILHOUETTE ROMANCE...VIBRANT, FUN AND EMOTIONALLY RICH! TAKE ANOTHER LOOK AT US! AND AS PART OF THE CELEBRATION, READERS CAN RECEIVE A FREE GIFT!

YOU'LL FALL IN LOVE ALL OVER AGAIN WITH SILHOUETTE ROMANCE!

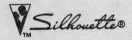